The Heart

of The

Sword

His World Ablaze

Franklyn Thomas Jr.

THE HEART

OF THE

SWORD

HIS WORLD ABLAZE

AUTHOR'S NOTE:
This is a work of fiction. Names, characters, places, and incidents either are the product of the author's imagination and experiences or used fictitiously, and any resemblance to actual persons, living or dead, events, or locales, or divine beings, is entirely coincidental.

CHAPTER ONE

With an army bent on its annihilation closing in, the people of the village prepare to fight to keep their freedom. In search of Sanch and the sword known as Shallin, Alshin will stop at nothing to keep Sillack from failing again. For this time, it may cost him his life. Young heroes positioning themselves behind the opposing army find they are greatly outnumbered, but press on, hoping to be joined by a greater force.

Back at the village, Ralyn, Kess, and Thrant await the pending danger that will soon be at their gates. Will they be ready? Will Sanch, Menis, and the daughters of the village? Traveling through the treacherous Thorn Forest with all its dangers, Kess holds onto her husband. He kisses her on top of her head, taking in the flowery smell of her hair. She closes her eyes and whispers a prayer to the Gods for Bethany's safe return.

"Do not fret, my love. Our little girl will make it back home to us." Ralyn held his wife to his chest.

"I just hope we still have a home for her to return to," Kess said.

Ralyn looked down at his wife. Her honey-colored skin and light brown eyes contrasted against the darkness of the forest. He could see her full lips curving downward, into a frown. He brushed a lock of hair from over her right eye. He wanted nothing more than to tell her that everything would be ok, and at the end of this day, everything would be just as it always was. They would all go back to their lives as it had been.

"Let us see how Thrant is doing reintroducing himself to Kanten's sword," Ralyn suggested.

Kess and Ralyn made their way to the marble table where she thoughtfully laid out Thrant's old armor and his brother's sword. The armor was a matted gray. His family crest was etched into the breastplate. The guards on his shoulder were scaled plates that protected but were still flexible enough to move as he did. The armor that covered his legs pointed upward into a spike. It came in handy to impale the enemy. It all was held together with thick leather straps fastened with silver buckles. Quietly approaching from behind, they both stopped and looked on as Thrant removed the sword from the table. A great sword that his brother, Kanten had swung with deadly accuracy.

"You know, Ralyn, Kanten would never have let me touch this thing no matter how much I begged him." Thrant brought the blade up to eye level and looked at the straightness of its edge. A smooth beam of light entered through an open window, bouncing off of it. The pommel was made of a strange stone that he and Ralyn acquired as boys while out hunting. Thrant found it after falling on it as they were running after deer. He loved it so much that he built it into the pommel of his big brother's sword. The hilt went out to a point on either end. They were weapons all their own. It was a two-handed sword that had been balanced in a way that it could be wielded with one. The blacksmith made one identical for Thrant, except for the pommel. Sillack had it taken from him when he imprisoned him.

"Yes, and if he knew you had it now, he would probably kill you," Ralyn replied as he scratched his salt and pepper beard.

"I do believe he would not be too happy with me, but now my greatest problem is fitting into my old armor. Stay close, I may need some help getting into this old thing." Thrant patted his small round belly.

Both Kess and Ralyn laughed and moved in closer and helped Thrant put on his armor. Some straps were worn but still strong. The dents from past battles still proudly showed themselves. Right along the shoulder piece of his armor was a clear and deep sword slash. Proof the armor worked. Without that piece of armor,

Thrant would be missing an arm. When they were complete with their task, to their astonishment, the armor fit well!

"Now, Thrant, are you ready?" Ralyn turned and faced Thrant.

Kess placed her hands on the shoulders of the battle-readied men. "Are you ready to face your people in a time when they need you the most? You may not know this, but your presence will make a difference, and give them true and real hope for victory. Let us see who has returned and will stand and fight with us. We are wasting what little is left of daylight." Kess dressed herself for battle. It was lighter armor that gave her unlimited movement so that she could send her arrows flying straight and fast.

They made their way to the stables and mounted the newly rested horses, then rode off to the village gates, where they hoped they would meet an army. When they arrived at the gates, they did not meet an army; they met people who would stand and fight to keep their homes and land free from Sillack and whatever evil he planned to unleash onto them.

Out front stood the young man who earlier swore to fight at Ralyn's side. He possessed a thick build and was wearing armor that was clearly not made for him. It fit loosely in some places, and tight in others. But it was secure enough and would protect, as it should. Hanging at his side swung his grandfather's sword. His grandfather would fight himself if not for being blinded in the final battles with the Xyles. Caught in the eyes by shards of bones hacked loose from one of the creatures, he was one of the many men who fought in that noble battle against such great evil. Now his sword would join other swords that would share its honor. They would share the honor of defending their people from a new enemy threatening their way of life.

His grandfather's sword had some wear on it, but from first glance, it was clearly a warrior's blade. The handle was swathed in black leather. The pommel was flat and resembled a hammer. The hilt stretched out with two more hammers, one on each end. Evian was trained with a sword like all other boys his age in the village, but a seasoned warrior, he was not.

"Evian, I see that you have returned. I feel at rest now knowing I will have a warrior fighting with me," Ralyn said as he approached the multitude.

Kess jumped down from her horse, her quiver of arrows settled on her back. She made her way over to Evian. Just as she did for Thrant not too long ago, she did the same for Evian. Kess adjusted his loose armor to fit and protect better. She, like the others, was a warrior, but a mother first. It showed in the care she took with straps and buckles.

"Did you think there would be so many that returned, Ralyn?" Kess asked as she walked back to her horse.

"No, my love. I thought it would only be the four of us."

"The four of us? What do you mean?" Thrant was confused as to how Ralyn came to the count of four.

Yes, us three and Evian. I knew that young man would wait here for us if no one else would join us in this fight. In his eyes, I saw fight and the need to protect his people and his home. This is indeed more than I'd hoped for. We may just have a chance after all."

"Our village has grown since I was here last." Thrant's eyes worked their way through the crowd, looking for familiar faces.

"Thrant, you have been gone for too long, but it is good to have you back," Kess said as she stroked her horse's neck, giving him a firm pat.

"Thank you, Kess. I just hope you still feel that way when this is all over." Thrant pulled back his dark brown hair lined with gray streaks.

"Why would the outcome of this battle change the fact that you are welcomed? This has, and always will be, your home," Kess said.

"Why? Look what I have brought to you and this village, my home. This is all because of me, the things I have done, and the poor decisions I have made in my life. Now, the guiltless people of this village will be forced to pay for all I have done." You could hear the breaking in the old warrior's voice.

"All that we are is the first to fight one battle of many more battles yet to come," Ralyn said, trying to comfort his old friend.

Ralyn then rode out amongst the multitude, drawing their attention to him.

"We are all here for the same reason, and that is to fight for the people of our village—the people we so love and who can't take up arms themselves. My friend here thinks he has brought this upon us, but I do not see it that way. My friend, our brother, has given us the chance to set the stage for a war that was destined to start with or without him."

All eyes were now on Ralyn.

"Thrant brought us something. He brought us hope. He brought us Sanch, The Son of Lackshin, who now wields the sword known as Shallin. Sanch is only one boy, and we are a village of warriors Alshin will meet when he arrives here. Out of the two and a half thousand people of the village, it looks like fifteen hundred of you that can fight have answered my call to arms. For the ones that are not here, I know it is because they are too old and have seen too many wars and wish not to see another. The others are too young and need not see war now. I hope they will never see war in their lifetime. The ones of us that are here will see to that. Our elders have seen their last battle. Now, let us prepare!"

Ralyn then rode over to where he left Thrant and Kess. They still had to devise a plan to keep Alshin's army from overrunning the village. There was only one direction in which they could attack: the front gate.

Some of those who came to fight were women who had come to the village with Kess years ago. Their homes had been destroyed at the hands of Daren and the Xyles that followed him.

Like Kess, they were welcomed. They became wives and mothers and made sure the art of fighting was shown to boys and girls alike. The men and women were trained to fight with several weapons and now have risen to use those skills.

Turning to Kess, Ralyn started a plan in motion. "Kess, get four of your sisters' bows, then take them to the village walls. Devise the best plan to keep our walls safe. Thrant, Evian and I will take the men, partition them into units, and prepare them to defend against a frontal attack. We must find several horses to ride into battle, and we must hurry, for we have little time."

Thrant and Ralyn rode off toward the armory.

Ralyn was correct. Alshin and his army had been closing in on him and his people. It was dark and morning was still hours away. The night's cold air brought thick fog with it. They prepared and hoped that Sanch and the others would make it before dawn when this attack was expected.

CHAPTER TWO

The darkness had been slowly devouring what little light remained. Cold air blew in from the north, bringing with it a nefarious chill. Sanch and the others approached the Thorn Forest that would take them to the base of the mountain that overlooked the valley. Alshin and his army would have to pass there on the way to the village. They suspected they would probably set camp in the valley below. They looked down on a vast, empty valley. Fires were still smoldering where camp was broken in a hurry. It was clear they were too late to do anything that could disrupt Alshin or delay his attack. They were gone now, and clearly on their way to the village.

The valley had a faint fragrance of fresh soil churned up by galloping horses. Some campfires were still smoldering. Some still had carcasses of half-eaten animals hanging from spicks. Tents were pitched but vacant. By the look of things, there had been a much larger force than they expected. Sanch tried to keep his composure and turned away from the valley, his lips tightly pressed together. Heat filled his face. If it could turn red, it would have.

"Bethany, did you not say they would be here? Where are they!" Sanch roared, not sounding like his normally soft-spoken self. "Alshin and his men!"

It felt as if a bottomless pit had grown in her chest. The army was gone, and Bethany knew her home was where they were heading.

"I thought we had more time. I did not think they would attack before dawn. A night attack will prove more difficult for our people, Lisha," Bethany said, feeling as if she let her people down.

"Everyone here knows the plans," Lisha interrupted before Sanch could say anything else that would make her cousin feel any worse than she already did. "We still plan to get there just as they do. Them being in that valley or not does not help our chances any less. There are still just a few of us, and our attack from the rear has the same chances it had a minute ago. So, if we are done wasting time ..." Lisha turned to look at Sanch. "Son of Lackshin, are you ready?" Her honey brown eyes reflected the sun setting in the distance.

"Yes, yes," Sanch said. He closed his eyes and shook his head. "You are right." He bit his lip. "I have a date to keep, and I do not intend to be late. I am certain Alshin has missed my smiling face as well as the edge of my sword. And you all know I do not want to keep him waiting." Sanch then turned to Bethany with sorrow-filled eyes. "Lead the way, little princess." A little calmer, his voice returned to its normal tone.

Bethany gave an accepting node. "This way." She motioned her head to her left.

They followed Bethany down the path that she knew would help them catch up with Alshin and his army. They picked up the pace, moving with purpose. The darker it got, the colder it became. With the speed in which they moved, sweat found its way on their brows. They knew they might not get to the village at the same time as the army, but they were determined not to be too far behind. Now, all that was left was for Dagger and the Elargun army to join them to help even the odds. They hoped the added force would give the village a better chance of survival.

Sanch played his earlier actions over in his head. He always had a bad temper, but still prided himself on control. He thought back to when he interrupted Sillack's men trying to have their way with Helen on the way into town. The rage he felt when he saw that showed in his actions but stayed hidden on his face. Sanch watched Bethany as he tried to find the right words. He noticed the discomfort in her walk. At sixteen, Bethany was considered a woman in her village. She carried her weapon of choice; a tempered bow staff that was as strong as any sword. Ralyn and Kess both insisted she also carried a sword. Although the staff was an effective weapon in battle, the sword had always been the better tool for killing men.

Sanch increased his stride to catch up with Bethany. He chewed on his bottom lip for a moment before he spoke. "I did not mean that," he whispered. "I did not mean to shout. I am sorry." He glanced briefly at her. The light brown, almost hazel eyes of Sanch showed his shame. Shame from what he brought to these people. *Her* people.

"What was that?" Bethany asked. She had not intended to let him off easily. "You did not mean to do what?" she asked, acting as if she hadn't noticed him looking at her with those eyes of his. Sanch had thick ebony hair that was locked and hung down right above his shoulders. Being only a little shorter than him, Bethany looked over at him just to get a quick look at those eyes of his.

"Shout. I am sorry that I shouted at you. That was wrong of me to do. I hope you can forgive me," Sanch said humbly.

"Is it that you are sorry, or is this an attempt to keep me from mentioning your outburst to my mother?" Bethany let a half-smile creep onto her face. Her green eyes glittered.

"No. I am sorry for that. It is truly unlike me," he quickly replied.

"Do not worry," the little princess said as she increased her speed, leaving Sanch behind.

"Now that you mentioned it, I don't see reason to say anything to your mother about what took place," Sanch said nervously.

"Afraid of my little aunt, Son of Lackshin?" Lisha asked, overhearing all that had been said between him and her cousin. Lisha used the conversation as a chance to speak with Sanch. She placed her hand on the small of his back to get his attention without others taking notice. "Do you feel we can trust them?" she whispered. "What do we even know about them?"

The Elarguns resembled men just fine, although their scales betrayed them to actual men. Green, blue, gold, and shiny gray scales covered them from face to tail. Their hair had been just as colorful and beautiful as their scales. Their human features showed best when the sun was no longer in the sky. Darkness hid their true appearance.

"I do not know, Lisha, but what choice do we have? Let's just hope they were loyal friends to my father, and can now be loyal friends to me—to us."

"Let us hope," Lisha replied.

CHAPTER THREE

In the cave, the darkness was as thick as melted gold. It seemed the deeper they descended, the darker it became. Dagger moved through the darkness with confidence and without hesitation. He was in his element in these caves, in this dark. He was at home here. Silma continued to suppress her glow to keep them hidden from what else could still be out in the thick of it. The one Dagger dubbed with the name "Hush" held Silma in one hand and kept the other firm around his bone-handled short sword. They came to a cave that had a faint light flickering at the end of it. Hush tried to adjust his orange eyes to the first light he had seen in a while.

"Is that a light I see?" Silma asked Dagger as she spread her wings.

Dagger's yellow eyes glowed from the small beams of light cutting through the darkness.

"Welcome to the Elargun City. Here is where we will need to convene this land's greatest army to come with us," Dagger proudly bragged to Silma and Hush. "Follow me. We must quickly find my father."

Silma was annoyed and confused why they needed to stop for family visits. "Dagger, for what reason must we stop to see your father? How is he going to help us get this army you speak so highly of?" Silma fluttered over to him.

"Why? Well, because only the king can order the army to be called to arms and to go off to battle."

"Why would he allow you to take his army off to war, a war that may never find you and your people down here?" Silma inquired.

"There are two reasons I think he will allow this. For one, The Son of Lackshin is the man who calls for his army. Then there is the most important reason that will ensure our involvement in this battle."

"What is this leverage that you hold that is going to compel your king to allow his army to join us?" Silma asked the Elargun boy.

"His son, the heir to the throne, is already on his way to this battle."

"Are you saying that Deem, your brother, is the king's son?"

"Yes," Dagger said, nodding his head. "And that is why this battle not only has to be fought, but it must be won. We must ensure the safety of our prince. I must keep Deem safe so that one day he can be king." Dagger picked up his pace. "Hurry, you two. Come on, this way." Dagger motioned for them to follow. "We must make haste. I do not want this battle to be over before we can get there. Deem will never let me live it down."

Silma and her protector stayed close behind Dagger so as not to lose him. The closer they got to where the king was, the more guards they encountered. Each time, Dagger had to give them the okay to allow Silma and Hush to go further. When they passed the last four guards, they entered a room that seemed to be illuminated by the rocks in the walls themselves. The ceiling of this vast chamber had rocks that shined as bright as the midday sun. It was simply a world of its own. Statues of kings long gone decorated the path leading to the throne. Each statue looked down with glowing eyes. There were glow stones set inside of them. As they got closer to where they expected to see the king, they saw a figure advancing on them instead. It was clearly one of Dagger's people. The closer the Elargun got, Silma and Hush realized it was the king. What took place next was not what they expected. Dagger turned to his guest.

"You two remain here. I will be right back." Dagger's eyes reflected the lights from the eyes of his ancestors.

Dagger continued towards the approaching figure that now had his weapon drawn. He closed his teal green hands firmly around the handle of his daggers. The sound echoed when he removed the two curved knives from their place of rest. Dagger picked up his pace. He jogged slowly which soon changed into an all-out sprint.

Hush and Silma, as well as the guards at the entrance of the throne room looked on, amazed by his speed and agility. It was as if he would disappear and reappear in his next location. The figure was now moving faster toward Dagger with two very unusual weapons. His weapons resembled swords, but how he held them was peculiar. The handles curved down and around and ran parallel with the blades. He held the sword along his forearm, using it as a shield. The other he used was almost like a normal sword. Dagger's opponent wielded these eccentric weapons as skilled as anyone with a traditional blade.

When their weapons finally met, it was a sight to behold. The sound they made was of two fine-tuned instruments harmonizing. The sound of their song rang through the astounding chamber. They matched each other move for move. The dance went on and on with the song playing off the walls, making the rocks glow stranger with every new strike. Dagger had agility over his challenger. He used the cave itself as a weapon. The other appeared to have more discipline and moved with grace in his movements. Dagger held his agency with every strike. With one leap, Dagger was airborne in an attempt to position himself behind his foe. That proved to be his undoing. With one swift motion, his adversary's tail swatted him out of the air like an insect. Laying there flat on his back, Dagger accepted his defeat. He looked up at his victorious opponent.

"Again, father, I lay here looking up at you. The only difference is Deem is not on the ground with me," Dagger said as he was helped to his feet.

"Son, where is your brother and who are your friends?" the king asked.

"Well, that blue glow is Silma, and the big hairy quiet guy is her protector. I just call him Hush. He has not pulled my head off thus far. I deduce he does not mind the name."

Both Hush and Silma fell to one knee, giving the king his respect.

The king smiled and signaled for them to rise. "Now son, tell me why you and your friends require my audience?"

"Father, we are here to ask for the army to be made ready and available immediately to me so that I can take them and join Deem and Sanch in a battle against Sillack's men. We ask in haste, for we have not much time."

"Who is this Sanch you are willing to take our men to battle for?" the king asked with curiosity.

"Father, Sanch is the Son of Lackshin. He is who we follow into battle," Dagger humbly replied.

"How is this so? It was said he had been killed as a boy. How do you know he is who he claims to be? He could be playing us for fools."

"Father, this boy has with him the sword of Lackshin. He carries Shallin with him." Dagger wanted to quickly gather an army so he could hurry to his brother's side.

The king's soft orange eyes widened. His face donned a strange look of hope. He lowered himself onto his throne.

"So, you are telling me that the Lackshin heir is not dead, and also has Shallin, the sword of his father?"

"Yes, father," Dagger replied. "The Son of Lackshin leads this fight and I mean to join him in it."

"Son, you will have your army."

After the king spoke, it was time for action. The king brought those of the Elargun army and ordered two of his personal guards be sent to protect Sanch. Esaab knew Sanch was the only man that could stop Sillack's hold. They put together an Elargun army of a thousand men, with the others preparing to follow shortly after with an even greater force. They prepared their horses. Not typical horses, but horses that had adapted to the dark underground environment the Elarguns had been forced to live in.

The Elargun City went on for miles underground. It made these horses necessary to get around faster. They got Dagger, Silma and her protector, and the king and his army to the magical exit to the outside world as fast as they could. No time was wasted. The larger force took longer to get to the subversive city than the three of them. Silma had to muster up the strength and magic required to get not only herself, but Dagger and Hush through the gate. She now had an army of a thousand Elargun men, and two of the king's guards.

"Your majesty, how will the others follow if I am not here to open the pathway out? How will they find us on the outside?" Silma beseeched the king.

"Silma, do not fret. We have other ways to enter the upper world. As far as finding your whereabouts, we know of this village you go to protect." The king reached for Silma. Now holding her in his hands, he whispered to her. "Go. You should have no worries. Your father knows why he sent you through this mountain, and if Sanch is anything like his father, you are on the winning side of this battle."

Then Esaab handed Silma back as well as a shield that was made from Elargun scales.

"I do not know your name or where you may have come from, but if Sanch gives you his trust, then so do I." He nodded. "This shield I give you has been made for his father, but he never returned for it. Now I want you to give it to Sanch. It is made of discarded scales of Elargun kings passed. It will protect the boy as it was supposed to protect Lackshin. Please, see that Sanch gets it."

The king, without a doubt in his mind, knew this creature would see to Sanch's safety. Something about this creature reminded him of someone. He just could not remember whom.

"Father, we must go now. Deem is out there and I need to be at his side when this battle starts," Dagger said as he rode his horse closer to the exit.

"Yes, son," replied the king. "You need to be with your brother. Every good leader needs his best man at his side. Go with speed, my son, and look out for him. I know he will look out for you. I'm sending out two princes and two is what I expect to return."

"Silma, are you ready?" Dagger asked.

"I hope so, Dagger," Silma said as she looked up at Hush.

The creature looked back at Silma, gave her a nod, and pulled her in close.

Before Silma started her mantra, she told the creature one last thing. "When that gate opens, ride out and stay to the side until everyone is out." Silma looked to Dagger. "I do ask that you stay close to us. I do not know how long I can sustain this gate open, and I want you to be on the outside of the gate in case it closes early. We are going to need you on the outside."

Silma took her place in the silent creature's hand and her chant once again started. Silma glowed a blinding shade of blue. Rocks glowed to match her brilliance. It was now time for the Elargun army to join the fight waging outside the protection of their mountain home.

CHAPTER FOUR

Everyone worked diligently preparing for dawn's welcome. The people of the village were on edge waiting for Alshin's army to arrive. The sounds of swords scraping on wet stones filled the night. Bows being strung sang out their melody. Seasoned fighters and those newly trained stood together this night. Older warriors showed the young boys how to form a strong shield wall. Those who could not fight were taken to the most fortified building in what can only be described as a small castle. At one time, Ralyn's family lived in that castle, but when his father died and Ralyn became lord, he left the castle and moved into a nice but modest home. That left the family castle empty for years. Women, children, and old men and the sick were among those taken there just in case the village became overran by Alshin's army. Twenty of the soldiers were ordered to stay behind as the last defense to protect them. Four archers were placed on different towers of the castle to give support to the soldiers on the ground.

Unbeknownst to Ralyn and Thrant, this army would soon be at their gates with the objective to annihilate anyone who stood between him, Sanch, and Shallin.

Kess prepared their first line of defense by strategically placing herself at the village wall. Her sisters in arms were dressed as she was. They wore light leather that had been stretched and beaten, making them flexible. They were sturdy, but much lighter than chainmail and steel armor. Their lightweight armor made it much easier to draw, pull and launch their arrows with deadly accuracy. Their hair was cut short or put back to ensure it would not interfere with their tasks. Kess made sure they had enough arrows to last for some time. Ralyn and Thrant were able to arm all the men and place them in platoons. Three platoons were led by Ralyn, Thrant, and Evian.

Before placing everyone in their assigned position, Ralyn had one last request. He ordered Evian to go to his and Kess's home to bring back Sanch, Menis, and Lisha's horses. Evian, being eager to please, ran with great haste to do what his lord had asked of him.

"Ralyn, what am I to do with the horses," Evian asked, curious to know what his lord's plans were.

"Release them," Ralyn instructed. "The four of them are going to need horses to ride into battle." He quenched Evian's curiosity.

"How are they to find one another out there?" Evian enquired, thinking that the horses would probably get lost.

"Somehow, I think Sanch's horse will find him just fine and the others will follow," Thrant said, seeing what Ralyn's plan was.

"Why would you think that, my lord?" Evian asked Ralyn.

"It seems like there is some sort of union between Sanch and this horse." Ralyn rubbed Sanch's horse behind its ear. "I feel they will have no problem finding one another out there. Let us go. We still have much to do before our guests arrive."

They all went on to prepare their units and inform them of their individual tasks. Thrant and Ralyn had the two larger forces that would be located outside of the village gates, the first line to prevent Alshin's army from entering the village. Evian led the smallest of the three forces. Their task was to stay inside the gates as the second line of defense against their attackers if they made it past Ralyn and Thrant. Kess, other women, and a few men were already in position on the village wall looking out for the impending forces. They shared flasks of wine while they waited. Many believed wine improved their aim. Now with the village on full vigilant, the women who were not to fight, the children, and the men who had seen many winters as well as wars were safely hidden away from where the fighting was to take place.

Now, with everything done, there was nothing to do but wait. Men and women alike told stories of past battles to pass the time. The archers listened while wrapping arrows with ripped rags and dipping them into oil.

A thousand hooves trampled earth. Horses carried Alshin and his men to the village of Quiet Waters—a once peaceful village that did its best to stay out of the conflicts of the outside world. Being far enough from Sillack and the land he ruled over made it easy to steer clear of all his evil. Only on occasions did the world outside their gates make it as far as their home. For the first time in years, they had to take up arms to defend themselves.

CHAPTER FIVE

A thousand men moved in sync with one goal among them. There would be murder, plunder, and some with worst deeds in mind. Alshin rode in front with the mounted infantry. The pikemen marched close behind, keeping instep as they advanced on the village where Alshin believed Sanch and Shallin has taken refuge. Alshin sat high on his warhorse, an already tall man. On foot, he already stood six foot six; his long sword on a lesser man would drag on the ground. The solid man's armor, normally shiny silver steel, looked dull in the darkness when the clouds allowed the moon to show itself. His thin, blond hair cut short above his shoulders bounced as he rode. Once a knight of the crown, he was tasked with the job of killing innocents if the fight came to that.

The force that Alshin commanded was more than both Sanch and Ralyn were expecting. The way it looked, they would be outnumbered, three to one. Alshin was not expecting there to be too much of a fight when he arrived at the village. He expected not to face much of an opposition. He figured when they saw the overwhelming force he brought with him, they would turn Sanch and the sword over to him to avoid a fight. Alshin could not be more wrong. He rode steady, not wanting his men to become exhausted.

Cutting through the dark was two of his scouts returning with their report. Neither of them looked more than eighteen or nineteen. Both thin boys rode much smaller horses than the others. Smaller horses made less noise when they were scouting. They carried short, lightweight swords and both had small daggers. Quiet killing made them effective scouts. They rode up next to Alshin's great steed, making it look like they were mounted on ponies.

"Sir, they are not expecting us," the scout with short, unkempt whiskers reported. He was young trying to look older than he was.

"The village is in darkness. Few homes had fires going. Sir, the village sleeps and there is still several hours before dawn," the younger scout added. He could not yet grow facial hair, so his face was smooth as the palm of his hands.

A faint smile made its way onto Alshin's face. "They will not know what is going on until it is too late to do anything." He motioned for the scouts to fall back in.

"No, Sir, they will not," the younger scout replied.

"March on!" Alshin shouted to the men on foot. "Follow me!" he ordered the men mounted on horseback. "I want Sanch and that sword in my hand and a village of slaves before dawn breaks."

Alshin's army moved out in full force. They were to be at the village well before sunrise. It was to be a night attack, after all.

With Sanch and the others on foot, the distance between them and Alshin made it seem like the odds were still tipped in Alshin's favor. He had more men—fighting men—ready and willing to kill on command. Some even took great pleasure in killing and looked forward to getting their chance to do just that to unsuspecting villagers. He had hundreds of mounted men and double that in infantry. He kept the archers in the rear. Archers were not known for their skills with a sword and only wore swords in case they had to do some fighting. More times than not they would drop their bows and scatter. Archers are fine when their enemies are far away, but any closer, they take to foot. Sillack didn't take too keenly to cowards. He would hang any archers caught after running. The choice was die by their enemies' sword or by Sillack's noose. It had gotten hard to find good archers after a while, so they stopped hanging runners and just started whipping them.

With the reports from his scout's, Alshin's pace increased. Maybe his confidence was the reason for the increase in his speed, or he just wanted to be at the end of it all. As a knight of King Patrick's court, Sir Alshin Barga was sent out to deal with any uprising that had broken out in the kingdom. He would ride out and deliver quick and decisive victories for his king. That earned him the title of head knight. He fought at Lackshin's side and even gave commands. He went on to win battle after battle, showing why he was the king's most trusted knight.

Known as a man of honor, it had shocked the kingdom when it was rumored that Sir Alshin Barga had betrayed Lackshin along with Sillack. Even King Patrick himself could not believe it to be true. Sending Alshin out to fight in the name of the crown was the king's chance to hold on to some honor after closing his gates on his people. The king hoped to hold on to his throne after all had ended. He would be able to say he sent his best man forth to take up sword in honor of the king. After getting the news of the betrayal, the king locked himself away seeing no one but the Obeah-Man and turning away even the queen for a fortnight. When he did show himself, he commanded that the gates remain closed except for trade that was to be closely controlled by men chosen by him. The king changed because of the act of one man—of one knight. Why Alshin decided to side with Sillack and kill Sanch's father is still a mystery to many, including Sillack himself. Now, he rides to face the son of the man he traded in his honor to betray.

CHAPTER SIX

In some way, they were gaining ground thanks to Bethany's knowledge of the terrain and the area. It gave them the edge they so desperately needed. It made the difference between being on time or being too late.

Are you sure this way will help us catch up to them in time to stop them or slow them down?" Menis asked, concerned that time was not on their side.

"They will be at the village before us, but we shall not be far behind. We will be there in time to make Alshin sorry he ever made his way to my home," Bethany replied, now worried and unable to think of anything but her mother and father.

"Sanch, let me send two of my men ahead to scout what kind of force we are to face when we arrive at this village. That would better prepare us for what is to come?" Deem asked, once again offering his assistance.

"Can they do this and go unseen? The last thing we want is for Alshin to know that I'm not in the village," Sanch said.

With a smile on his scaled face, Deem answered Sanch with confidence, "Yes, Sanch, my men can go forth undetected and return with their findings."

"If that is so and you can do this, then yes. Please, anything to find out what we are to face. Pick your men and send them on."

Deem, wasting no time at all, gave two nods to the chosen men. Soon, they were on their way.

Deem walked over to Sanch. "Now watch this, Son of Lackshin."

Deem's men moved like nothing Sanch had seen before. The Elargun scouts flew by Sanch, Lisha, Menis, and Bethany in a blur. Dust kicked up as they vanished into the darkness. Deem and his men had chameleon-like abilities, and Sanch, being the man he was, saw the advantages of that. They continued not slowing. A battle awaited them, and time was not in their favor. Sanch was clearly in a state of mind that Lisha and Menis had not seen him in before. He had become overly relaxed, yet focused. It was like nothing Deem had seen before, and he could not wait to see what would stem from it. Deem was used to seeing young warriors agitated and fearful.

It did not take long for Deems men to return. It had been only a little over an hour before his men appeared almost out of nowhere. It was amazing how fast they moved. Coming at them was what looked like a moving cloud of dust.

"What is that?" Bethany asked, squinting her eyes. "It looks like a dust storm."

"That is not a dust storm," Deem replied. "It's my men and they're moving as if something is terribly wrong."

As they got closer, they returned to focus. Falling in, in front of Deem, they started their report. Sounding out of breath, they began to speak.

"Deem we have not much time. The men will be at the village gates in less than an hour." They turned to Bethany. "I have a feeling that your people are going to make them sorry for stopping by. Your army seemed to be at full readiness, and a fine army they appear to be." The Elarguns had very good vision in the dark and were able to see more than Alshin's men had.

Bethany looked to Lisha. "Cousin, we do not have an army, I know not of what he is talking about. We are a peaceful village that never had need for an army."

Sanch, with that smile on his face, let Menis know just what was on his mind.

"They do now," Menis said as he rested his large hand on Bethany's shoulder.

"Yes, that is so," Sanch added. "Let us be on our way and see this army that awaits its two princesses." Sanch admired Bethany's face in the moonlight. Almost long enough to forget the task that awaited them all.

"We don't have far to go." Bethany pointed ahead to break the awkward silence. "Just over that hill."

"It would be nice if I had my horse," Lisha said, walking between Sanch and her cousin.

"That would help us make it there much faster," Menis added.

"Stop," Sanch quietly ordered. "Something is moving over there." Sanch firmly gripped the handle of his sword.

Bethany pulled her bow and Menis drew one of his axes. Deem and his men readied their strange weapons. They all moved slowly toward the sound. Bethany and Menis stood ready. When they got close enough to see what was making the sound, they stopped and laughed before turning to look at the others.

"Sanch, I think there is someone here to see you," Bethany said.

Both Sanch and Lisha rushed over.

"You two are not going to need those," Menis said, looking at their weapons. "These are friends, not foes. They may make it easier to get to the village in time."

As he came closer, a smile crossed Sanch's face. It was truly a friend he so missed. It was his horse along with Lisha's, Bethany's, and Menis'. The tide had just changed. Sanch put away his sword and greeted his friend by stroking his face against his. You could see that he was now feeling better prepared for this fight. Things were now going the way he needed it to go. Sanch looked at the others and by the look on his face, they knew things had just gotten bad for Alshin. They all knew they were still a good way behind. The darkness would cover their approach on Alshin from the rear. Sanch turned to Deem and his men to ask him how he would like to proceed.

"Now that we have our horses, we can move a lot faster. I saw your men run, but I do not know if they will be able to keep up with horses in full gallop." Sanch's horse pushed him with its head.

"We are fast, but we will not be able to keep up with you on horseback. We will not hold you back, but we will be there before the first blow is struck. I will fight at your side, Son of Lackshin, you can count on that. Go. We have a battle that awaits us and a village to protect." Deem approached Sanch's horse slowly. The horse turned his head giving Deem permission to stroke him.

Now mounted on horseback, the four warriors rode off toward the village and Alshin's army. Not knowing what difference the four of them could make to any of this, they rode with the confidence of victory in their minds. Sanch had no plans of letting Alshin leave this fight alive. This was to be his last dawn. Sanch was going to see to that. The young heroes now on horseback unleashed the speed that was theirs now to control, and that speed was just what they had prayed to the Gods for. The closer they got to the village they could hear the sounds of a marching army. They were close. They not only saw fresh tracks, but the noise of the army in the near distance could also be heard. Lights from the torches were visible. Sanch motioned for them to stop. The only thing it could have meant was that the village walls were nearby.

CHAPTER SEVEN

❝My lord, did I not tell you they did not know of our coming? The village is asleep and unprepared," a scruffy young scout said.

"Let us wake them up," Alshin demanded. "Bring me one of my archers, we are going to give them light."

Alshin had one of his archers light an arrow. "Notch, draw, lose!" Alshin's second commanded a flaming arrow to be launched into the village.

"That should get their attention," Alshin said, a smirk resting on his face.

The archer's arrow flew at the village. To Alshin's surprise, the village was not asleep at all, but ready and waiting for him and his army.

"Shield!" shouted Ralyn as the flaming arrow made its descent over them.

"Light!" Kess commanded from on top of the walls.

Two arrows were set ablaze and launched off the wall, landing into two piles of wood placed on either side of the village, which revealed Alshin and his army.

Sanch and the others watched from a distance. They had stopped on a cliff overlooking the rear of Alshin and his men just in time to see it all come alive.

"Bethany, look. There is your homecoming. Is that not a sight?" Sanch asked as he looked at Bethany.

"I think our chances just got a little better," Menis added. "We are still outnumbered, but help should be on the way."

"Something is going on down there!" Lisha pointed at Alshin.

"Give me the boy and the sword!" shouted Alshin as he rode out in front. "I am here to obtain the one called Sanch and his father's sword, Shallin!" His voice became more aggressive. "Give them to me!"

"Why would we give you The Son of Lackshin?" Ralyn replied, sitting high on his horse, his green armor looking almost black in the dark. Only when he passed close to the flames could you see the splendid color of it.

Sanch heard a voice coming from behind, spun his horse around, and reached for his sword. He quickly noticed who it was.

"Have we missed all the excitement, or are we on time?" Deem and his men appeared out of the darkness.

"No, you are just in time," Sanch replied, turning back to face the night activities. "Alshin and his army just arrived and got a bit of a surprise when the lights were turned on."

"Look, Alshin is moving closer to the walls." Lisha pointed.

Frustration filled the air when Alshin shouted more demands.

"I did not come here to fight a battle with old men and boys. Even though I am certain my men would enjoy the practice of killing you all, I am simply here for the boy and the sword. There is no need for bloodshed. Hand them to me, and we will march back from whence we came."

"Then why have an army if you have no intention to bring harm to my people?" Ralyn asked. "Why bring such a force with you if death was not intended?"

"If you do not hand him over, we will have no choice but to take him. The lives that will be lost will be the lives of your people." Alshin gave his last offer.

Atop the wall, Kess had all she was willing to take of Alshin's offers. She climbed to the very top of the walls with bow in hand. She reached down and grabbed an arrow from one of her sisters. Notching the arrow, she drew back.

"Who is that woman on the wall?" Deem asked.

Lisha, Menis, and Sanch looked over to Bethany. "Her mother," they answered together.

"Oh," Deem said as he looked with anticipation.

Kess released her arrow. The hum of the arrow was deep as it flew and ended its journey right into the chest of the rider mounted next to Alshin. It rang as it cut through the man's armor sending a crushing sound filling the night. Its impact knocked him well off his horse onto the men standing behind him knocking his shield and spear from his hand. The rider lay dying on top the foot soldier; the loud sound of air came gurgling from his open mouth. The soldier shuffled back freeing himself from the dying man.

Kess stood there with the bowstring still quivering. "Now, there is a life taken!" she shouted. "Now can we now move on? Know this, you will not leave here with that boy or his father's sword. Make peace with whatever gods you pray to for you will not be leaving."

Seeing what just happened brought a smile to Sanch's face.

"Bethany, your mother is some kind of woman. But I cannot let her have all the fun."

"Sanch what do you have in mind?" Deem asked.

"You and your men do that thing you guys do. There is no reason for them to know how many of us rode out to meet them. I think it is time for Ralyn to know his little girl is home." Sanch smiled at Bethany.

Now in a rage, Alshin signaled his men to move on the village. Like a cool chill on the back of Alshin's neck, he heard a voice he had encountered once before.

You can look all you want in that village, but you will not find me, nor will you find my father's sword!" Sanch shouted "Sorry, Kess, I'm a bit later than I had anticipated, but not too late to see what you can do with a bow."

"Do you still have something of mine?" Kess asked.

"Yes!" Sanch replied. "Bethany and Lisha are safe with me, and I will be more than happy to give them back to you."

"That is enough boy!" shouted an angry Alshin. "Do you think you will be allowed to make it back into that village through all of my men?"

"Not without having to kill a few first. You can save yourself the trouble and leave now while you still have the chance!"

"Sillack wants you and that sword back at his castle by week's end. I am here to see to that," Alshin said.

Sanch took Shallin off his back and undressed it out of the dark gray cloth it was wrapped in. Lisha turned to Bethany and signaled her to watch and be ready.

"Is this the sword that Sillack wants?" Sanch held the shiny black sword firmly by the handle with the blade pointing behind him. He spoke to the whole army and not just Alshin. "If any man wishes to possess my father's sword, all you have to do is pull it from his chest." Sanch pointed to the rider on the other side of Alshin, then released Shallin. She flew straight and true into the chest of that man throwing him off his horse and onto the ground. The horse reared up from its rider's sudden departure. The men knew this time to not stay behind this rider. He lay in the wet grass pulling at Shallin, still shaking from the sheer force of it. With every pull, his arm got weaker and weaker. All the men stood watching but none helped. The shock held them like newborn babies.

CHAPTER EIGHT

The cold, brisk morning air kissed his cheek. The dry hay crunched under every step he took quietly as to not alert anyone of his plans. He nuzzled the mare comforting her and calming her from his earlier than normal visit. "Shhhh, it's ok, girl." He stroked her soft fur ever so gently. He walked over to where his saddle now sat alone, when normally it had company. The leather was cool and stiff to the touch as he lifted it from its place of rest. Cold air entered quickly while he made his way back over to his trusted mare, her hooves shuffling in anticipation.

"What are you doing, Unghell?" she asked, standing there with hair as black as ebony with a touch of white near the roots, showing her age. Startling him, she entered the stables. The horses shuffled the hay. The smell of the animals became more pungent as the beasts stirred. "Where do you plan on going? You don't even know where to start looking," she said, as she walked toward him, her powder blue frock sweeping the hay behind her. Already knowing the boy's plan to leave, she grabbed a strap on the saddle bringing him to a firm stop. "He can be anywhere by now, and he would not want you out there risking everything looking for him." She looked up at him with her piercing brown eyes. She could always tell if they were lying about the mischief they had gotten into. "And does your father even know what you are up to?" She gave the strap a soft tug, hoping that hers was not the first voice of reason he had heard.

"It has been almost two months since he left to chase a fight that is not his to finish." His words grew louder as he spoke each one. "The great Lackshin could have ended himself with one swing of that sword. As children we heard so much about him in the stories men told, but he left war for his son to fight." Unghell turned to face Vera. He stood over six feet tall looking down at her. Wearing the closest thing he could find to make him look like a warrior, he had only used his sword in practice, and had never really been in a fight; unless you count the fights he and Sanch got into with the other boys over Sanch not having a father. He could have easily wrenched the strap free of her hands, but he would dare not. He stood strong and at her mercy.

"Quiet," Vera said, looking around to ensure that they were alone. "Do you want everyone to hear you? He entrusted you with his secrets. Do not forget that." She pulled hard on the strap. "I like it much less than you do. It has been over two months today," she said with tears welling in her eyes. "No matter what you or I like or dislike, it is his fight to end. I did not wish this for him. He was not ready to leave, but his nightmares were coming more often. He was not getting more than three hours or so of sleep a night, and that was a good night for him. Do you not think I wished he had taken you with him? His most trusted friend?" She stroked his firm but still boyish face. He was much taller than Sanch was but only a year and a half older.

"There have been talks of dragons in the sky since stories of Lackshin and his fight to rid the world of the threat of Xyles. Before then there had been no dragons seen for hundreds of years. And those were the last talks of dragons," he said trying to convince her that his diction to follow Sanch was just.

"Shallin," Vera whispered under her breath knowing of the dragon he spoke of.

"All of which I am sure were nothing more than rumors anyway. Stories drunken men told women, children, and anyone who would listen." He tried to convince himself that these stories were nothing more than just that, stories. "Now battles are breaking out all over, but we have yet to hear a word from Sanch. Tell me why no one here has been sent out after him? I am his best friend, his brother." He beat on his chest making Vera jump ever so slightly. "And I can no longer sit by hoping he is stay alive out there. As for the secret of who he is, I will keep that one. Him being Sanch Allen, no one will hear that from me." Unghell firmly pulled the strap from her hand.

"I am not your mother, but just as Sanch is like a brother to you, you are like a son to me, Unghell." Vera put her hand softly on his shoulder. "When we had nothing, you and your father made us family and said nothing of who we were to anyone." She tried to discourage him from following after Sanch.

"He will not listen, my dear," a deep voice filled the stable. "I spent our entire hunt yesterday trying to talk him out of going after his brother." A figure stood at the entrance of the barn. "Boy, I told you if you insisted on doing this to be gone before she noticed you were missing." Unghell's father opened the barn door wider. The morning sun illuminated the dust around them. There was no longer a need to be quiet. The possibility of leaving without notice was now gone.

"So, you knew of his plans to slip away as Sanch did?" The anger in Vera's voice consumed the room. "Do either of you remember how upset I was when Sanch left without a word, without as much as a goodbye?" Her voice cracked as she spoke. "Me, waiting for him to return that entire week thinking maybe, just maybe he needed a little time away to think as he had done several times before. Now here you both are, doing the same thing." She turned to face Tris. "You knew of what he was planning and said nothing to me." Her eyes narrowed. "You two take me for just a woman, a mother, and nothing more?" She eyed Unghell's sword that leaned on the wall. "Did you both forget who showed Sanch what he could do with a sword before you took him as a son?" She glared at Tris. "And you at first not wanting him as a brother nor me as a mother. I, myself, wanted to ride out after my boy. But I did not. I stayed here knowing firsthand what is out there waiting for him."

"Yes," Unghell replied. "You stay here because your fight has ended. Sanch's has just begun, and my place is fighting beside him. Wherever he finds this fight, and whomever he finds this fight against, is where I should be. The Gods only know whom he has out there looking out for him. I can no longer ask that question. I can no longer wait for an answer that is not coming. Please understand, I can no longer stay here with him alone out there." Unghell placed the saddle on his horse. "No, I did not want him as a brother, but now that is exactly who he is. And what kind of big brother would I be if I did not look out for him?"

Vera picked up Unghell's lonely sword. You could hear a leaf drop when she did that. Her temper was unmatched and her plans with the sword were anyone's guess. Unghell could very easily find himself with a horse needing to be put in the ground.

"What are you going to do with that sword, my love?" Tris asked Vera nervously.

She walked over to her Unghell. "We have no right keeping you from your duty to your brother." She handed him the sword, fighting back tears.

"Thank you, mother." Unghell leaned down and kissed her on top of her head. The rowdy hairs tickled his nose. A lone tear crept down her face. She had tried to be a mother to him.

Hearing his son call her mother brought a smile to Tris' face. When she and Sanch first arrived, she became like a mother to Unghell even with a young son of her own that needed a lot of attention. When Sanch had food, so did Unghell. With Unghell's words, they were now truly a family.

Tris walked over and placed his arms around Vera's waist. He could feel her shivering at the thought of both the boys out there in a world of death and unfairness. She let another tear escape the fortress of her eyes.

"So, we all agree now that he should go find his brother," Tris announced as he held her close.

"We do all agree," Vera replied as she squeezed his hand mercilessly.

Now with help from his mother and father, Unghell prepared for his journey—to where exactly, he was not sure. They had traveled outside their village into nearby towns to do business with their father, but never alone. This would be his first time venturing out on his own without either his father or Sanch at his side. Being Sanch's big brother was a lot of work. Sanch on the other hand, would always set off on his own whenever he felt he did not belong around Unghell or any of the other kids, which was very often. Like his big brother, he was tasked with finding him and bringing him home.

After spending entire days looking for Sanch, Unghell would go home tired, frustrated and hungry, just to find Sanch on his second serving of supper looking up at him as to say, "Where have you been?" To punish Sanch, they would have him spend extra time with his sword. Of course, it was Unghell out there with him practicing for those extra hours of punishment.

"Now that we have a moment alone, I have a few things to tell you that will be of help out there." With Vera preparing food, Tris took that time to quickly speak with Unghell. He placed his hand on his boy's shoulder and stepped in close. "Sanch would have most likely headed to a town North of Har."

"You always told us never to go there," Unghell quickly replied. He looked nervously at his father.

"I know, and for good reason," his father said, firmly squeezing his shoulder. "That town is greatly occupied by Sillack's men. It is dangerous, especially for Sanch, and now for you since you wish to follow your brother. There is a place you may be able to find a friend. There is a tavern in the town owned by a man that fought alongside Lackshin in the war against the Xyles. Hopefully, your brother was able to find this man. If Sanch did find this man, he would have helped him. He will also be able to help you, and tell you how to find Sanch, and also how to stay out of the way of Sillack's men while doing so." He looked around making sure they were still alone.

"How shall I know this man who you speak of?" Unghell asked. "Should I not just stay to myself the best that I can?" He scratched the bit of hair that was sprouting from his cheeks.

"You are going to need help finding your brother. After two months, he truly could be anywhere by now." Tris tightened his grip on his son's arm. He did not want him leaving, nor did he think it wise, but he knew there was no stopping him. Unghell's mind was made up. All he could do at this point was do his best to give him a fighting chance. "This man will be missing part of his earlobe. A scar he got when a Xyle had gotten too close."

"Do I then tell him who I am?" Unghell asked, his heart beating rapidly. He doubted his decision to leave the safety of his home. He wanted to go soon before his courage took its leave. He had been so sure of himself before Vera surprised him. The words of Sanch's mother, his mother, were now echoing in his head like a bird's song outside an open window.

"No!" Tris replied. "Telling him who you are will do nothing for you. Anyone can walk in and claim to be another man. Poison can call itself drink, but only show itself when its victim exits this world. You will have to prove to him you are my lad." He pulled Unghell's dagger from the sheath on his hip. "The words on the handle will show him who you are." He pointed at the etching on the handle. "This will pay for your food, room, and the information that you will need."

"Family above all else," Unghell read aloud. He had never noticed the etching before. "What does it mean?" He ran his finger across the words.

"It means the words are true for you and your bother, and you truly belong at his side," Tris said proudly, stepping back to take a good look at his son of barely nineteen. Unghell wore a mat black leather vest over a dark gray top. His boots came midway up his calf. He was not a knight as his father had been, so he did not have armor. But even if he had armor, it would not have been wise to ride out in it with Sillack's men scattered everywhere looking for anyone that may look like they would be trouble for their master. He would currently attract more attention than would be good if he were to be found dressed as a knight from a different kingdom. Now that word of The Son of Lackshin had been heard, there had been movement all over that land. Lords have been sending their knights out to see if these rumors were of any merit.

The years after Lackshin was killed and Sillack stood unopposed, the first thing he did was dispose of any Lackshin loyalists. More and more lords backed away to their lands and behind their walls, leaving those that had no walls to hide behind to fend for themselves. The Allens, Archers, and Skeritts simply did not care after Lackshin died.

When the son of Isaac took up arms to fight, only then did the other lords send men of their own to fight at Lackshin's side. It wasn't just those three noble families, but others that were bound by words to help. The Parsons sent men to assist with the fight. The Nores sent their great mounted force to show that they were not cowardly people and could fight along with other great families.

The people of Tegra, after their show of betrayal to the Allens and Archers, were not trusted to fight beside the other families. Therefore, they were left to fight alone and were quickly pushed back to their lands. Only some that held the words spoken as their honor-bound duty stayed and fought where they could and endured the shame their people brought upon themselves.

"I will make you proud, father." Unghell looked up and over his father's left shoulder. "And I will bring my brother back, mother." The word "mother" flowed from his mouth like an object freed from his throat. Now breathed easier.

Tris turned around to see his woman. Her hair was pulled back and anchored with a long thin dagger as she often did when she would prepare food for him and his sons. She would never say where she obtained such a thing. No matter how many times she was asked how she came into possession of it, the story always changed. Many came to know that she was toying with them with every story she told. The boys could not get enough of the tales. Tris hoped that they would do a better job in actual war than when they played war as children. Unfortunately, this was a war of friends fighting friends, and brothers killing brothers. The thought stuck in his chest like cold steel. He swallowed his thoughts deeply. They both walked over to her, standing high and enduring her stares of disapproval. She held a well-rapped bundle of cloth. In it, she packed loaves of bread, wedges of cheese, apples, and dried salted beef. She brought him three skins of water, and one of wine for his travel.

Vera packed it all in the leather bags that hung from his steed. They covered Unghell with a heavy hooded cloak that hid his sword as well as the dagger that would surely give him away. Anyone that would have knowledge of the old family's symbols that they wore would spot him for sure. Unghell said his goodbyes while fighting back the tears he felt pool in his eyes. Vera pulled him down, as she always did and kissed his forehead. Every other time, he was reluctant, but not this time. This time he welcomed the affection she gave him. He wanted and needed that kiss from her.

"Be safe out there, son," she whispered, still holding him in an awkward position. "Bring him home to us." She kissed him once again.

Warm tears fell onto his forehead. Here she was again crying for another son leaving to face only the gods knew. Tris looked up at his son mounted high on his horse. The proud father held a lump in his throat as he gave a nod of approval. Unghell returned the nod, turned his horse around, and started a slow trot. He dared not look back in fear that the look on his mother's face would make it impossible to fight back his own tears. Tris held Vera as they watched until their son was out of sight.

CHAPTER NINE

Alshin sat atop his horse infuriated. His two first generals lay dead with their chest leaking life. Killed by a woman and a young boy, they both openly threatened his life in front of his men. Alshin angrily raised his hand and signaled to his men to prepare to move forward. His men were still reacting to the two dead brothers in arms. The second man still twitched. The first man smelled of waste from soiling himself when the arrow ripped through his armor.

Alshin called back to his rear flank. "Turn and ready yourselves to protect our rear from that boy, Sanch!" His horse shuffled around. "Archers!" he shouted. "Ready your bows!" His words brought his army to life. At first, the men believed this would be a simple invasion with little to no opposition to speak—until they saw the force that awaited them.

Sanch knew he needed to still the movement of this army to give Dagger and the Elarguns a chance to join the fight.

"I'm glad to see that you did not forget me," Sanch mocked Alshin. He drew his sword and the others followed suit. Bethany drew her bow, Lisha her sword, and Menis one twin axe. As Sanch continued to distract Alshin and his men, Deem and his fellow Elarguns had already surrounded Alshin's army, ready and waiting for the right time to attack.

Ralyn noticed the movement of Alshin's men and ordered his men to hold their position. He sensed that his men were a little anxious. Thrant gave the same order as he rode his horse through his ranks. He knew they had an advantage.

Kess and the other archers were perched on the wall. She made her way across the wall giving her archers the order to keep arrows notched and ready. Their plans to fold that army started with Kess and her archers.

"Take out the middle ranks and that will cut off their advance and most of all, their retreat. Make sure to give Sanch and the others as much cover as you can. They are few in numbers and will need all the help we can give them. Do not forget your sisters are out there and need our help to make it home safe."

The archers had their orders. They sat notched and ready. It was still dark out, and the moonlight faded in and out as the clouds moved. The sun was still some time away. Kess hoped for the sun to rise hours early. A night battle would make it more difficult for their untested army. These were mostly fighting men, but many had never fought at each other's side. Their army had heart but no rhythm. Kess lit her arrow and gave the order not to release arrows until hers was overhead. Her flaming arrow climbed like the hush before a storm. The sound of crackling filled the air and the sheer brightness of it drew the attention of Alshin's already uneasy men. When the arrow was overhead, they heard the snap of bows as if only one was released. It has begun the first of many battles to come.

Sanch heard the deep ping that the strings made, and motioned Lisha and the others to follow him. As they made their way down the hillside, the arrow Kess shot into the sky started its descent. It revealed the shower of arrows that rained down on Alshin and his army. For some of Alshin's men, it was too late to do anything. They tried to move, but where could they go? They were in a tight formation that did not give them many options.

"Shields, shields!" Alshin shouted. "Shields up, you fools!" Those of the men that carried shields and were able to put them up in time were spared from the barrage of arrows. The others weren't as lucky. They took arrows to the chest, face, shoulders, and legs. One man had an arrow that found its home in his eye socket. He walked around confused, bumping into the other men that were moving out of his way. Another man was pinned to the shield of the man behind him. One man cried out in pain. The other men looked on confused until they noticed that both his feet were pinned to the ground.

Just as Kess had planned, the middle ranks were now useless from all the confusion. The barrage made it hard for them to make an advance, as well as cut them off from falling back.

Now vexed, Alshin shouted to his men to move forward. He knew if he waited any longer the archers would pick them off one by one until none remained.

Kess and the archers continued their rain of arrows. Ralyn and Thrant's men prepared their shield wall for Alshin's attack. To their rear, the men had Sanch and the others to contend with. Riding hard, they quickly closed in on the rear flank. Only a small, mounted force rode with Sanch, but it was a force to be reckoned with just the same. One by one, the men were being killed. One soldier had his throat opened from a dagger that appeared from thin air. Another had the tendon on the back of his feet cut sending him down into the dirt. In the confusion, some of the men swung their swords around wildly at things they could not see. A man got his head lopped clean off with a blind swing of an axe. All the chaos from the carnage caused Alshin to spin his warhorse around clumsily to see what was going on at the rear.

Deem and his men started to strike, making waste of Alshin's men cutting a path for Sanch, Lisha, Menis, and Bethany, and the others to ride through. This battle would surely be the start of the war between Sanch and Sillack, and a deadly war it would become.

With Sanch leading the charge, the mighty four now showed themselves in battle. To prepare for the attack coming from the rear, Alshin's men turned to fight but being under attack by an invisible force made that difficult. At full gallop, the four young warriors hit the line like a stampede of bulls. The men who were able to turn to face Sanch's attack were no match for him, Lisha, Bethany, and Menis. They cut them down with little trouble, but they still had an army to push through before reaching the village gates. In an instant, the battle became more intense. Menis, Sanch, and Lisha had no issue killing anyone that stood in their way.

Bethany, on the other hand, had never taken a life or faced anyone in battle. Her sessions with Kess and the village's man-at-arms taught her how to swing a sword, but not how to take a life. Bethany, unlike the others, killed no one, just incapacitated them. With the intensity of the battle growing, her leaving men alive on the battlefield was not wise. Deem and the other Elarguns were pulling men from their mounts by a force they could not see.

The four young warriors made their way to Deem and his men in the center of the rear battalion where the Elarguns were wreaking havoc on Alshin's men. Some of the warhorses started to buck and seemed to become wild. A horse kicked one of the men so hard that it crushed his breastplate knocking him down leaving him lying there trying to suck in air. Deem and his men were able to acquire the horses of the men they killed. Sanch noticed the horses were now under control, so he ordered everyone to regroup on his position. Bethany, Lisha, Menis, Sanch, and twenty-nine horses cut an exit path through what was left of the men. Ralyn saw what was taking place and thought it was time to order his attack on Alshin's army that had already been closing in on the village gates. Thrant noticed the same and gave his men the same order and together they started their offense. Swords were drawn and spears lowered, horses reared, and battle cries rang out on both sides. The sounds of gallops thundered through air.

Kess kept the shower of arrows coming as she and her archers joined in battle cries. Thrant and Ralyn did not attack Alshin forces head-on; they came in on an angle to their right and their left. Being outnumbered three to one, a frontal assault would leave Alshin with the advantage. By doing this, they forced Alshin's army to separate in order to defend themselves on both sides. On the other side of the village gate, Evian and his force could hear all that was going on. Evian kept his men ready to spring into action at a moment's notice. He kept his hand gripped firmly around the handle of his sword and waited for that order to attack. The leather on his handle was cold at first but as he waited the heat from his hand changed that. Sanch, seeing Ralyn and Thrant closing in, recharged his desire to get back into the fight.

With what looked like rider-less horses next to them, Bethany, Lisha, Menis, and Sanch mounted a second attack on an already badly battered rear flank. With the rest of the army busy defending against a frontal assault, there was little chance for reinforcements. Even with reinforcement, Sanch and the others would still be outnumbered.

"I think it's time we rejoin this fight. We can't let Thrant and your father have all the fun, Bethany," Sanch said as he tried to shake his sword dry.

"Yes, this is exhilarating!" Bethany said.

"Deem I think it's time for you and your men to let yourselves be known. When we get closer this time, show yourselves. Elarguns appearing on horseback should get a reaction from them."

Menis looked over at Bethany. It was as if she could not stay still. She had a look of thrill on her face.

"Bethany, are you ok?" asked Menis. "It seems as if you can no longer stay still on your horse."

"No, I can't! We are going back in are we not? They're going to need us."

Seeing Bethany's enthusiasm, Sanch smiled and gave the order to attack. Again, they were back at full gallop. Alshin's army was now being attacked both from their front as well as their rear. Even though Alshin had them outnumbered three to one, they were taking a beating.

Just as Sanch and his small force collided with Alshin's rear flank, Deem and his men materialized right before their eyes; the horses now had riders. The small Elargun force had revealed themselves.

"Is that Elarguns?" shouted Ralyn. "I thought they were no more. Were they not all finished at the hands of the Xyles?"

"I do not know my lord. I have not seen nor heard of the Elarguns since the final battle against Sillack," replied one of the older of Ralyn's men who looked as if he had seen many a battle. His long gray beard blew in the wind as he swung his morning star.

"His father did it before him, now he has done it as well. Sanch has made them our allies once again. He is truly the Son of Lackshin."

Thrant, on Alshin's left flank, shouted, "Sanch has done it. He brought help!"

His force joined in with a battle cry as they ran through the left flank. Thrant remembered once again how it was to be in the heat of battle. With his brother's sword in hand, his old armor was dampened by the men who tried to stand in his way. Still outnumbered three to one, they advanced through Alshin's men.

Oddly, Sanch and the others seemed to be having the time of their lives. No longer on horseback, the four young heroes continued to cut a path through a greater force than their own. Their skills were unmatched. In the thick of battle, Sanch noticed Bethany was badly injuring the men but not killing them.

"Nice going with that stick, but does that sword you carry not dislodge from its sheath?" Sanch shouted to Bethany. "You plan not to stain such a willing blade? It cries out for a drink. I can hear it from here."

"Yes, cousin, give it a drink." Lisha laughed as she kicked a man loose from her blade.

"Leave her be!" shouted Menis. "She will have her time, and a time I feel it will be." Menis cleaved a man's head from his shoulders sending it flying in Sanch's direction.

Lisha and Sanch looked at one another and could not help but laugh.

"Thank you, Menis. I am not quite ready to detach a man from his life."

"Sanch!" Lisha shouted. "We are still outnumbered. It seems like for everyone we cut down, two takes his place."

"Just a little longer my friend. Help is near," Deem reassured the others.

Unlike Deem and his men, Sanch and the others could not hear the Elargun force closing in behind them. For now, Deem and his men keep fighting strong, and in a way never seen by those who opposed them. It was almost as they were performing a dance as well as using the men's weapons against them. With his two short swords in hand, Deem faced off with three of Alshin's men. They were confident that they had the advantage, but they were going to see what the prince of the Elargun's could do.

It was like a well-choreographed dance; he did not move, but flowed with little to no exertion. The first man that made his move was quickly introduced to the hilt of his sword. He didn't kill him but made him very uncomfortable and continued to the other two. They were not as lucky as the first man was. One was impaled with Deem's armor-tipped tail and the other no longer had the burden of carrying the weight of his head. Standing there slightly spent, Deem looked to Sanch, who was not far away. He gave Deem a nod showing his appreciation for such a display of swordsmanship.

Sanch now decided that he was going to cut his way to Shallin as well as meet with Alshin and his axe. A soldier with his mindset on glory wanted to be the one to kill the Son of Lackshin. The large man ran up to Sanch with a huge broadsword over his head. The impact of the two swords when they met sent a shock that ran down Sanch's arm. Sanch pushed the long sword off to his left throwing the large man off balance and twisted himself free of the big man's attack. The man caught himself and came around with a wild swing almost catching Sanch's midsection. It was so close that Sanch felt a breeze rush into the opening that the huge man's sword cut into his shirt. Smaller and much quicker, Sanch used that to his advantage. He knew he could not take direct strikes for too long. It was like a hammer every time his sword came down onto Sanch's. It had to end soon if Sanch was ever to make it to Alshin. He figured if he bested Alshin, his men would most likely turn and run and that would bring this battle to a much-desired end and could lessen the chances of more lives being lost on their side.

Sanch prepared himself to take on another heavy blow from the beast of a man and his ridiculously large sword.

As the five-foot-eight boy stood ready, Lisha could only look on helplessly. The man let out a grunt when Sanch stepped into his swing letting it come down behind him. A splash rang out as the man's entrails spilled out from under his armor. Sanch noticed that every time this man raised his sword over his head it revealed an opening in his armor rendering his soft parts unprotected. Sanch regained himself and once again started cutting a path through the men.

Alshin noticed Sanch was attempting to reach him and ordered men to converge on Sanch's position. Menis and the others were in no position to follow. They had their hands full with their own struggles and were cut off from Sanch. He'd barely get done with one fight before he was again heavy in battle and becoming overwhelmed. All at once, they felt a slight vibration moving their way. Sanch was doing well for himself and made little of the men bent on stopping him from his goal. As Sanch was defending from an attack, he stepped back against a rock that caused him to lose his footing and fell to the ground. The men saw that as their opportunity to finish off Sanch.

Lisha turned to see what was going on and started toward Sanch's position. "Menis!" Lisha shouted as she pointed to Sanch. "They mean to kill him!"

Lisha tried to reach Sanch, but Alshin's men fought to keep her from him. On his back fighting for his life, from the corner of his eye, Sanch saw a disc-like object flying towards him with what looked like a blue light accompanying it. All of a sudden, Deem heard a familiar battle cry fill the air like thunder. It was Dagger and the Elargun army.

The Elargun army was moving in fast, the ground vibrated beneath everyone. Dagger and his Elarguns rode creatures not of the surface world. They resembled horses at first glance, but after a closer look, all the differences were there. They had thicker and slightly longer necks. Their frames were more or less the same as regular horses except for hairy tails which were more like the tail of a dog or a wolf. Some would say the biggest difference would have to be how these creatures' eyes glowed a haunting white in the dark. In front riding hard was Sanch's silent friend with that strange bone-handled sword. He was eager to partake in the fighting. Sanch was still holding on to his fight and Lisha was still trying to make her way to his side.

Sanch's every attempt to get back to his feet was met with another man seeking glory. One man found himself on the point of

Sanch's sword. Sanch had to turn to his side and use his knee to push the man free. He barely had time to defend against the next attack that came down on him. To his right, the object was still closing in and the glow became larger and brighter. It was Silma. She had fight in her eyes and a sword in her hand. Seeing her put a smile on Sanch's worried face as he gave the fight all he had. He only had to hold on just a little longer; his angel was on her way.

As Silma was flying under a disk of some kind, she reached down and slightly grazed her hand across the shoulder of one of Alshin's men rendering him unconscious, giving her the strength to do what needed to be done. One of the men finally gained the edge, pinning Sanch's hand under his boot before coming down with the fatal blow.

"SANCH!" Bethany's voice echoed across the battlefield.

This was to be it for The Son of Lackshin. As the soldier's sword cut through the air, they all looked on helplessly. In a flash of light, the blow came down. Lisha, Menis, the Elarguns, and all of Alshin's men, covered their eyes from the blinding flare. Kess and the archers on the wall could see what looked like an explosion from where Bethany, Sanch, and the others were last seen fighting.

Is that what it looks like when a hero is killed? Menis thought as his sight slowly returned to focus.

When the light diminished, in the mix of it stood a human-sized Silma holding a sword and a shield. On the end of Silma's sword was the man that seconds ago had glory in his eyes. Now he hung impaled on the sword of a Sprite.

"Silma, you're big," Sanch said.

"Yes, it's a little thing I do," Silma replied.

"Is Guardian with you?" Sanch asked.

"Who do you think threw up this shield? Now, excuse me while I join this fight. Oh, and I have it from here if you want to take a minute or two down there," Silma said.

Sanch did just that and lay back down on the damp grass. He took a minute he so well needed.

Leading the charge of the Elargun army was Guardian, planning to cut a path through to Sanch and his traveling companions. Alshin's rear flank saw the approaching forces and tried to form back into their ranks and defend against the Elargun army. Bethany, Lisha, and Menis saw Silma standing over Sanch cutting away at the men that still were converging on him. She gave quick deaths to all that ventured too close. They could not believe what they were seeing. Silma moved gracefully in a blue haze.

Now that Sanch was in Silma's care, the others concentrated their efforts on keeping the army unprepared for the approaching Dagger. Those three, along with the small force of the Elarguns that traveled with Deem were already with them. They made it hard for the rear flank to get back into formation. Alshin turned to see his rear flanks about to be overrun.

"To the rear!" Alshin pointed with his axe ordering his reserves to reinforce the rear.

"Sanch, are you going to rejoin the fight?" Silma asked as she slowly returned to her normal size.

"Silma, you've shrunk." Sanch returned to his feet.

"Did you think I was going to stay that way?" Silma handed Sanch his shield.

"What's this?" Sanch asked as he examined the shield. "What is this made of?" It seemed almost weightless in his hand. "Can it stop a powerful blow?"

"There is only one way to find out," Silma said as she stepped aside and revealed Sanch to a powerful downswing from a large and hairy man.

Sanch covered himself with the shield, successfully blocking the powerful hit, answering his inquiry about the object in question.

"Silma, did you save me just to have me killed?" Sanch shouted.

"You are a big boy. You will be fine," Silma replied, taking flight.

Guardian was still plowing his way through, destroying anyone that opposed him and his blades. The Elarguns hit Alshin's rear line like a moving wall. They were no match for Dagger and his men. A soldier with a long spear tried to hold his ground against Guardian finding out the hard way how bad of a decision that had been. Guardian deflected the spear with his bone-handled sword. He then ran it down the length of the spear, cutting the man almost in half, leaving both his arms free from his body while still holding firm to the shaft of the spear.

"Deem!" shouted Dagger, appearing with Deem's ride.

"I see you brought my transportation, brother, and not a moment too soon."

Deem released the beast to find its way to its master. It trampled the men in its way and left destruction in its wake. Deem grabbed the reign and vaulted himself onto the saddle.

When Lisha saw Deem on this creature, she found that he looked more comfortable than he or the others looked on horseback. The other Elarguns greeted their brothers, ready to join the fight. These powerful animals maneuvered gracefully yet commanded great power under their hooves when they galloped. Still outnumbered even with the Elargun army joining them, the power of the creatures and their riders turned the tide. Alshin saw this and commanded his reserves to move in and directly attack the Elargun army as he pushed forward trying to overwhelm the force keeping him from the gates.

Sanch regained his momentum and continued on his way to reclaim his father's sword and make his long-awaited date with Alshin.

"Now that we have the chance, we should finish this battle once and for all!" Ralyn shouted to Thrant.

"Agreed!" Thrant said. "This needs to end, and soon! They are getting too close to the walls!"

"I know how to bring an end to this. To kill a snake, the head must be removed, and the body will wiggle to a stop." Thrant rode off in the direction of Alshin.

Kess shouted to Thrant. After Thrant did not slow his mare, she shouted to archers atop the wall. "Archers clear his path!" Kess pointed to Thrant with the arrow she held in her hand.

She and the others rained down a barrage of arrows on the line of men that thought they would try to block Thrant's path. Following Thrant was a handful of his men attending to Alshin's men that were filling in the path that Kess was making. Both Sanch and Thrant were converging on the same destination. It didn't matter who got there first; they both had the same intentions. One of them would bring this to an end by removing the snake's head. As Thrant rode into the thick of it, Ralyn kept his force in position along with Thrant's men. They kept the frontline from advancing.

The fighting became fiercer now that the enemies of Sanch knew this was not as easy a fight as they thought it would be. They did not think they would find an army waiting for them in a village that was said to house no warriors. To get there and not find the boy or his father's sword in the village, but to have the boy show up behind them outside the protection of the wall was not expected. They now knew that Sanch was not a coward. He would not hide behind walls or its people; he would meet them in open battle. He would face them head-on and fight them hand to hand, matching them sword to sword, one by one until he got the ones he sought. They came to this village and found two of its heroes, and the men and women that followed them into battle. These men and women would willingly give their lives to protect their village from Sillack. Now, with the Elarguns, their chances of winning the battle had just gotten better.

CHAPTER TEN

Sanch and his men closed in on Alshin's position. Alshin noticed his old commander as he rode in, and a smirk crossed his face.

"Cut him off that horse!" Alshin shouted as he wrenched his axe free from the skull of one of Thrant's men. His men tried to make Thrant's ride more difficult, but Thrant, being the warrior that he had been, made little work of the men that came to stop him.

Sanch was still trying to remove Shallin from the man's chest it was buried in. Lisha, Bethany, and Menis were not too far behind Sanch, but still had their battles to fight along the way. Guardian had nothing in mind other than making it to Sanch's side where he felt he belonged. His strange impulse to protect Sanch was still a mystery to all of them.

Silma pelted the enemy with a barrage of arrows of light, throwing men off their horses. Her attack was small, but powerful. For the first time, these young warriors saw what a real war was like, and they held themselves well.

Sanch's journey to his father's sword seemed more challenging than he had anticipated. Several of Alshin's men attempted to unsheathe Shallin from the warrior's chest before Sanch could retrieve her, but none were successful. One of the men who tried to pull the sword free had his hand instantly freeze all the way to his elbow. He shattered like glass; only a jagged stump remained. That man was known for his coldness on the battlefield, and brutality to women and children during village raids. He would have mothers watch as he killed their children and would make men witness as he took their wives and daughters. Another man grabbed hold of Shallin and was consumed by flames leaving nothing but ash. He was famous for setting villages on fire and burning people at the stake just for the joy of hearing them scream. After one person was dead and no longer screaming, he ordered men to put another on the fire as he drank ale and laughed wickedly.

Sanch continued to push forward, killing man after man trying to make it to Shallin. Suddenly Sanch noticed Thrant galloping through on his way to Alshin, sword in hand, ready to engage.

"Change of plans, Lisha!" Sanch shouted. "Look!" He pointed his sword to Thrant.

"What is he doing?" Lisha asked.

"I do not know, but we need to get there first!" Sanch said.

"That is going to be hard to do," Menis chimed in. "Thrant is on horseback, and we are on foot."

"Then we need to hurry!" Bethany said.

"Sanch, are you not going to get Shallin?" Menis asked.

"Shallin will be there when I go for her. Besides, they look to be having fun trying to remove her from that poor man's chest," Sanch replied, a smirk dancing across his face.

Lisha had no problem joining in the charge. She spilled fluids of many that stood between her and her uncle. Alshin's men formed a wall between the four of them and where Thrant was to meet Alshin. Both were still riding full speed at one another with weapons drawn, shield's up. The thunder of Alshin's warhorse gave the battlefield its heartbeat. Grass and dirt churned up behind him sending earth flying. The sound of the impact of steel against a wooded shield rang out. Alshin came down with such a swing with his axe that it nearly split Thrant's shield in half. It almost knocked them both off their horses sending the beasts into a tangle.

"What do you think you're going to accomplish here, old man?" Alshin asked Thrant, pulling his axe free. "Are you tired of living?" Alshin pulled the heavy beast around for another assault on Thrant.

"I plan to end this thing so we can all go home, and to do that, you need to die." Thrant pulled on the beast's reins and faced Alshin.

Sanch dawned a horrified look wanting nothing more than to be in Thrant's place. He was fighting hard, but for every man he took down, it seemed like two would take his place.

"Lisha, can you get through?" Sanch asked.

"I am getting the feeling they do not wish us to get through to Thrant. These men are getting on my nerves," Bethany said as she threw a man twice her size to the ground and then proceeded to step on his chest and face.

Alshin was mounted on his dark brown horse. The horse's coat had a glass-like sheen. It was no longer night. Dawn had come and they had been fighting for hours. Thrant's sword was red from the men he had faced that night.

"What is it that you think you are going to accomplish here, old friend? If you think you are going to be the man to finish this, you may want to turn that animal around and take your leave from this battle."

"We will see, Alshin," Thrant replied as he prepared to launch another attack.

Thrant raised his sword and galloped toward Alshin. His sword grazed off Alshin's shield. Alshin countered with another swing of his axe that again struck Thrant's shield. This time, the sheer force of it knocked Thrant off his horse. He quickly rolled to avoid the hooves of Alshin's great beast and sprung swiftly to his feet. Now, without his horse, Thrant dug in, bracing himself. When the trusted horse noticed her rider was no longer with her, she turned to retrieve Thrant, but it was too late.

Alshin had already started his charge on Thrant. With his axe high over his head, he came down with the full strength of it. Thrant braced himself. Everyone around saw the sparks as the axe struck the mettle straps that held Thrant's shield together. It was like lightning on a clear day. Thrant ducked under his shield letting Alshin pass him. Taking his sword, he cut Alshin's saddle straps with precision, nicking the warhorse and sending the beast into a frenzy. Thrant did this and never once lost his footing. Alshin did not get far before him, and his saddle came free from his horse dumping him and his shield onto the ground. He barely held on to his axe as he tumbled in the mud. Thrant rushed to where Alshin landed and came down full thrust with his sword in hopes to land a fatal blow, but his sword was met by Alshin's axe. Alshin put his feet against Thrant's chest and pushed him away, giving himself time to scramble to his shield and stumble to his feet. Thrant put his shield up and waved at his horse. That brought her to a full stop.

"I see you have moved up in the world. Sillack gave you my old rank. I remember the first time I saw you. You were just a foot soldier desperately trying to please your commander." Thrant taunted Alshin.

"Yes, but that commander turned out to be a traitor, and now instead of pleasing him, I plan to kill him." Alshin came down with his mighty axe.

Thrant countered and blocked the blow with his shield that sent splinters flying. Using what was left of his badly beaten shield, he pushed Alshin back and when there was an opening in Alshin's defenses, Thrant thrust his sword forward. Alshin brought his shield down and with the edge of his shield deflected Thrant's sword. Alshin replied with his axe down at Thrant's head. Thrant barely avoided what would have been a fatal strike. When the axe fell short, Thrant took the opportunity and swung in with his shield hitting Alshin in the face, throwing him off balance. Thrant remained on the offensive and pounded him back with swing after swing with his sword.

"That is not good!" Sanch shouted back to the others. "He is being led!"

"But he is winning," Bethany said.

"No, he is right," Lisha agreed with Sanch. "How long is Alshin going to lead him? We need to get in there now!"

As the four continued to cut their way to Thrant, Guardian fought his way to Sanch. The strange creature he rode plowed down and trampled the men that stood between him and Sanch. On his hip was the unusual blade he unleashed inside the mountain—a blade that looked to be older than Shallin. Guardian desperately tried to get to not only Sanch, but also Thrant.

Thrant fought feverishly as he tried to end it all. *The snake's head needed to be taken off*, Thrant thought to himself as he hacked away at Alshin with a barrage of attacks. Left swing, right swing.

Thrust, thrust, crash, crash! Thrant made every swing count. Now, it was Alshin's shield those shards of wood flew from. Thrant saw an opening and made a move that looked like it would do what he intended. Thrant hooked his sword under the blade of Alshin's axe and used his shield to give himself an advantage.

Menis, Lisha, and Bethany watched and felt a small sense of relief, what happened next was brutal. As Thrant swung around to land the blow that was to end this battle, Alshin pulled a dagger placed strategically behind his shield and victory was his. Alshin plunged upward, violently picking Thrant up off the ground. Alshin slowly lowered Thrant to his knees. As Thrant slumped down, it was as if the battle stopped, and the air thickened.

Sanch's face lost all emotion. Bethany fell to her knees. Menis ended the man in front of him with his bare hands. Lisha's body filled with rage. Her anger brought on a strong wind blowing through, and when it stopped, so did the heart of many of Alshin's men. Moving in an eerie silence, the four young warriors destroyed the wall of men that stood between them and Alshin.

"Thrant did not kill Alshin, but in his defeat, he had ended this battle," Kess whispered on the village walls as her eyes filled with tears of anger and loss. "Prepare your arrows, sisters, they will soon be needed!" Kess shouted with a small but clear crack in her voice.

Ralyn, leading his force on the other side of Alshin's army, saw the whole thing. He was helpless to do anything to help his old friend. When Thrant's men saw him fall, they became enraged. Even though they were outnumbered, they found motivation and made Alshin's men pay for his action. An infuriated Ralyn signaled Kess to send a downpour of arrows as soon as the enemy was in range.

"Fall back!" Ralyn shouted. "Move back to the walls! There are too many of them!" He let the enemy chase him and his men into the archer's range.

"Fire!" Kess shouted. One by one the men were removed cleanly off their horses. The men riding out front tried to pull back, but the foot soldiers following closely behind made that difficult. Some on horseback trampled over their men to escape the arrows.

Now, with these men falling over one another, Ralyn could redirect some of his men to assist Thrant's forces in what had become a fiercer battle. From his position, Alshin continued giving his men orders as he engaged the men who followed Thrant in. With not very many men remaining between him and Sanch, he shouted for a horse.

With Sanch leading the charge, the horse was not going to make it in time to make a difference. Sanch moved cold and swift toward Alshin. The four still moving in silence made little work of the men in their path. Alshin saw that Sanch would soon be on him. He prepared for the attack. Following close behind Sanch, Lisha punished the men that still thought they could stop her. When she saw that Sanch would make it to Alshin before her, Lisha broke the silence.

"Sanch!" Lisha shouted.

Sanch looked at Lisha. Without words, Sanch knew just what she asked of him. Now he was in sword range of Alshin. He continued forward fast and cold. Menis looked on as he made his way to that same location and noticed that Sanch was not looking at Alshin nor engaging him. Sanch was only defending himself from him, and even when there was a chance to strike, he did not.

"Are you not going to fight me? Have you lost your nerve, boy?" Alshin lashed out at Sanch.

Sanch let out a cold sounding laugh, leaving those around him confused, sending a chill down their spines.

"Are you not here to fight? Is this not what you were waiting for? Here I am! Fight me! Or now that you've seen what I've done to the traitor, you no longer have the stomach for it?" Alshin ridiculed Sanch.

"No, I am not here to kill you, Alshin," Sanch replied.

"Then what are you doing here?"

"I am here to make sure you do not get away. Trust me when this is all over, you are going to wish I was the one you fought."

Now realizing who Lisha must be, and whom he just killed, Alshin knew she was not just some nosey little girl.

Closing in at an all-out sprint, Lisha did not miss a swing. She let Sanch know what side she was coming from. Lisha threw down her shield and shouted, "Sword!"

Sanch heard her and stepped back. He went down on one knee, placed his shield behind him at an angle, and held his sword up, handle first. Alshin braced himself, not knowing what to expect.

"He is all yours," Sanch said as he looked up with a smile that sent Alshin's insides cold.

When Sanch felt the impact on his shield and a tug on his sword, he stood up and let go of his sword. Lisha catapulted, flying gracefully through the air. She wielded both her and Sanch's sword. She came down with the weight of her father's revenge for his brother, and her anger from not getting the chance of knowing her uncle. The blow to Alshin's shield pushed him back, throwing him off balance. Lisha kept on with the bombardment of sword strikes on his shield, giving him no chance to retaliate. Alshin's men saw what was happening and started moving to protect their leader from Lisha's angry attack. Sanch saw this and shouted for the others to hurry to his position. He knew he could only hold the men off for a short while.

Ralyn ordered his men to follow him into the center of the army's ranks to disrupt their charge on Sanch and the others.

Thrant's men rushed to him and pulled him out of the way of danger. Thrant was not dead yet, but he was fading fast. The whole time he was saying the same thing over and over. Thrant repeated, "He has friends in the clouds, find the winged ones, they will join the fight. The Xyles are unleashed and need to be stopped. They followed his father they will follow Sanch."

Weakened, Thrant leaned back on his shield to rest and save his strength. Only armed with a shield, Sanch defended Lisha as best he could. Bethany was closer than Menis and arrived first in rare form. The men that were trying to keep her from Sanch and Lisha met great suffering at her beautiful hands.

After arriving, Bethany took her place at Sanch's side and assisted him in protecting her cousin. The battle between Lisha and Alshin became more intense. Alshin regained his footing and was now able to fight back with great skill. Lisha gracefully matched his every move, surprising him with her expertise.

"You are quite the young warrior. Too bad Thrant did not put up as good a fight as you. I see you last longer than him, but not by much." Alshin taunted Lisha.

Alshin then attacked with an aggressive swing of his axe. Instead of trying to avoid the blow, Lisha stepped in and blocked the axe with Sanch's sword. Lisha was able to place her sword against his right side and used the force of his axe as leverage to push off and cut his side deeply. He let out a deep cough.

Surprised that such a young girl could fight in such a way, Alshin had to ask, "Who are you and who taught you how to fight like this?" The life leaked from the gash in his side.

With a devious smile on her face, Lisha replied, "I am Lisha, daughter of Kanten, and that man you just injured and may even have killed was my uncle." Lisha proudly made it known to Alshin.

Close enough to hear Lisha, Sanch could not help but allow a smile to creep on his face.

"You are the daughter," Alshin said. "You are the daughter of Kanten?" He leaned back; the blade of her sword pressed to his side. He turned to look at her. "That explains your skills with a sword. Nonetheless, I cannot allow myself to be beaten by the likes of you." Alshin composed himself and prepared to make another attack.

"It's good that you feel that way. It would be no fun if you gave up now. And so that you know, the man dying over there is why you will soon be dead, too." Lisha pulled her sword free and swiftly moved back in with both swords swinging.

With Alshin's men still attempting to break through Sanch's shield, he and Bethany stayed them off the best they could.

"Bethany, all you are doing is slowing them down. It's time you stop them!" Sanch shouted.

"This is how I choose to do it, Sanch," Bethany replied.

"Well, I hope they show your cousin the same kindness, because I think they mean to kill her if they get past us."

Bethany glanced back and saw her cousin, Lisha, fighting. Not only for her life, but also for the lives of their people. Bethany holstered her staff on her back and drew her sword. She opened the next man that stepped in front of her. She was not going to let anyone make it past her and Sanch. Just then and not a moment too soon, Menis made it to Bethany and Sanch to find Bethany's sword drawn, covered in a thin pink mist. They were four once again, fighting for the same goal. This is why they set out the night before, made a journey through a mountain, and recruited the prince of the Elargun's and his army. Now if things were done right, it would only take one more life to end it all. Cut the head from the snake and bring this battle to an end.

CHAPTER ELEVEN

The moon was now a memory and all that remained was the sun in its place. There was no longer a cloud left in the sky, but there was a strong breeze blowing in from the east, bringing along with it some menacing-looking weather. Locked in battle with Alshin, Lisha showed no mercy, nor did she seem to tire. Alshin fought strong in spite of the ingress caused by Lisha. Her attacks never weakened, but he held his own. With every swing, Lisha hacked off chunk after chunk of Alshin's oak shield. He could not tell if this was just how skilled she was, or was brought on by what he did to her uncle? Here he was, a skilled and seasoned soldier, and even once a knight, being bested by a child.

Lisha continued to rain down abuse on Alshin's shield, which was on the same side as the wound she inflicted. Sanch defended himself with only a shield after surrendering his sword over to Lisha. He glanced over to see Menis's other axe still strapped to his back. Menis was almost in reach of Sanch, and Sanch could almost reach the axe. Sanch fought his way closer to Menis trying to get hold of it.

"Menis!" shouted Sanch. He held up his shield and his empty hand to show Menis he had no sword.

"Hey, Sanch," Menis replied. "Nice shield. Where did you get it?"

"Do you not notice something?" Sanch asked, as he blocked a sword strike. He kicked the man to the ground and used the sharp edge of the shield to sever the man's head from his body.

"Sanch why are you not using your—" Menis stopped before finishing his statement. As he drew his axe and threw it to Sanch he shouted, "All you had to do was ask!"

As the axe flew through the air, Alshin's men tried to prevent Sanch from caching it. Still, Sanch gave those men no choice but to pull back their attack or be liberated from their earthly form.

Sanch caught the axe in such a way that he used the momentum from Menis's throw to clear every man at arm's length. He could hear the battle between Lisha and Alshin rage on behind him. Alshin shouted curses and insults at Lisha and had his insults answered by her sword. Still emotionless, she was cold and detached and fought automatically. Her moves were without thought.

As Ralyn and his men closed in on Sanch's position, the village leader was able to get a better look at what was going on. He was able to better see the fight between his niece and the man who would see them all dead. Ralyn was in full gallop with sword in hand. A strong eastern breeze carried the scent of roses from a field on a hillside not too far away. He could see that Lisha had the advantage and could bring it all to an end with the simple strike of her sword.

"Finish it!" Ralyn shouted. "He is already dead, and you know it, Lisha. You can end this battle with the edge of your sword!" he added. "You just need to let him know what you already know!"

Lisha heard her uncle's faint shout in the distance. Lisha slowed and became aware of what she was there to do. It was time to stop cutting away at him and end him. She backed off, and dug her feet in, bracing herself. Alshin took this as she was tiring and saw it as an opportunity to attack. She used the weight of his advance against him and threw him off balance.

With both her sword and Sanch's, Lisha stopped for the first time since that fight between her and Alshin began. The look on her face said it all. She was cold and without feeling, her face gave no expression. Whatever feelings she may have had were not revealed or shown in her eyes. The strong winds pushed her jet-black hair straight back revealing her cold face. The dirt of the battlefield dulled her olive skin. The breeze suddenly increased, and her lips tightened as she corrected the grip on the swords. As if both took place at the same time, her lips relaxed, and the breeze stopped blowing.

Before her hair made it back down to her shoulder's, she was on her way to engage Alshin again. He attempted to defend himself, but she was too fast. He was able to get his axe over his head, but that was as far as he got with it. With Sanch's sword, she stopped the descent of his axe and with her own sword, did just as she was told. Lisha ended it. She looked up at Alshin for the first time through the fight. As she looked into his eye's she leaned in and placed her face against his, whispering softly into his ear, "You should thank me."

A confused look covered Alshin's face as the life flowed out of him, down her sword, and onto her hand.

"Yes, you should thank me for letting you live as long as I did. Because Sanch would have killed you quickly just so he could get to the next man. As for me, I wanted you to see that I could have killed you anytime I wanted. The great Alshin killed by me, a lowly girl. What would the world have to say about you? The songs they will sing about you?"

Lisha leaned back to look into his eyes once more and watched as the life left his face. Just before he took his last breath, she wrenched the sword free of him and turned to walk away as he fell free of its embrace. She refused to bestow on him the honor of watching him die. The men that were close by saw their leader fall in battle. They tried to pull back, but Silma stopped them with a volley of her arrows of light. Those of Alshin's men that were farther away, didn't know he was defeated until one man shouted, "He has fallen!" The man mounted a mare as it trotted by him. He rode, again shouting, "He has fallen! Alshin is dead! The battle is lost!" He rode past and over his own men.

Those of Alshin's men that had still been on horseback, stared at the man announcing their leader's death. It started with a few and turned quickly into a full retreat. Dagger and the Elargun force were at the rear cutting down as many as they could, but not all were stopped. Several made it past, escaping back the way they came.

Now with her task complete, Lisha ran over to Thrant's.

"How is he?" she asked. "Is he going to be okay? Does this village not have an Obeah-man? Call him!" Lisha demanded an answer from the men that tended to him. Down on his knees one of the men looked up at Lisha, and from his dim green eye's she could tell her uncle was not to see another dawn. Lisha turned to rejoin the others in the fight. She had seen a lot of men die, yet she could not stand and watch Thrant die and not be able to do a thing about it.

"Lisha do not leave," Thrant whispered. "There are some things I need to tell you that will help Sanch in his quest. Sillack has a great army, and now that he has released the Xyles he will be unstoppable." Thrant coughed violently. "Unstoppable unless you find allies."

"We have the Elarguns now fighting with us, and they seem to be very powerful and have great fighting skills," Lisha said, trying to comfort her uncle. "I think we are going to be alright."

"Yes, the Elargun's have a powerful army, but they're not going to be enough. You're going to need more. You need to find Ygen. His father stood with Lackshin, and he will stand with Sanch, I am sure of it." Thrant slowly started drifting away. He held his niece's hand tightly.

"Where do we look?" she asked, resting his head against her chest, trying somehow to give him an ounce of her own life.

"Look to the clouds, the black wing." Those were his last words.

Thrant was no longer. His dark brown eyes slowly closed as he became no more. Lisha returned to her feet and with both swords in hand, she turned to join the fighting again. Some of Alshin's men still did not know he had fallen by the edge of her sword, but it was time for them to know the head had been taken from the snake.

"Alshin has fallen!" shouted another of his men who were close enough to see what had taken place. He tried to ride out and to tell the men still pushing forward at the village gates. His ride was short-lived. Ralyn quickly quieted him.

"Sanch, it is time for this fight to end!" Ralyn yelled over the sound of swords clashing, horse's galloping, and body's hitting the ground.

"I agree!" Sanch shouted back. "It is time!"

"Sanch, head for the gate! We need it opened! We have one more surprise waiting on the other side!" Ralyn pointed to the village.

"Lisha, take my place, I have a ride to catch and a gate to open," Sanch said as he returned the axe to Menis. Lisha fell in beside him still carrying both swords. She created a pink mist with the first man that greeted her when she returned to battle. She looked over and saw her cousin no longer fighting with a staff, but with a sword covered by a thin layer of memory of lives.

"Bethany!" Lisha shouted. Looking down at Bethany's sword, "What happened? Your sword is covered with—"

Bethany interrupted, "What kind of friend..." she paused. "What kind of cousin would I be if I let them get you before you had your way with their leader?"

"Good point," Lisha replied. "And good work." She gave her cousin a proud nod before turning her attention to Sanch. "It is up to you now, Son of Lackshin. End this thing."

"I would very much love to, and it would be a little easier if I had a sword," Sanch told Lisha.

Lisha realized she still had Sanch's sword "Oh, I am sorry. I do still have it. Here you go. It does feel good in the hand. Amazing balance." She threw it to him. "Catch!" She donned a partial smile as she engaged her next opponent.

Riding at a full gallop, Guardian headed toward Sanch while leaving a trail of battered bodies behind him.

"Oh, look. Here comes my ride." Sanch holstered his sword and prepared himself for pick up. "It will soon be over. Stand fast," he ordered as he was abducted by Guardian still riding full gallop. By just looking at them you would not believe that the two of them did not grow up together mastering their technique. They worked as if their minds were one. They headed to the village gates at an amazing speed, challenged by Alshin's men the whole time. Waiting patiently was Evian and his small band of men that stood ready and anxiously waiting to join the fight. Guardian stopped and let Sanch down a couple of feet in front of the gate.

"It is I! Unlock the gate!" Sanch shouted.

Still atop the wall, Kess looked down and saw Sanch standing outside the gates waiting for it to be unlocked.

"Evian, he is who he says he is. Unlock the gates!" Kess commanded. "Men stand ready."

Sanch heard the locks on the gates being released and started pushing them open. Like last time, Ralyn was again amazed at the strength of this young man. When the gate had been fully open, Evian ordered his men to move out. With his sword drawn, Evian lead the charge. Now inside the walls, Sanch shouted to Kess, "I did what I said I would!"

"What is this promise that you say you kept?" Kess asked the boy.

Sanch, feeling sure of himself answered back, "I have returned your daughter to you."

"She is not yet inside these walls. I still have not embraced her. Your task is not yet fulfilled. When you retrieve Bethany, do make sure Lisha is with you as well. Now, Sanch, make your way back out there and retrieve my daughter and niece!"

Sanch stood with a crooked smile. He nodded and left to catch his ride out to re-join the fight. Evian and his men now had the chance to face those that came to harm the ones they loved. They charged out of the gate, announcing themselves with their battle cries. Once protected behind thick walls, Evian and his legion joined the fight. Evian instructed the five hundred men left under his command to get in formation, but not yet engage.

Evian sat tall on his horse. His sword still shined, for his blade had not yet tasted flesh. With the soft texture of the wind blowing across his lips, he felt the heat from the sun right above them in a cloudless sky. He tilted his head to the right and squinted his eyes, trying to get a glimpse of what was coming from behind. He could hear a strong gallop closing in on his right.

Evian looked to see the creature that delivered Sanch to the village gates stopped beside him. Standing on the back of the horse-like creature, his left hand firmly gripped the shoulder of Guardian as they rode to join up with Evian.

"What is your name, friend?" Sanch asked.

"My ... my name is Evian, my lord."

"Well, Evian, it is an honor to meet you," Sanch said. "I'm…"

"Yes, I know who you are." Evian swallowed nervously. "You are Sanch, Son of Lackshin. From what I am told, you are the only one that can stop all of this."

With an uncomfortable smile on his face, Sanch replied, "That is what they tell me." He looked at the battlefield. He saw what was taking place and could not help but to think this was all caused by him and his quest for revenge. With the strong wind blowing his hair, Sanch turned and looked at Evian. "I think this has gone on long enough. Ride with me, my friend. It's time we stop this madness."

Evian signed to his men to follow close at a slow trot, as they rode out to the battlefield where no one seemed to want to tread. It became clear to Evian where Sanch was leading him and his men. Sanch was going for Shallin, still firmly embedded in the man's chest and partly into the ground. As it had been in the belly of the volcano, Shallin could feel Sanch's desire to retrieve her from her place of rest.

Again, Shallin started to sing a song of welcome to the son of her friend gone, but not forgotten. The song began to fill the air; those who were well away could faintly hear it. Men that were close by became overwhelmed by her singing. Some of them even dropped their weapons so that they could clutch their ears to protect them from the intensity of the sound. As Sanch, Evian, and Guardian got closer, Sanch became entranced by it.

As the gap between Shallin and Sanch grew less and less, Evian and his men were affected and had to fall back. Sanch and Hush seemed unaffected by the sound Shallin resonated. It seemed to be coming from everywhere and yet nowhere. It could not be stopped. When they arrived at Shallin, Sanch sprung from the creature's back. When he landed, a thin cloud of dust was released and then slowly descended back to the earth.

As he walked, smaller clouds followed and marked his progress. The grass beneath his feet was soft, and for a second preserved his footprints as he walked glidingly, sheathing his sword as he moved to greet an old friend of the family.

As Sanch approached where Shallin landed, the song was now loud across the nearby hillside. He stood over her and reached out his right hand. With his thumb facing down, he grabbed Shallin. When his hand closed around Shallin's hilt, the body where she spent the better half of the day turned to ash and blew away with the wind leaving nothing but an ashy reminder the man ever existed. The song of Shallin ended suddenly, leaving an eerie silence that blanketed the battlefield. Breaking the silence was the voice of Sanch who sounded more like Lackshin than the boy they saw.

"It ends now!" shouted Sanch. "Alshin is dead. Your leader is no more, and if you choose wrong, you can share his fate. These are the choices that you have. You all can leave your swords where they lay, claim you're dead, and return to Sillack and fight alongside the evil that he has released. It's an evil he cannot control and will eventually turn on you all. They will kill with no mercy. Your other choice is to join us and help stop the evil that will eventually threaten your family and the ones you love. The last choice that I give is to reclaim your weapons and continue this fight. But know this; if you wish to fight, I give you my word that we will escort you all to the underworld where you will surely find your leader. So, what say you? Do you leave, stay, or die?"

Sanch turned and walked to his horse that now stood next to Guardian. With his father's sword in hand, Sanch leaped onto the back of his trusted friend.

"What will it be?" Sanch asked as he settled into his saddle. "Will you die by our hands today, or do you wish to see another day?"

Menis stood over one of the men with his axe raised above his head. He looked to the man for a decision. As Menis better positioned himself over this man, a smile slowly crept across his face. Off in the distance, a man loyal to Sillack shouted, "We will fight to the last man!" Those were his last words.

On the village wall, the only proof of the arrow's origin was the vibration from Tasha's bow. Kess looked over at Tasha. Her braids dangled carelessly in front of her left eye. Tasha brushed them from her face, and looked back at Kess as to say, "Why not kill him?"

Menis prepared to land the finishing blow when suddenly…

"We yield! I yield!" the man shouted.

Menis buried his axe in the ground next to the beaten man's head kicking dirt into the man's face. He retrieved his axe and cleaned it on the man's chest and walked away.

"So, what do we do now?" he mumbled as he walked away.

Sanch looked back at the village wall to see where the arrow came from. There he saw Kess looking back at him slightly thrusting her head to her left where Tasha stood. She shrugged her shoulders, put her bow away, and stepped back from the wall. Sanch turned and he and Guardian rode to where Lisha and the others were re-grouping. Menis walked over with both his axes slung over his shoulders. Sanch and Guardian climbed down from their horses and walked over to them.

The five warriors stood there looking at one another. In the opening between Guardian and Bethany, and in the space between Menis and Lisha, and footprints appeared. Suddenly Deem and Dagger emerged in full Elargun armor. Flying into the center of the circle was Silma. She took her place on to Sanch's shield, which hung on his back. Deem looked at Sanch and uttered under his breath, "You are indeed the Son of Lackshin."

CHAPTER TWELVE

The red-eye beast casted an evil shadow. Steam rose from its nose, heating the cold air around its face, and making it look as if it were breathing fire. Its mane was still sticky from its last victim. The coat shined an evil black. This animal was not of this world.

"Taddayuse, come over here and steady my Rinnis!" Sillack demanded as he removed his helm.

"Yes, my lord," the young warrior obliged.

Tired from the long ride from hell itself, the warrior approached the agitated beast. As he got closer, the beast could smell the stench of the Xyles that Taddayuse killed. Some of the remains were still on the boy's armor. As soon as he got close, Sillack's Rinnis turned to make Taddayuse his last victim of the day. Noticing the animal's sudden movement toward him, he threw up his left arm and blocked the attack from the beast.

Snap, snap, scratch! The beast's teeth scraped at Taddayuse's shield.

Normally, Sillack would allow his extraordinary Rinnis to indulge himself and dismember the young warrior. In this situation, Sillack felt this young man's skill would show itself useful in the future. Sillack thought he might have to put Taddayuse's forces to the test against the forces of the son of his enemy. Sillack dropped his helmet and grabbed the rein with both hands and pulled, forcefully backstopping the attack. Fillip approached with his hand gripped tightly on the handle of his sword. Even knowing that it would most likely cost him his life, he was still willing to attempt to stop the beast. Luckily for Fillip, Sillack brought it to an end himself without Fillip having to intervene.

"I think she likes you, boy," Sillack said as he climbed from his Rinnis. "You are lucky that I need you to lead a group of my men."

"What do you mean, my lord?" Taddayuse asked.

"I need strong men to lead, and with what I have seen of your skills, you are a man I can use. I will have Haygen hand pick you a hundred good men, and I will have you take twenty Xyles with you."

"My lord, I do not think that would be necessary I think the men and I will be just fine without them accompanying us," he replied, gracefully declining Sillack's offer to have the Xyles join them.

"For this task, I need to make sure you have all that you will need. Now, go rest yourself. You will be told your assignment soon enough. Oh, and get that stuff off your armor. The smell of it drives her insane. She loves it so much." Sillack turned and walked away with his rabid beast close behind.

"Are you ready for that?"

"What do you mean, Fillip? Do you think I cannot lead?" Taddayuse asked, hoping for reassurance. "Do you not think I am ready?"

"That is not it at all, boy. I'm asking if you are ready to fight alongside these creatures that you were told stories of? Stories of the destruction they caused and the lives they needlessly took. Lackshin was your hero when you were a boy. Now you fight alongside the man who killed him? This same man is trying to do the same to his son who now wields Shallin, the sword that could rid this world of Sillack. Taddayuse, are you sure you are on the right side of this war? Are you fighting for the right man?" Fillip put a hand on Taddayuse's shoulder.

"How is it you ask me this as you stand here in the same armor I wear? Fighting for the same man you stand here and warn me about. Why fight on what you call the wrong side?" Taddayuse forcefully replied. "I had no choice. I put on this armor to keep my family out of harm's way. I do this so the ones I love can live in serenity, away from the same man I fight for. We had nowhere else to go without having others look down on us. I am ashamed by the actions of my people, but these were actions I was not alive to see happen. Do you not think I have thought about all you are telling me? Do you think I have forgotten all the stories I heard as a boy? And now, I am asked to fight alongside the same things that killed so many people. I know where I am, and it is on the wrong side of all of this. I need to find my way to where I can stop what is about to be unleashed. Then I will join my people." He turned from Fillip, pulling his shoulder free of his hand. "You should get some rest, old man."

"Why is that, boy?" Fillip inquired.

"As soon as I get my orders, you will get yours. I plan to keep you with me, friend. We both have better things we could do with our swords. Death will find me before I bring shame to my father. Get some rest. I shall see you soon enough."

A smile found itself on Fillip's face as he turned and went his way. He knew now that what he saw in Taddayuse was not just in his head; it was real, and the boy just may be his way back to the right side.

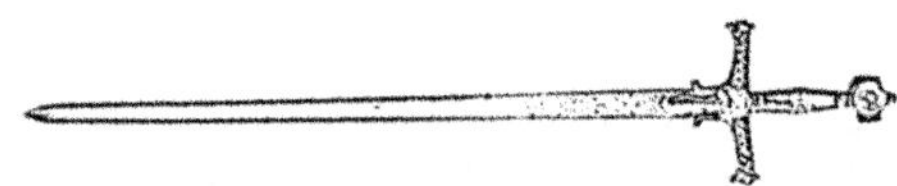

SILLACK MADE HIS WAY UP TO HIS THRONE ROOM, loosening the wet leather straps that held his armor on. The throne was a big hall with six large pillars on either side holding up the balcony overlooking all below. On a clear day, large windows would let in a great deal of light. His second in command followed close behind.

"Haygen, have you heard any word back from Alshin about the boy and that blasted sword? Does anyone know what is going on? If not, someone needs to find out and let me know within the hour!" Sillack made his way to his personal chambers in the tower above the throne room.

"Yes, my lord. I will look into it," Haygen agreed. "I will see if we received anything on the wing."

"Send in that Obeah-Man turned wizard. I have questions about these Xyles and how better to control them." Sillack swung open the heavy doors of his throne room.

Haygen stopped halfway up the steps where some may say evil lives. He then retreated down the steps and made his way toward the courtyard. After he located the wizard and gave him his orders to report to Sillack, Haygen stopped at the tavern to see what the men were talking about and what was on their minds. When he entered, it smelled like sweat, ale, and less than honest women. In the tavern, he found the young man Sillack deemed worthy to lead his group of men.

Haygen took a seat in a dark corner and beckoned for a bottle of wine. From there he could observe Taddayuse, who sat alone drinking. The boy was having a modest meal of half a chicken and bread. He could tell by the look on the young man's face that he had a lot on his mind. He could also see a veil of uncertainty over the boy.

Taddayuse looked around the room at other men enjoying themselves and telling their different accounts of what happened out there. As he listened, he thought to himself that they did not know what manner of evil was now among them. These are men that had not heard the stories of what these creatures are capable of. They were wild animals that killed for pleasure. However, how could these men not know? There were still lands that had not yet recovered from what was done to them. Now, these same things were what they were supposed to fight alongside and entrust their lives to in battle. The thought of all these things filled Taddayuse with rage and when he could take no more, he slammed his mug down and quickly exited the tavern, leaving most of his food untouched.

Following close behind was Haygen, curious to know his reason for leaving so abruptly and in such haste. Taddayuse did not go too far before he noticed that he had someone following him.

He tried not to let on that he was aware. Taddayuse walked on for some time to be sure he was indeed being followed. After he was certain, the young warrior slowly placed his right hand on the handle of a dagger he always carried. He then heard a voice coming from behind that he had heard several times before.

"There is no need for that. If I wished you dead, you would have been several moments ago, so you can slacken the grip on that blade."

"Have you come to give me my orders?" Taddayuse inquired when he saw it was Haygen.

"Not yet," Haygen replied. "We have not heard back from Alshin. We do not know the outcome of his campaign to retrieve Sanch and his father's sword from Ralyn's village. We will give him until sundown to get word to us. By then, you should have your orders. For now, you get your rest, and I will help you choose the best men to help you do Sillack's bidding."

"Yes," Taddayuse responded, then asked, "What of the men that were left back at the cave entrance?"

Haygen smiled and let out a little laugh. The tall man turned and as he walked away, he said something that helped Taddayuse make up his mind. "The men at the cave either are there to greet the Xyles or feed them. Not something you need worry about."

As Haygen walked away, he left Taddayuse to think that these men they so easily turn their backs on are the same men that he shared meat and ail with the other day. Now, they were nothing more than expendable. All he could think of now is what he and Fillip spoke about earlier. Now he knew Sillack must be stopped. He was willing to release such destruction just to destroy one boy, one boy, and his father's sword.

"He must be stopped before this destruction goes any further," Taddayuse uttered to himself as he made his way to his quarters.

Unbeknownst to Haygen and Taddayuse, off in the shadows, Fillip was liberating his grip on his sword. Being around as long as he has, he knew Haygen's reputation. If Haygen ever felt threatened by any of the young warriors that showed promise, these men always mysteriously ended up dead. Some simply just went missing and were deemed deserters. Sillack openly showed interest in Taddayuse's skills with a sword, and that worried the seasoned in command. Fillip somehow knew that this boy from Tegra was going to play a big role in the fight to stop Sillack from doing the same to the son as he did to the father. Alternatively, maybe Taddayuse himself needed to be stopped, depending on what way the wind blew. Either way, Fillip would stay close to him.

AT THE HIGHEST AND DARKEST POINT OF THE CASTLE, Sillack's chamber overlooked the courtyard on one side. On the other side was a door that opened to the mountain the castle was built into. You could walk out the doors and find yourself on an enormous cliff with a hundred-foot drop straight down onto jagged rocks below. The room was illuminated only by light through the open door, in addition to the fire that burned in the fireplace. Sillack gazed off into the distance as he loosened his armor. He required his squire to help him with the buckles he could not remove himself and hated having to rely on someone dressing him for battle. There was a faint rap on the massive steel doors that separated Sillack from the rest of the castle. It was a knock from someone that truly did not want to enter.

"Come in wizard!" shouted Sillack, annoyed by the disturbance.

It took some time for Daren to push the doors open, for his strength was his magic and did not lie in his physical feats. The guards posted outside Sillack's chamber would never assist the Obeah-Man turned wizard. They found it funny to watch him struggle. Slowly entering the room through the small opening he managed to make for himself, the wizard walked in and stopped at the edge of the light that was entering the evil painted room.

"You called for me, my lord?"

Quickly getting straight to the point Sillack asked, "I need to know how."

"What do you mean, my lord? You need to know how to what?" the wizard responded.

Sillack asked again, "I need to know how to control these creatures. I do not plan on losing control the same way you did! So, I ask once more. How?"

"My lord, you have what you need to control them. The ruby claw controls them, and you have that."

"Then how is it you lost to Lackshin? How did he stop the Xyles if you had them under control?" Sillack moved closer to the wizard as the questions became more intense. "I was there. I saw it all. It looked to me like you had no control. Why is that?" Sillack stood over Daren.

With the power of Sillack glaring down on him, the wizard could only give one name and one explanation. "It was Shallin. That sword he wielded."

Sillack stepped back. "You're telling me this sword the son now carries made you lose control of such powerful creatures?" Sillack threw his shield across the room.

Now uneasy, Daren chose his words wisely this time. "I don't know what it was, but every time Lackshin and his sword was around, the Xyles were harder to control. Only when he was almost overwhelmed by the Xyles was I able to regain control."

Sillack walked over to his chair and stood looking at it. He turned with his head still down and his fist clenched. "If I cannot destroy Shallin, then the boy must die. Bring Haygen to me and find out what has happened to Alshin. We should have heard something by now. I think I have a mission for my new commander, and you are going to need to get the Xyles ready to accompany him. Now, go find Haygen!" Sillack shouted.

"Yes, my lord." The wizard hurried out of chamber.

ON THE OTHER SIDE OF THE KINGDOM, A SMALL BAND of female warriors trained. Haygen hoped to enlist some of them to help with a plan he was putting in motion. First, he would have to find their leader to see whom she would recommend for what he had in mind. Haygen found the first cherub and asked her where he would find Deidra? The young cherub only reached Haygen's hip and carried two short swords. She led him through their camp to where Deidra was conducting a meeting with her commanders in her tent. She turned to see Haygen standing outside.

"Haygen, to what do I owe this visit?" Deidra asked as she dismissed the five that sat around the table. Her long black braid hung past her butt. Her brown eyes looked at him knowingly.

"Sit with me and tell me what the great Sillack wants from us. What is this that I hear that this madman has liberated the Xyles from the hell they belonged in?" She leaned in closer to Haygen, not wanting to miss anything that may leave his lips.

"Yes, the Xyles are once again amongst us," Haygen answered, emotionless. "He needs them to defeat The Son of Lackshin."

"So, what you are telling me, Haygen? Sillack felt it necessary to release the greatest evil these lands have ever seen for one boy? Do you not think your master has gone too far this time? Do you not think this is more than he needs for just one boy?" Deidra did nothing to hide her agitation.

"Sanch is not just some ordinary boy; he is the only man that can wield Shallin. Do you know what that means? Sillack is our king. He must eliminate any threats."

"He is not my king. He will never be a king. I have made that very clear to you all, and that is why we have been left to ourselves. Is that not clear to you?"

Haygen looked away.

"I know what that means, Haygen. I have also heard the stories about the sword that can end great Sillack's miserable life. That sword was said to have been destroyed, but it is now in the hands of this boy, Sanch. Tell me what it is that Sillack wants from me and my cherub?" Deidra sat back in her chair.

"I am not here on Sillack's bidding. I am here on my own accord. I have a mission and I would like your help. I require five of your best warriors," Haygen informed her.

"What do you want my girls for? What part will they play in your mission?"

"They will be my eyes and ears out there. I need them to report back to me and only me. Do you have such a five?"

"I have five in mind that would serve your intention. How long will they have to prepare themselves to leave?" Deidra stood up to leave.

"The man leading this mission and the men joining him are resting and will be for the next eight hours. Your girls have nine hours to be in the courtyard and ready to ride. Tell them their objective is different from the others."

Deidra was puzzled. "Then what is it?"

"Taddayuse is their objective."

"Who is Taddayuse and why is he so important?" Deidra asked.

"This boy is Sillack's new pet, but I do not trust him because I cannot read him. I want your girls to keep an eye on him and report back to me. His father fought at Lackshin's side, and I need to know where his devotion lies. If it does not lie with us, they are to kill him where he stands. As for his family, I will kill them myself."

"I will go find my girls," Deidra said as she walked away. "I will make sure that they are on time for their task. Oh, and if harm befalls them, Sillack will be in need of a new right hand." She caressed the handle of her sword.

"So be it," Haygen replied. "Till we meet again."

"Another thing. They report to me. I will tell you what they bring back. That is how that works my friend." Deidra left to inform the cherub of their commitment.

Haygen handpicked a small band of men of his own to join Taddayuse, just in case the cherubs were unable to get the job done. As he got closer to Sillack's castle of evil, layered in darkness and reeking of despair, he could hear the curdling cries of the Xyles, and the stench of the decaying remains of men rotting in their fur. It was now midday, and the men only had an hour or so before it would be time for them to report and prepare for the task at hand.

CHAPTER THIRTEEN

The candle flickered and made the wood on the ceiling look like rippling water. Fire from the fireplace provided the heat to his normally cold living quarters. Despite the comfort from the fire, Taddayuse did not get a moment of sleep. He just lay there and pondered the resolutions he would soon have to make. It was getting closer to that time. He thought he should ready himself. He got up and sat on the edge of his bed and looked at his sword he had cleaned earlier. As he sat there looking at it, he noticed a spot of Xyles on the hilt.

"Great, now I may never be rid of them." He stood and walked over to where his armor hung. He knew that when he stepped out the door of his room, he would no longer be just Taddayuse, the boy from Tegra—he would be the leader of a small division of men whose loyalties may be greater than his own. He could no longer hide among the faces of the other soldiers—he would now be upfront leading. Looking at his armor reminded him of the disgrace he felt when he dawned Sillack's evil mark. An evil that his father once battled against alongside the father of the man he is now to look at as his enemy. His sword was still the sword his father gave him as a young boy. Made of Croyanite steel, it was the one thing that gave him pride. He unsheathed it and attempted to clean what remained of the Xyles off its hilt.

After Taddayuse took care of the only friend he felt he had, he started putting on his armor of shame, and prepared to go pick the men he was to lead. Ready to leave and not knowing if he will ever return, Taddayuse packed his tote with everything dear to him. He strapped on a dagger his mother had made for him when he started sword lessons. When she gave it to him, she told him not every fight required a sword, and for those that do not make sure to have your dagger. Taddayuse opened the door to his quarters only to see Fillip in full armor leaning on the wall, waiting to join him.

"I pledge my sword to you, young Taddayuse, and I will fight and die."

Taddayuse quickly interpreted what Fillip was about to say.

"I am not sure what you think my plans are but dying or any form of death is not a part of them. So, if you wish to throw yourself down on the first sword you see, I have no need for you. I am not afraid of dying, nor am I handing out easy kills to anyone. The man who kills me will die shortly after. I promise you that, Fillip. Now, we have men to lead, and I say *we* because I know not what I am to do."

Fillip looked at the young warrior and smiled. "We will make sure not to let them know that little piece of information, my boy."

The two walked through the courtyard in silence. Never once was it mentioned what Taddayuse may have to do and what it may cost him when he is forced to do it. As they walked, they noticed five girls walking towards the courtyard from another direction clearly dressed for battle. Neither Fillip nor Taddayuse thought twice about it. They figured they were there for an audience with Sillack. Fillip and Taddayuse continued on their way.

"Have you given any thought to which of the men you wish to have join you? Many men are very loyal to Sillack, and they are not the ones we are going to want to come with us." Fillip pointed. "You are going to want men you know, men you have fought with. Soldiers that will give you their loyalty.

"I know," Taddayuse said. "I intend to pick the younger of the men. The ones that have not yet been completely made to believe the lies that they are being told. That way, I have a better chance of either having them join me or just have them leave me to my choice. What do you know of Haygen? What kind of man is he? Is he someone that I need to worry about? Is he someone with great power?" Taddayuse tried to feel out his situation and what he may have to face.

"We now have three great evils inside these walls. The Xyles, Sillack, and Haygen, and in that order. He is an evil man, but that is not what makes him so dangerous. What makes him so dangerous is that he does not trust anyone. He will be watching you very closely, especially since Sillack has taken a liking to you. That makes you a threat to him. Haygen has never been a man that liked threats. The men that were with us have not stopped speaking of your way with a sword, so he has heard a great deal about you. Be prepared for anything, because I am sure he has plans for you," Fillip warned Taddayuse.

"Yes, Fillip, I will watch Haygen. Now, let us choose my men. I think the men I went through training with would be our best choice. I know a lot of them, and some are as unsure as myself. If I make a move, they will either join me or just return and not pursue me."

"Don't you mean us, Taddayuse?" Fillip asked.

"Yes, friend, us. It will be up to us to figure out a way to make this work when we find Sanch."

"Try not to let him kill you when you meet, and in turn, try not to kill him. Do not forget he is the only one that can wield Shallin, and only Shallin can vanquish Sillack." Fillip questioned the boy's true intentions. "How many of your men do you think Haygen is going to let you pick for yourself? He will not leave that completely up to you. He'll want to have some control over that."

"I would not have it any other way," Taddayuse said, smiling as he stepped into the courtyard. He looked around for some familiar faces—faces of men he went through training with—men he hoped he could trust and count on. As Taddayuse looked around the courtyard, he tried to assess the men he was to choose. He walked through quietly, trying not to be noticed as he moved amongst them to see who was who, and what they had to offer him on whatever assignment he had been chosen for. Fillip stayed close to Taddayuse. The old warrior kept an eye out for Haygen. Fillip knew he would not be far from something this very important to Sillack. Fillip had been around long enough to know what makes a powerful man worry, and as far as he could tell, Taddayuse made Haygen do just that.

As he walked among the men who were all preparing to ride out as soon as they were given their order, Taddayuse had yet to receive his orders from Sillack. Few people received their orders right from Sillack himself. When he reached the stables, he heard a familiar voice.

It was Haygen returning from the cherub's village.

"Fifty men?" Taddayuse asked. "I was promised one hundred men. What am I to do with fifty men? Have my orders been changed?"

"No, they have not. I will select the other fifty that will be assigned to you. Did you think I would trust you to pick every man for such an important task?" Haygen asked.

Taddayuse, with his hand resting on the pommel of his sword, looked at Fillip and smiled. All the men in earshot turned to see what was happening. Most of them had never seen this much of Haygen, much less seen him speak to one of them. Till this day, Taddayuse went unnoticed by all but a few, but that would no longer be the case. Now he had been singled out by Sillack and brought to the attention of Haygen and the other men. Taddayuse knew he could not show this man any kind of weakness. He kept eye contact and did not release his gaze. With all eyes on them, Taddayuse and Haygen stood in the middle of the courtyard, now embraced in a stare.

Turning away from Taddayuse, Haygen walked to the stairs that lead up to Sillack's throne room. He called back to Taddayuse, "Are you coming? Lord Sillack would like to speak to you about what he would like you to do. I'm not sure what he sees in you, but my lord does not like failure, so I would advise you not to fail him."

"I'm sure I will do fine. But thank you for informing me of that," Taddayuse replied with confidence.

He followed Haygen up the dark stairway that led to Sillack's chamber.

Sillack spent most of his time practicing his sword skills. His skills seemed to be unmatched. Sillack was said to be immortal, yet he feared death. Now that he knew the one who could kill him was out there somewhere looking for him, he grew more and more paranoid.

As a nervous Taddayuse approached the large doors to the throne room, he made sure to stand ready. He did not know what to expect. As Taddayuse walked thru the heavy doors that lead into Sillack's den, the first thing he noticed when he entered was the empty room. There was little to no light in there. As he walked into the dimly lit space, he felt a change in the air around him. There was a slight vibration in the bricks beneath his feet. As his eyes were adjusting to the darkness, he saw a slight reflection. With one smooth motion, he stepped clear and drew his sword, blocking Sillack's perfect strike.

"I lose more good men this way, but I am glad to see you can handle yourself. Haygen, I think this boy's reaction to my strike may have been better than yours was," said Sillack.

"I doubt that," Haygen replied.

"No matter, here we all are. Are you interested to know what your assignment is going to be?" Sillack looked at Taddayuse.

"Yes, my lord. But I am most interested in why the first thing I had to do when I walked through the doors was to fight for my life? Is this my mission or is there more you would have me do?"

"Watch your tongue, boy," Haygen warned. "I can end it for you now if you would prefer!"

Taddayuse, still gripping his sword, looked at Haygen with no fear. "Feel free to try, but I promise you it will not be a simple task." He smiled. "Now, my lord, am I to be bombarded with more threats, or will I be briefed on this task in which you would like me to tend to?"

"Yes, this is a great task in which I want you to take. Taddayuse, have you heard of the one called Sanch?" Sillack walked deeper into the darkness.

Taddayuse followed close behind. "I have heard mention of him. Who is he, and what does he have to do with my task?" Taddayuse was unsure how he was to answer. Of course, he knew who Sanch was.

"He is the Son of Lackshin, and I want him found and brought to me," Sillack instructed the young warrior. "He is looking for me and I wish to find him first. He has something that interests me, and I want it."

Taddayuse felt safe enough now to sheathe his sword. "So, you want me to take one hundred men and go find him?"

"Yes, that is what I am asking of you. Do you think you are up to the task? Can you find him and bring him here?"

"I am not sure this boy is up for this. Look at him," Haygen said.

Taddayuse turned and smiled at Haygen. "I will do this as long as I get to pick the other fifty men that will be joining me." He turned back to Sillack. "My lord, how do you wish me to bring him to you?"

"I need him alive, but if he puts up too much of a fight, dead will do just fine as well. As for you picking your fifty men, that is fine, and you will have Xyles joining you."

"I would rather not have Xyles with me on this," Taddayuse said.

"You will have the Xyles," said Haygen. "And you will have a small team of cherub with you as well. Just a little more help for you on your mission, boy. You should be thankful for that."

Taddayuse thought back to what Fillip was telling him Haygen would try to do.

"Who are these cherub you speak of? Why do I need them joining me?" Taddayuse turned to face Haygen. "Is this your way of watching me?"

"Instead of asking things you can do nothing about, I think you should be picking the men. You do not have much time. You will leave at dusk," Haygen said, pulling rank.

"You two leave me now. You have your mission. Go on your way. Taddayuse, I do not reward failure, so do not fail me," Sillack ordered.

"Yes, my lord." Taddayuse turned and made his way out.

"Wait for me, boy! I will come so I can show you to the men I have chosen for you; good men loyal to Sillack."

They both walked down the dark stairwell leading out to the courtyard.

"Why me?" Taddayuse asked.

"Why you what?" Haygen replied.

"This quest he is sending me on … why is he tasking me with it?"

"I do not know. He must see something in you that I do not. As far as I can see, you are not the man for this. You are just a boy with a sword looking to make a name for himself." Haygen scratched his thick black beard.

"I will try not to disappoint," Taddayuse replied, smiling. "Oh, and Fillip will be my second."

"Why would you want that old man as your second? Can he still hold a sword, much less swing one? I will assign one of my best for your second, " Haygen insisted.

"That is what I am afraid of. I do not want one of your best. I want a man I can trust." Taddayuse didn't hide the fact that he did not trust Sillack's second. "And I have the feeling anyone that you trust I should make it my business not to. Thanks for your offer, but I will be giving Fillip responsibility, or you can tell Sillack why I will not be leading this quest."

Taddayuse stopped and looked at Haygen, waiting for his response. When Haygen said nothing, the boy turned and took his leave. Haygen stood inside the gate leading into the castle, glaring at him as he walked out into the chilly evening. "I thank you for showing me out. Tell your best I will not need his service. Maybe next time."

Fillip did what his young leader expected of him. Taddayuse's horse was saddled, ready and waiting for him. The men Taddayuse told Fillip to round up were also ready.

"Fillip, are we ready?" Taddayuse shouted across the courtyard. The heat of his breath rose in a white mist from his mouth.

"Yes, we await your orders," Fillip informed the nervous Taddayuse.

"How was it in the den of our Lord Sillack? Are there really devices of torture on the walls?" Fillip inquired.

"It was like no other place I have ever been. It smelled and was badly lit, which worked out for me."

"How so?" Fillip asked.

As Taddayuse climbed onto his horse, he looked at Fillip and smiled. "That bad lighting saved my life."

Fillip shrugged his shoulders and mounted his steed. He followed closely as Taddayuse road to greet the men he was not acquainted with. Taddayuse tried to see if he recognized any of the faces of the men Haygen embedded in his ranks. He was not sure what a cherub would look like or what they did, but all he counted was his fifty, and the fifty of Haygen's men. Not even the Xyles that were to be assigned to him were there yet. As far as he was concerned, he would be fine without the likes of those things. He told Fillip to order the men in formation and prepare them to move out. The first fifty complied, but the fifty that Haygen handpicked did not comply, and did their own thing and ignored Fillip and his orders. Taddayuse saw this and did not plan to stand for that in any way. He heard one of the soldiers mumble under his breath.

"I will not take orders from a boy and his old man."

Taddayuse acted fast. He pulled a dagger and ended the soldier. His horse reared from the sudden yank of the reins, almost kicking another man off his mount. The other soldiers fought to keep their horses under control. Taddayuse jumped down from his horse and walked over to retrieve his dagger from the man's throat and cleaned it on the man's clothes. He leaped back onto his horse and looked at Haygen. With a smile on his face, Taddayuse shouted, "That makes it forty-nine!" He turned back to Haygen's men. "Are the rest of you coming, or would some of you like to stay here with him?" Taddayuse pointed his dagger to the man that still lay on the ground clutching the hole in his neck.

The rest of the men did not hesitate to fall in.

The Xyles that were to join them had not shown up yet. Taddayuse attempted to leave before those things showed up. He now had all his men in formation and was ready to move them out. He and Fillip took the lead. Just as he was ready to give the order to move out, Daren ran out in front of Fillip's horse.

"What do you want, wizard?" Taddayuse moved his horse forward, almost pushing Daren to the ground. "Do you wish for us to run you down, because it would be my delight to do so?"

"I am sure it would be, boy," Daren said.

"Say what you must and be gone with you," Fillip ordered him.

"I am here to assign you your Xyles and give you what you will need to control them." Daren pushed his way clear of the horses.

"What do you mean control them?" Taddayuse asked. "You want me to take these beasts with me, and then what?"

"I am not asking you to do anything. Your lord Sillack is telling you that these Xyles will be joining you on this. I am just here to give you what you will need to control these creatures."

"Hours ago, I was killing these things. Now you want me to fight alongside them. I hope these things do not hold a grudge. So, what is this thing I will need to control them?"

Daren reached into a bag and pulled out a bracelet with an odd shine to it.

"As long as you have this on, they will do your bidding. That is, if your bidding is that of Sillack's wishes," Daren added.
"Thank you, wizard. And if that is all, we will be on our way." Taddayuse ordered his men to move out.

The five cherubs were not there yet, but Taddayuse was not waiting for them. He saw it better not to have more people that answered to Haygen riding with them.

"There are more you must wait for," Haygen announced.

"We leave and we leave now!" Taddayuse ordered.

After his last display of what happens when he is disobeyed, the men did not hesitate to follow. They rode out with Fillip and Taddayuse in the lead Taddayuse was unsure what he would face or what kind of man Sanch would be. The young leader tried to show nothing but confidence in his mission. He dare not show his insecurities. He led with his head facing forward. His goal was to find Sanch, but not for the reasons Sillack wanted him found. Taddayuse wanted to see if Sanch was a man he should join and fight alongside. The boy wields the sword his hero once used to stop the creatures he now traveled with. Xyles were vile, filthy animals that killed without cause.

Shortly after they were on their way, they heard what sounded like horses galloping hard behind them. The young leader wasted no time. He shouted, "Stand ready, men!" He turned and rode out toward the sound of the incoming gallops approaching at their rear.

As he got closer, he could see the outline of five riders, none of which looked large enough to be ominous.

"These must be the ones Haygen was expecting," Fillip said as he came upon Taddayuse's right.

"Yes, that must be them," Taddayuse agreed. "That is just what we need. More people we cannot trust and will most likely kill us if given the chance."

"Let us make sure not to give them that chance," Fillip said.

As they got closer, Taddayuse searched for the leader. As he looked, he noticed out of the five there was one of them the others rode behind. That was the only thing that Taddayuse could see that made one stand out from the others. They were not like women he had seen before. They were exceptionally small.

"Fillip, what do you know of the cherub? What are they about? Do they stand for anything, or do they just blindly fight for whoever will pay?" Taddayuse asked.

"I hear their leader does as she pleases and is a force to be reckoned with when she has a sword in her hand. As for the ones she commands, we will know soon enough. Do not show them your hand, let them show you theirs," Fillip instructed.

Taddayuse did not order his men to stop. He took his place back in the lead and they rode on, making the cherubs have to catch up with his forces. He did that for good reason. It showed them he could do with or without them. He did not want them to feel like he needed or wanted them. Their horses were extraordinary; they were catching up with little to no effort. The redhead that rode up front looked like she would be the one in charge. The others rode behind her, but not too far behind, showing that if she was the leader, she had not been for long. The others still felt her equal. As they got in range, one of them shouted.

"Taddayuse!"

They pulled up and around on his rear left flank. They pulled their horses in front of him, forcing him to stop along with everyone behind him. It was their show of aggression and their willingness to bring it all to a stop.

The smallest of the five did the talking. "Which one of you is Taddayuse? We were told that we are to report to him." The lead cherub looked at Fillip. "Are you Taddayuse?" she asked.

"No, I am not," Fillip replied. He looked at Taddayuse and corrected her. "He is the one in charge. Ladies, this is Lord Taddayuse. He is the one who leads us."

"I've never heard of Sillack putting someone so young in command before. There must be something about this one."

One of the other girls rode up closer to Taddayuse and took a good look at him. "I guess we will have to see what he can do.

The smallest of the five added. "Yes, we'll just have to see. I will be keeping my eye on this boy." After she said that, she and the others rode off and joined the formation.

"Lord Taddayuse, do you think they will be any trouble?" Fillip asked as he took a better look at them.

"First thing you need to do is stop calling me lord. Second thing is I think the little one likes me." Taddayuse smiled.

CHAPTER FOURTEEN

The brightness was overwhelming to most the first time they entered the throne room. The large, high windows lined with gold reflected the sun inwards onto the marble ceilings, making it look like the sun was always over the throne. The tapestry on the walls showed the great deeds of kings past. One showed King Patrick, who was just a prince at the time fighting the battle at the foot of Hell's Doorway. His small force was tasked with holding back his father's enemies and keeping them from flanking his force. The line of Meadows Kings had been known as fearless fighters except for a few that were simply cruel and had others fight their wars.

They all demanded loyalty from all their subjects. And different kings earned that loyalty their own way. The better of the Meadows Kings earned it by ruling with strength and fairness. That was the foundation of their rule. The ones that did not pledge their loyalty like they were expected to would quickly and violently be dealt with. They believed in justice and would not stand for defiance. King Benjamin, knowingly or unknowingly to him, was also known as the "Cowardly King," although no one would dare proclaim that to his face. He was the kind of king that hid behind his walls when it came time to fight. He left it to men like Lackshin and Sillack to protect his people—men who came from great families that loyally served kings before him.

The council was called earlier than scheduled. The king had not been well as of late. That information was only privy to members of the council and the Obeah-Men tasked with his care. Obeah-Men are thought of by some as healers. But those who knew better knew them for what they truly were. The head knight, Sir Samuel Parson, was a man known for his honor. He stood honor-bound to the king even when he showed himself a coward. He stayed at his king's side when others of his family followed Lackshin into war against the Xyles. Even though he remained with his king, no one thought less of him. As a knight, he was expected to stay with King Benjamin and protect the "Cowardly King" with his life. Riding out with his two brothers to battle is what he truly wanted to do. But to him, a vow was a vow and meant to be kept. Sir Samuel stood over six feet tall, with broad shoulders and striking features. The women said his hazel eyes caused their garments to fall clean off them like magic. His locked hair hung past his shoulders, jet black in all their glory. His dark gray armor encased his body, fitting like another layer of skin but hard and cold to the touch. Unlike the warm soft feel of flesh, he smelled like sharpened steel. It seemed everything about him could cut you.

Jason Henry, a man whose story had not been clear to most, was short and heavyset with dark brown hair slicked back on his head. It looked greasy to the touch. His eyes were blue-gray, beady little things that hung close together on his chubby face. It had been said he was the son of a pirate who took his part of plunder and started a life in the great city, then slowly weaseled his way into the court. From there, he used his skills as a pirate and found himself head of the kingdom's bank. Just the thought of it made people laugh. A pirate in charge of the kingdom's gold? It was like putting a fox in a henhouse. He was not a man you wanted to owe money to. There had been a rumor that a backer could not pay his debt to the royal bank, so his two daughters were made to work off his debt with interest in a nearby establishment. Jason was also said to be the son of a lord that the king owed a great debt to and placed Jason in his position as parasol—payment to whatever was owed. Now, here he was on the king's council. One thing the court was not short of was rumors.

"Why are we here, knight?" the short banker asked.

He looked at Jason with contempt in his eyes. There had been no love lost between the knight and the pirate banker. "How am I to know, pirate? I was called here same as you," he said, looking down at the fat man.

"Maybe the king has finally figured out that you have been stealing from the kingdom and brought us here so he can accuse you and have me take your head where you stand." Sir Samuel rubbed the pommel of his sword.

"I cannot leave you two alone for a moment before you are serenading one another with words of affection." A tall, skinny man wandered in like he had all the time in the world to make it to the Sunroom. His yellow hair was cut short, but still long enough for some of it to hang past his ears. His purple vest covered his white shirt buttoned part way up. Gray trousers fit loosely but clung to his waist. A short sword dangled from his belt. The man known as Norris decided he would join the rest of the council at their early morning commons.

"Has anyone seen that Obeah-Man?" Norris asked as he nervously looked around. His head went left and right, up, down and around.

"If he comes out from nowhere, I will cut him in half again." Sir Samuel joined the search. His head now went to and fro as he looked for this Obeah-Man.

"Is that your way of solving every problem?" The fat pirate made his way to the table where the wine was kept. He poured himself a cup as he watched them prepare for this freakishly creepy man to show up from anywhere. "I think he does this to us on purpose," Jason said.

"He will not be joining us this morning," a deep voice bellowed through the throne room, followed by the loud sounds of heavy doors closing.

"Your Majesty." Sir Samuel Parson dropped to one knee.

Norris looked at Sir Samuel and shook his head. "Your honor will keep you on your knees." Norris walked past the knight toward the throne. "Where is your father, Prince Brook? When did you start calling council meetings? I thought only the king, or I could call for the council to assemble." Norris poured himself a cup of wine and drank. Patting the sides of his lips dry with a silk scarf, he took another go at the nineteen-year-old prince. "Are we playing at king again, boy? Have you not outgrown this yet?" Norris took another swallow of wine.

"To your feet, knight," the prince said as he glared at Norris. His blue eyes would have cut a hole through him if they could. Long, curly light brown hair hung down past his neck, tied neatly with a gold cord. The prince stood just short of six feet, dressed in parasol armor. A polished, blue steel breastplate reflected a blue glow from all the sun that flooded in from the windows along the walls. The long sword he proudly called "Whistle," hung brilliantly from his belt. A knight said that he swings the sword so fiercely that he could hear it whistle as it cut the surrounding air. The hilt and the pommel were made of the same blue steel as his breastplate. Its blade held a lighter glimmer of the blue, a faint reflection when the sun hit it just right.

"How are you still a part of this council, Norris? My father should have put you to the sword a long time ago." The prince squeezed the handle of "Whistle." His knuckles whitened as his grip tightened.

Norris smiled a crooked smile. "Your father and I were friends years before he released you into your mother. I am one of his most trusted friends." Norris drank the last of his wine. "So, if there is nothing more, I will take my leave." He turned to go.

"The reason the Obeah-Man is not here is because he is with my father. I am sure you all have been made aware that the king has not been in the best of health," Brook said as he sat in his chair to the right of his father's throne.

"What has happened to his majesty?" Sir Samuel asked. His hazel eyes widened as he stepped closer.

"Unfortunately, he has taken a turn for the worse. And to answer Norris's earlier question, no, it is still up to the king and yourself to call the council. I did not think my calling council this one time would be such a problem for you all." The prince paused, waiting for approval from Norris.

Norris turned and gave the prince a reluctant nod.

"Thank you." Prince Brook pointed to a table in the sunroom. There he had fresh fruits: plums, grapes, and pears, just to name a few. Warm baked bread was placed on either side of the table next to a tray of sharp cheeses and bowls of jam. A pitcher of red wine sat in the middle.

Prince Brook made his way down from his throne and sat at the head of the table with Sir Samuel to his right. Norris sat to the left of the prince, and Jason sat to Norris's left. Brook picked up a jar of honey and poured it into his cup followed by the wine.

Norris laughed. "When are you going to give up the honey, prince?" Norris poured himself a second cup. "When the prince was a smaller boy and wanted to drink with his father and I, he would always ask for some honey in his cup because he could not stand the taste of wine."

Clink, clink, clink. Prince Brook tapped a spoon on the side of his cup. It echoed through the room.

"Now that Norris is done reminiscing about my childhood, we can put some attention to the problem at hand," the prince said before taking a drink of his honey red. He nodded in approval. "What are we doing to find out more about the rumor of this boy claiming to be the Son of Lackshin?" The prince scanned the three, waiting for an answer.

"More stories of this boy again?" Norris shook his head. "Almost a year has passed since Sillack put him to the sword. The sprout of this man is probably dead, afraid to show himself, or does not even know who he is." Norris grabbed a fist full of grapes.

The knight pondered a moment as he poured himself his first cup of red. He took a long, heavy drink before he spoke. "My prince," he began, "some of my scouts have come back with some peculiar stories of late. The kingdom's quietly stir. There is no talk of unseating Sillack from his made-up throne or any talk of war. Yet, Sillack is sending out larger than normal forces to keep his peace. That is reason enough to be concerned," Sir Samuel informed the prince.

"It is probably him reacting to the same rumors that you have called us here about," Jasen said, sounding perturbed. He was made to get up much earlier than he had been used to. He preferred his feather bed much more than the cold wooden cheer he had been sitting on. "Do we not have men we can pay to kill this pretender?"

"You mean like an assassin?" the prince asked. "Looks to me that your solution to everything is to throw the kingdom's gold at it. Tell me, where do we find these assassins, Jason?"

"In these time's every other man thinks himself an assassin and would be more than happy to take a chance to prove himself," Jason said. He wanted to make this problem anyone else's but his. Like many who dare not say it, he had been sick of the tales of this boy every year or two. Jason ripped off some of the sweet bread. It was still warm to the touch and paired well with the tartest of cheeses on the platter.

The fat banker used his hand to tear an opening in the light brown crust and squeezed the two halves together on the cheese.

"There is always the Skeritts," Norris muttered under his breath.

"What was that?" the knight asked. "I do not think I heard correctly."

Norris cleared his throat, followed by another sip of wine. They waited for the silk to leave his lips. "I said there are the Skeritts. We could always employ them to find and eliminate this boy before this gets out of hand. Every time someone threatens to undo the power Sillack values more than a man, we all hear him declare Sanch as his trueborn brother." Norris' dark eyes remained emotionless. His eyes often seemed dead, making it hard to know if he meant to help, or meant to do you harm.

"The Skeritts? The ones that swear fealty to the Allens?" The prince made sure they were indeed speaking of the same family of assassins. "Lackshin's surname is Allen. That would make him family to the assassin you would have me dispatch?" Prince Brook angrily clenched his jaw.

Sir Samuel thought the prince would break a tooth or two if he got any angrier.

"Have you truly lost your mind, Norris?" Sir Samuel firmly said. "They would just as well kill one of us before turning on one of their own. 'Family above all else,' remember?'"

Norris stared at the knight with his dead eyes. "You know those words all too well, don't you?" A sly, crooked smile crossed his face.

"I will cut that smile straight!" Sir Samuel reached for his dagger.

The prince placed his hand on the knight's shoulder. "Leave his smile as it is Samuel. Those lockset savages..." Prince Brook caught himself and turned to Samuel. "My apologies, sir."

Sir Samuel humbly nodded.

"We all know that the Skeritts will stay loyal to this boy if indeed he turns out to be the true Son of Lackshin. Instead of having the Skeritts wander the city waiting, we will give them a reason to squeeze their hand around our throat in the name of this boy. We will be better off letting the pirate make a few would be assassins prove themselves. Best case, they get lucky and kill him." The prince drank the last of his honeyed red and got up and turned to exit the same way he'd entered.

The knight quickly stood.

"And the worst case?" Jason asked.

The prince stopped but did not turn around.

"The worst case would be?" Jason asked once more.

"Worst case would be this boy kills them and no one is the wiser that we had anything to do with this messy business," the knight answered for his prince.

"And that is why we call him Sir Samuel Jason." The prince pointed to the fat banker.

CHAPTER FIFTEEN

The battle had ended, and the sounds of combat had stopped. The only sounds were of the men from both sides collecting the dead and wounded. Down on one knee with his hand on Thrant's chest, Ralyn said farewell to an old friend. Standing with her back turned to everyone, Lisha held Sanch's sword in her hands, still dripping with Alshin's life. Bethany stood over her father with her hand on his shoulder as she looked at her cousin to see if she needed her to be there for her. Sanch, Menis, Silma, and the others looked on silently, not sure what to do nor how they could help. Some of Alshin's men came over to gather his body and were met with resistance.

"Do not touch him!" Lisha commanded.

"We are just here to prepare him to be moved," one man said.

"The first man to touch him will be put to rest right next to him," Lisha warned.

"You heard her," Bethany said.

"Do you not understand? Leave the body right where it is until she tells you otherwise," Sanch said. "Unless you truly wish to join him in death?"

The soldier saw Sanch standing there with Shallin in hand and that made it clear to them that the body was to stay where it was. They got the point when Menis and Sanch stepped up. Alshin's men left to join the others.

"Lisha, what is to be done with his body?" Menis asked.

Kess made her way to Lisha and Alshin's body.

"What is that in her hand?" Bethany asked.

Ralyn looked to see his wife with the fuel to light the arrows in one hand and a torch in the other.

"This is not going to be good," Ralyn said as he got to his feet. "Men, stand ready!"

Kess walked over to Alshin's body and handed Lisha the torch. Lisha stabbed both swords into the earth and took the torch from Kess. Kess then started to cover Alshin with the fuel, then grabbed Lisha's hand, pulling her back a bit. Lisha put the flame over Alshin's face and lit him up. His men who still had fight in them saw this and became enraged. They started making their way to where Alshin burned.

"Give them the order!" Kess shouted to Sanch. "They follow you!"

"But our men are close with them," Sanch replied.

"They do not miss!" Kess smiled. "Trust me."

Silma sat on Sanch's shoulder and agreed with Kess. "Give the order Sanch. Let's see what these archers can do!"

Sanch lifted his hand and gave the signal to fire. The arrows came off the wall in a familiar pattern. Every arrow hit its mark. One extra arrow landed at Sanch's feet.

A smile crept across Menis' face as he looked at that arrow. "Now, they're just showing off,"

With Alshin's body burning, things got eerily quiet across the battlefield. Thrant's men gathered around his body. No one knew what to say. One man walked over to Thrant's shield and picked it up.

"With your shield or on it?" the man walked over to his fallen brother.

The point made, they all worked together to get Thrant onto his shield and, with great reverence, walked him into the village. Now, with the loss of Thrant, Sanch saw how real it all was. He saw the lives of so many he held in his hands. He thought to himself, how many more will have to die over a war between two men that have never met. He wondered why his father did not finish the job when he had Sillack at the end of his sword. Could he have stopped Sillack? If his father was unable to finish him, how could a boy who knows nothing of war do it? Sanch wondered if he had what it takes to end all of this. If so, what would the cost be?

Bethany, already in the village, looked back and saw Sanch still standing there with an unsure look on his face. She broke away from the others and ran back to gather Sanch. Bethany approached him without a word and stood in front of him. She was only half a head shorter than him, but she still needed to tilt her head back to look him in the eyes. With his head down, there was no way he missed her standing there. She could sense that his body was there, but his mind was elsewhere. He had a lot to process.

"Alshin did this, not you. He was sent by Sillack to destroy us all, and with your help, we stopped him. This war started before the both of us. Its time was long ago, and we are still fighting. In their time, they followed your father, and he took them as far as he could. He saved as many lives as he could. In the end, it cost him his life. Do not think for a moment no one died under your father's command. Now is a new time, and we follow you. This ends with us. I have been told about this war since I was a little girl. We are what it will take to end it. Sillack knows this. That is why he has gone as far as he has to try to stop you. You are what this war has been waiting for all these years. None of us started this fight, but it has been passed to us to finish. We are not being given a choice, but we have to give others a choice."

Bethany looked at Sanch. She couldn't change what he had to do. He had to fight Sillack alone when it came time. All she could do was fight alongside him and the others that agree that Sillack needed to die. The evil that made its way to them had to be stopped.

"The day is yours, Sanch," Bethany reminded the battered warrior.

Sanch returned her gaze. Bethany put her left hand on Sanch's right forearm. The world went quiet as she ran her hand down to his hand where he held Shallin, and before they knew it, they were both holding Lackshin's sword.

"We should catch up with the others. We still have a lot left to do"

With his hand on her shoulder, Bethany and Sanch made their way over to where the others were on their way to enter the village. They were taking Thrant to where his body would be prepared and laid to rest. The war was over for Thrant, but the others knew there was more to come.

Ralyn and all the others that would play a big role in the outcome of battles yet to come met in the village meeting hall which doubled as war room. It was a large room with strips of wood carved with the history of many that came before them that hung the length of the great hall on both sides. Large windows also lined the top, allowing sunlight to shine down on the round tables that filled the room. There was one table in the center of the hall with five tables surrounding the first table with ten more tables surrounding those five.

Now and for several years, it had been used for celebrations, weddings, and births of children. They entered the great doors carved with the history of the village to discuss the events yet to come. Sanch could count almost twenty or more torches along the wall in cages holding flames in place to give each table light enough to see at night. The grand building smelled of the history of the world outside the gates.

"Do we wait for them, or do we ride out and meet them before they send a larger army to take the Son of Lackshin from us?" Ralyn asked as he wiped dirt off Bethany's face.

"We know they are out there, and we will not be their only victims," Sanch replied. "If we just sit here and wait, they are going to leave a path of destruction behind them. I will not stay here when they're out there killing in the name of finding me. Yes, you will be safe behind your walls, but think of what will happen to others that are not so lucky to have what you have. My mother is still out there. Unlike the others, she has me to protect her."

"What are you saying, Sanch?" Bethany asked. "Are you planning on leaving us? Are you planning on going back home to your mother? Without us?" She turned to her father. "We will not let him go by himself, are we, father?"

"We are not letting him go after his mother at all," Ralyn answered Bethany. "That is just what Sillack would be waiting for. He will have a great force sent there waiting for you, Sanch, and we can't have that. Besides, if Sillack knew where Sanch and his mother were all this time, he would have sent men to kill Sanch and his mother long ago. Why wait till now to use the information of his whereabouts? What we're going to do is send out two forces, maybe three. One small force will be sent to bring Sanch's mother and whomever else that will fight with us. We do not need to attract attention from Sillack's men, who will be keeping an eye out for us, and those that would join us. The other force will head to Sillack's castle. He needs to know we are coming for him," Ralyn growled.

"If you do not mind, uncle, I would like to go with the force to find Sanch's mother," Lisha said. "To get to the village, we will go right past my father's inn. I need to tell him of his brother and the return of Shallin." Lisha looked over at Sanch and added, "I will let him know of the return of the Son of Lackshin."

"That would be a great idea," Ralyn said, praising Lisha. "You, Menis, Deem, and Evian can take the force that will escort his mother back to us. And the other force will be headed by you, Sanch, Dagger, Silma, and your quiet friend over there."

Quickly adding to her husband's list was Kess. "And Sanch, Bethany will also be joining you and your force."

"Yes, I wouldn't have it any other way, my lord." Sanch tried not to make eye contact with Kess.

"How will we know your mother, Sanch?" Menis asked.

Sanch smiled. "If Sillack's men have gotten there before you, then she will be the woman with the sword standing over a dead man or two. The last thing you will want to ask her is if she is my mother, because she will most likely kill you where you stand. When you find her, just tell her I am being true to my sword. Then, and only then will she know I sent you."

"Sanch, what is her name? Whom do we ask for?" Lisha inquired.

"Her name is Vera, but I call her mother. Now that this much is decided, we all should get some food and rest before we prepare our loved ones to be put to rest and sent off to meet their god." Sanch looked somberly at Lisha.

"That sounds like a good idea, Sanch," Ralyn agreed. "We have a lot to get done before you all are on your way. Today has been the first battle of many to come, and you young warriors have shown yourselves to be very capable. This is not a war any of you started; this is your fathers' war. There is no doubt in my mind that you will succeed where we failed. Now, everyone go do what they must, and we will meet back at first light."

Evian nodded and took his leave to go prepare for the long journey from home. He had never been very far from the village, the place he called home. The people called it a village, but it was as large as a small city. It had always just been Evian and his little brother and his parents. He knew how to fight, but he knew nothing of war. Today was the first time he had to end a man's life. Now he must wonder what else he will face on the other side of the village gates past the land he knew. What atrocities will he face and what kinds of evils will he see? He walked through the village and saw many others doing just as he meant to do. They prepared to leave and meet Sillack's men. None of them wanted to go out and fight knowing the Xyles were out there and what they do to men or anything that stands in their way. No one wanted to leave their family behind, not knowing if they would ever see them again. Yet they all knew there was no other way to keep the ones they love safe. As of right now, no one knew if there was anyone out there to oppose the evil, and the destruction Sillack meant to carry out on the lands and the people living there.

As a boy, Evian grew up and heard from his father of the battles he and the other men of the village took part in alongside Lackshin and his best friend. He was told how two of them were unstoppable together, and how the Xyles had no chance when opposed by them.

Evian arrived at his home to find his mother and father nervously awaiting his safe return. He walked through the front door with a different look on his face. A look he had not had before. His mother knew not of this look. It was not her son's familiar face. His father knew this look all too well. It was the look of a man who had taken a life. It was not the look a boy came back with after his first time hunting with his father. This look was very different, dark even. His mother went to walk to him, but her husband held her back from advancing.

"He is going to need some time alone," his father whispered. "He is not the same man we said goodbye to this morning. He has changed from the son you have known into something else. A line has been crossed that he cannot come back from. He will be ok. We just need to give him a little time to himself for him to come to terms with whatever it was he had to do today, and the things he must have seen."

"But he is my son. I did not want him out there fighting a war that was not his. You men started this. Now our sons are going to be forced to finish it." Evian's mother fell into her husband's arms.

He embraced her to comfort her the best he could. Before Evian made his way to his room, he rested his hand on her shoulders and kissed her on the back of her head.

Lisha and the others were still at Ralyn and Kess's home. It was a couple of rooms shy of a castle. There, they were getting things ready to put Thrant to rest. Thrant had used his brother's sword in battle. A warrior could not be laid to rest without a sword of his own, so one had to be forged for him. Sanch and Menis were told by Ralyn to go to the blacksmith and commission a sword to be made for Thrant. They were told to walk toward the smoke that bellowed from the blacksmith's workshop.

Menis asked a question that had plagued him and surely some of the others. He turned to Sanch and asked, "What is that black stain on your sword, my friend? Is it an imperfection in the steel, or was it burned when it was being forged? I have never seen something such as that on a sword before."

Unsure himself, Sanch told Menis what his mother told him when he asked the same question, "It was made different than other swords. My father made it himself. My mother said he wanted me to have a weapon that works for me as well as his worked for him. What that means, I do not know, but my mother always told me to be true to my sword. She would say Shallin is my father's sword, and my sword is where I need to put my trust. So, she is my mother, therefore I do as she sees. Shallin is only needed when the time comes to end Sillack's evil hold on these lands. That is all I know of my sword's markings. The stained metal I know nothing about, but the first day I received this sword from my mother, it felt like it was a part of me. It is forever cold, and sometimes it feels like there is nothing in my hand. It is an extension of myself."

When Sanch and Menis arrived at the blacksmith, they proceeded to tell him of the sword they needed made for their friend that they had lost in battle this very day. The blacksmith had heard rumors of the loss of many of their own, but he did not know Thrant had been one of the fallen. He had been the same blacksmith that made Thrant's original armor and sword.

"Did my armor fail him? Was there a kink in his shield or was his sword not sharp enough?" the blacksmith asked.

"No," Menis answered. "He fell in battle against a great foe. He was wearing his brother's armor and wielding his brother's sword. That is why we need one made for him."

"We cannot send him off without a sword and armor, now, can we?" Sanch added." The sword you made him years ago has been lost, and that is why we need a sword made for him. Before this is all said and done, someone will give us back the lost one and the life that was taken from us today. Swords of Thrant's enemies will hit the ground in abundance. I am not ok with being the reason people are dying," Sanch said as he walked away in frustration.

"How much time do I have to forge this sword?" the blacksmith asked Menis.

"You have till dawn, because that is when the rest of us will leave and go our separate ways. There is much to do, blacksmith. I'm sure this sword is not the only one you will forge in days to come"

"What is with the young man?" the blacksmith asked as he looked over at Sanch.

"That young man is who we are all looking to end this war. He is the reason these swords will be needed in the days or maybe years to come. We will be back at dawn. We thank you for your help. This means a lot to us."

Menis walked over to Sanch.

"No one blames you for any of this. Without you, we would have no hope and you need to remember that." Menis walked away, leaving Sanch to ponder what he had said.

Sanch stopped and thought. He needed to hear that. He needed to know he did not cause the things that were happening, and needed to understand that this started before he could even hold a sword, much less take a life.

As the two made their way back to the others, few words were spoken between them. They both had their mind on things to come. Sanch worried about the safety of his mother. He didn't like that he was unable to retrieve her himself and had to trust others to do it. Even though he knew he left her in capable hands, he still worried. He understood what Ralyn said about them waiting for him to come for her, but still, he did not like it. He trusted his friends to protect his mother but were they going to make it on time before Sillack's men figured out what village they hid in all these years?

Menis's biggest fear was that he would let those who count on him down. He knew what was expected, and he just hoped he could do what it was they needed of him. He thought to himself that the men of his clan would be a great help in battles to come.

When the two boys arrived back to the house, they only found Ralyn, Deem, and Dagger going over some things. The girls and Hush had gone.

"Where have the girls run off to? Where is Bethany?" Sanch asked.

"Kess heard what they did for Silma in the Thorn Forest and thought maybe she should help them hone their power a little better. I do not know what you told Hush, but he would not let Silma out of his sight. Anyway, before you all arrived, she was helping Bethany bring her powers out to where it could be used," Ralyn informed the boys. "Kess's mother and my mother came from the same fighting clan of women. In their clan, some women are born with that glow you saw Bethany and Lisha use to help Silma in the woods. I am sure you can see how a power like that is needed now more than ever All you saw of their power is the healing part of it, but there is so much more to it. Those two girls have not even grazed on what they really can do with it. They're both young, and until the other day, Lisha had no idea she had powers of any kind. I'm sure you can see where they're going to need a bit of help with this."

"After you guys left the cave, the power that Silma was left with was amazing," Dagger added. "If they can do something like that to something that small, their power is definitely something we are going to need."

"In the meantime, we need to put together a plan of attack. They brought the first fight to us. The next one we will take to them," Deem said as a smile crossed his face.

CHAPTER SIXTEEN

"Lisha, focus your thoughts. You have to feel what it is you want to do. Do you want to help or hurt whatever you want to use your glow on? That is what you need to decide before you release your energy."

"It worked fine when Beth and I used it to help the little fly girl," Lisha said to Kess.

Silma did not take well to what Lisha had to say and had a bit to say herself. "Who are you calling little? Did you not see what I did on the battlefield? I got plenty big enough when it came time to throw down." Silma fluttered above hush's shoulder. The sun behind her no longer hung high in the sky. It was now mid-afternoon. "When you're ready, witch, I will show you just how I did it." Silma's blue became brighter.

"Now, you two, there is no need for that. You are both on the same side. As you saw in the Thorn Forest and in the cave, your powers work very well together. You and Bethany both should be able to do that alone and much more. In the morning, you will go in two separate directions and you both will need to be more in control of what you can do. Watch this." Kess walked over to Hush and gently picked Silma off his right shoulder and backed away far enough so the girls could see what she was doing. She looked at Silma with gentle eyes that glowed a soft blue. Her hand then glowed the same blue and transferred energy from herself to Silma. By doing so, her powers increased exponentially. "Now, Silma, do that thing you do. Grow."

The two girls and Hush watched in amazement as Silma did just that with little help from Kess. Silma grew like she did when she drew the life force from others. Her growing glow reflected off the trees that surrounded the clearing they stood in. Strange white stones surrounded them. Great big ones stood almost as tall as some of the smaller trees. Others looked as if they had carvings at one time, but were now worn to the point they could no longer be read. When they did not feel like standing, they sat on the stones to congregate. Those stones all faced a pulpit. The white ones turned a beautiful blue.

Now Silma stood five-foot-two with a four-foot wingspan. Her almost transparent, yet extremely strong wings were outlined with a glow all its own. She had done it before, but never like this. She looked and felt strong.

"Mother ... what did you ... how did you do that, and can we learn to do that as well?" Bethany asked. "That could be of great use if we ever find ourselves in a tough spot."

"I feel great! What did you do to me?" Silma asked Kess "I think this may last longer than the times before." Turning to Kess, she asked, "Can these two do the same thing?"

"They will be able to when I am done with them, I hope," Kess said with a smile. "Now, you two come over here so we can get started."

The two walked over, not knowing what to expect. Kess explained to them that the power could help as they saw with Silma, or it could kill. The same power she used could easily be changed into a deadly force, and even remove someone's life energy.

"You both were lucky you did not kill Silma in your attempt to save her. Beth, you knew what you were doing, but one wrong thought or an unintended change could have made a big difference in the end results. Luckily for you two, it worked just fine."

"Lucky for me, you mean?" Silma interrupted

"Yes, Silma, especially lucky for you." Kess smiled. "These two witches could have done some harm." Silma and Kess exchanged a look and a smile. "Do not worry, Silma. When we are done with them, they will not have to rely on luck. They will know what they're doing. Where we need to start is with your emotions and how to control then. You must focus them, and then release them. First, both of you need to find yourselves two roses and then we will begin."

As Bethany and Lisha looked for the roses, Silma and Kess had time to talk face to face.

"How bad could it have been, Kess?" Silma asked.

"Like I told you three, they could have killed you. Understand, apart, they are powerful, but together they're almost unstoppable. We do not want them mad because they could lose control. No good could come of that," Kess added.

"How is it that I can stay this size this long? My powers feel so much stronger than when I take the life force from someone."

"That is because what I gave you was pure life energy willingly given, and not that stuff you pull from humans. You pull life force that makes life. It will wear off, but not for some time."

"Can all the women in your tribe do this? Silma inquired.

"No. It has to be in the lifeline that makes us family. Lisha's mother and her father's grandmother had the glow. Ralyn and I, our mother's both had it. Since men can't wield this power, the power that was meant for their fathers was passed to them tenfold."

"Where did it come from? When did it start? How did it make it to all of you? I just think it's great, but please do not tell them I said that," Silma said.

"Don't you worry, I will say nothing," Kess said. "As for where these powers started or whom of us were the first to obtain them, I do not know for sure. There are stories, but nothing that can be proven."

Kess told Silma the history of the glow with the limited information she had. Her two students came to another clearing field with rose bushes, and with nothing said between the two, Lisha and Bethany went looking for roses they were to return with. It may have been because of them both being nervous that even though they looked together, they said not a word. In the search, they found four perfect roses.

"What do you think is to come of these roses?" Bethany asked Lisha, breaking the silence.

"One will be made to live, and one will die, I suppose," Lisha replied. "She said our powers can help and destroy, so two powers and two roses," Lisha deduced.

They went through and avoided the thorns as they picked their roses and started back to join Kess, Silma, and Hush in the clearing where Silma began to slowly return to her normal size.

"He does not say much, does he?" Kess asked as she examined Hush. "I have not heard a peep out of him. Does he understand us?"

"I don't know about us, but he understands Sanch just fine. Sanch ordered him to keep me safe, and he has been doing just that." Silma stroked the fur on the back of his neck.

"He is a handsome beast. I am happy to have him with us," Kess said as she offered Hush some of the fruit she brought with her. He gave a little smile and received it graciously.

"Oh, there they are!" Silma shouted. "What took you girls so long? How far did you have to go?"

"Roses don't grow wild around here," Bethany replied. "But we managed to find a rose bush not too far away."

"What would you have us do with these roses, aunt Kess?" Lisha walked closer to her holding the spoils of her search out in front of her.

"I am going to show you girls how to focus your powers. You both have shown that you can use your glow, but focus is the key to using it to its full capacity. For example, you both got lucky when it came to saving Silma. Bethany, tell me what you were thinking when you were using your powers on Silma in the Thorn Forest?"

"Well, mother, I have seen you use it, so I went with that as a guide. I have even used it for healing thoughts to help little animals. I did the same with Silma."

"Why is it you asked Lisha to help?" Kess asked curiously.

"Well, I've heard you all talk about the power her mother possessed and thought maybe cousin was like me. Being that Silma was not some small animal, I thought I could use the help if it was to work at all."

"Well, thanks for seeing that I was not just some small animal," Silma said.

"No problem, little friend." Bethany smiled.

"That was smart, Bethany, but very dangerous," Kess said as she handed Hush another piece of fruit.

"Why is that?" Lisha asked.

"Because you know nothing of your powers, so I do not know if Silma is lucky or if you are just that good. Lisha, what were you thinking about when you were healing Silma?"

"Not much. I was just surprised with all that was going on." Lisha twisted her face showing her confusion.

"That must be what protected Silma," Kess said. She took the roses from the girls' hands.

Silma went over to Hush and realized she was still too big to sit on his shoulder. Instead, she opted to put her head there.

"I need you both to stand in front of me and hold out your hands." From the look in her eyes, Kess could tell that Bethany's mind was somewhere else.

"Do you have something on your mind, Bethany? Is there anything you want to share?" Kess asked, moving a lock of jet-black hair from over one of her eyes. "Cause if there is, I need you clear-headed for this."

"No, it is nothing mother," Bethany replied. "I am fine. I am ready."

"Ok, let's begin. I want you to kill these roses I place in your hand."

"But how do we do that?" Lisha asked.

"You need to aim your negative energy through your body into your hands. What you will be doing is pulling the life from the roses through, therefore killing them. Find your anger and direct it to your center. Hold it there, but not too long. Then release into your hand. Now comes the tricky part." Kess put a hand on each of the girls. "Slowly pull it back into you."

The cousins prepared their thoughts. Both closed their eyes and visualized something hurtful to them—a thought that would make them angry. Both lucky and unlucky for Lisha, she had something fresh on her mind to help her do that. They both got started at taking the life of these flowers. A soft white glow came over the two of them, starting in their face and slowly flowing through the rest of their body until it consumed them. The soft white glow slowly began changing and became a dull, bark gray. The roses began gradually losing their luscious red color and wilted. You could see the life of each petal as it left the roses and entered Bethany and Lisha's fingertips to the point where their face took on a glow the same color of the roses.

Suddenly, Bethany's face lost its red and energy started flowing back into the rose. Her rose changed from its lifeless state. She gave it back life, but not only that, she changed it. The rose was no longer a red; it was now a soft dark brown. Both Silma and Hush got up to get a better look at what was happening. Now Lisha was holding a dead flower and Bethany a very alive flower that no longer shared the color of a normal rose.

Recognizing the new color, Kess smiled and ordered the girls to stop and open their eyes. "I want you both to look at your rose."

Lisha's dark red rose resembled death, but it was very much alive.

"What is wrong with my rose?" Bethany asked. "Is it dead or what? It looks dead."

"Bethany, are you ready to tell me what is on your mind yet?" Kess asked. "It is very important that you have your mind on the task at hand for this to work."

"Yes, I have something ... someone I am worried about," Bethany reluctantly admitted.

"Who is this someone?" Kess asked.

Not sure what was going on, Lisha looked on curiously.

Bethany did not know how to put words to what she was thinking. She hesitated, but then explained. "I am worried about Sanch." She looked down at her feet.

Lisha smiled. "I could tell it was him you were thinking of. What have you noticed about this flower you made?"

"Nothing other than I killed it. Roses are supposed to be red, but this one is a funny brown." Bethany pushed at the petals with one finger.

"No, it's not a funny brown, it's a brown you can't get out of your mind." Kess made it clear to Bethany. "I have only seen this brown in two places, and one of them is here with us. Do you still not get it, my child?"

Silma, catching on to what Kess was saying, turned to look into Hush's eyes and started laughing.

"Quiet, Silma." Kess held back laughter.

Now being close to her original size, Silma flew over to Lisha and whispered something into her ear. A stunned Lisha turned to Bethany.

"Really cousin?" Lisha smiled at her.

"What is it? What am I missing? What is with this flower?"

"Bethany, look at Hush's eyes and look at the color of your flower. Do you notice anything about them both?" Lisha still cradled a dead flower in her hands.

"They seem to be the same color, which is a little strange. I don't understand why that is. Why would my rose end up the color of Hush's eyes?" Bethany shook her head.

"Bethany, Sanch's eyes are the same color as Hush's." Kess turned his large head to Bethany so that she could take a better look. The creature's eyes held the same softness as Sanch's.

"Bethany, I think you have strong feelings for Sanch." Lisha said.

Bethany quickly realized what had happened and why the rose was the color it was now. All this time, Bethany thought there might have been something between Sanch and her cousin. She quickly turned to Lisha. "I am sorry. I did not mean to. I know he is yours..."

"Mine?" Lisha said. "He is not mine. We are friends and we fight great together, but I am more into the strong silent type."

Just then, everyone looked at Hush.

"Come on, I am talking about someone else, and since the color of my rose did not give up my secret you all will just have to wait and see."

"Bethany, I will take this flower and put it away, and we will go on with our training. You still have a lot to learn."

Silma quickly stepped up and volunteered to hold on to the rose and keep it safe. Flying back to Hush, she could not see the look given to her by Bethany.

"You know she can't wait to get those roses back so she can show Sanch, right?" Lisha looked over at her cousin. "She will not let this go, Bethany. She is going to tell anyone that will listen. You know this, don't you?"

"Yes, Lisha, I do. Try not to look so happy about it, will you?" Bethany's face turned as red as Lisha's roses.

Lisha leaned over and gave her cousin a hard kiss on the side of her head that nearly pushed Bethany off her feet.

"If you two are done here, we still have a lot to do and a lot to learn. My little girl can bring life back involuntarily, but that is not good enough. You will not always have the thoughts of Sanch's eyes to focus your energy on."

"Mother, you too?"

"Sorry, Beth. I just could not let that one go. I am good now. That was all I had. Or is it?" Kess winked at Lisha. "Anyway, can you pour some of your dead roses in your cousin's hand? Since we only have one dead rose, we will do it a little differently. We are going to bring two roses back using the remains from one. What I am going to need you both to do is bring your mind down to almost no thought at all. That will put you where you need to be to refill yourself with what you need. You will then think of what that rose was and what it needs to be again. So, when you are both ready you can begin."

The girls took some time before they began the task that was asked of them. With the day they both had—from Lisha losing an uncle she was just getting to know and grow to love—to Bethany, just a little girl that knew nothing of combat and the ways of war—to now a woman that has taken lives of men.

Clearing their minds was not an easy task for either of them. Lisha and Bethany took a deep breath, closed their eyes and tried their best to think of nothing. After finally clearing their minds, they thought of something that would give them the positive feeling to resurrect the dead roses. Try as they may, neither of them had enough good thoughts to bring about what they needed to do what was being asked of them. The longer they tried, the weaker they both got. Kess noticed that neither of them was making any progress and both were becoming weak. She felt it was time to end the exercise.

"Ok, girls, I think that is enough. It is not working. You both have had a long and rough day. Finding something good may not be the easiest thing to ask of you right now, nor is it fair to ask you to try." Reaching out her hands, she asked them to pour what was left of the dead rose into her palm, then had them put the last remaining rose in her other hand.

"When you both have learned to use your powers, this will be nothing for you to do." Kess effortlessly held out both of her hands. In the hand with the dead rose, life flowed powerfully back into that rose, while in the other hand, the opposite happened. The dying rose slowly lost its color and then wilted rapidly. She was giving life and taking life at the same time, but she did not stop there. She brought life back to the rose she had just killed. She stood there holding two beautiful roses in her hands.

"That was amazing!" Silma flew over to get a closer look. "Will these two eventually be able to do this?"

"As soon as I get them trained. They both already have the raw power and what it takes to do what I just did, but with all that took place today, it is going to be a little time before their minds are where it needs to be to learn what I am teaching them."

Over Kess's left shoulder smoke billowed from the chimney of a large house in the village.

"What is that?" Lisha pointed to the smoke.

Kess turned and saw something she had not seen for some time. The smoke was coming from the blacksmith's house. Until now, the blacksmith only made shoes for the horses, nails, and things of that sort. All those produced a different kind of smoke; not the thick, dark smoke that you get from forging swords. Until today, everyone who needed a sword had a sword. As for everyone else, they had no reason to have a sword and just learned to bow in order to hunt for food for the village and their family. Now these were different times where everyone was in need of a sword.

"That is the blacksmith, Lisha," Kess said as she turned to look. "He is making swords. We should go."

Kess ordered them to gather up everything. Silma made sure to remind them to bring the Sanch flower. A red-faced Bethany knew that her feelings for Sanch would no longer be a secret.

"Do not worry Silma, this rose is going right next to her father's. This rose will no longer need sunlight or water. This flower will live on love alone."

"But what if he does not feel the same? What then?" Bethany asked.

"He could not keep his eyes off you when we first got here, cousin. Your mother had to make him take you along with us." Lisha put her arms over Bethany's shoulder. "I know him, and if it were up to him, he would have locked you away till the fighting was over. Trust me, The Son of Lackshin likes you a lot, and I will prove it when we get back to the boys."

"Please don't. You are going to embarrass me," Bethany begged as Lisha led her like a lamb to slaughter.

CHAPTER SEVENTEEN

"As soon as Thrant's sword is made, we will lay my dear friend to rest. He is now at peace. We must fight on." Ralyn held back the pain.

"What are we going to do with all the prisoners we have? We do not have the men needed to hold them indefinitely, and it is also dangerous to keep so many of our enemies inside our gates. Who knows what they could plot while in there?" Deem ran a rag down the length of his blade before putting it back in its place of rest.

"That is a good point, Deem," Ralyn agreed. "We have never had so many prisoners, nor are we equipped to hold them indefinitely."

"Then we need to find something to do with them," Dagger said.

"Do what?" Sanch uttered. "Maybe not all of them need to remain prisoners."

"What do you mean, Sanch?" Menis asked.

"Some of them were eager to lay down their swords when Alshin was killed. Some even looked relieved." Sanch looked over his new shield.

"How do we know who will stand with us to end this, and who is still loyal to Sillack?" Deem asked.

"We ask them." Sanch shrugged as he tapped Menis on the chest. He stood up from the large marble table and started out the door to a day of cloudy skies with the sun peeking through, giving the day just the right amount of light. The grass was finally dry from the morning dew, but the smell of wet air still lingered. Sanch was making his way to where Alshin's men were being kept. He knew with the death of Thrant, things needed to change. He could no longer just be the son of a great man. He himself had to become a great man—a leader like his father. To do so, not only did things need to change, *he* needed to change.

As Sanch, Menis, Deem, Ralyn, and Dagger made their way to the prisoners on the other side of the village, they could see off to their left Kess and the girls walking back to the main part of the village. As they got closer, Kess saw Sanch's eyes focused on her little girl. Her long, black hair was still messy from the battle she took part in hours ago. Kess could truly see the color of the rose in that boy's eyes. There was no doubt about it.

"There are the girls." Ralyn pointed. "Maybe they should come along. They are going to need to be a part of this as well."

"Yes, that is true." Sanch changed direction to intercept Bethany and the others. When they got close enough, Sanch noticed Lisha's arms around Bethany's shoulder. He also noticed the red in her face. Sanch's pace increased, making an obvious path to Ralyn's baby girl.

"Are you ok?" Sanch gently cupped her red face in his hands. "What's wrong?"

"Really, Sanch?" Lisha said as she made her way past him. "By the way, I am fine too. Thanks for asking."

Kess walked over to her husband.

"That is an interesting colored rose," Ralyn said, placing a gentle kiss on his wife's forehead.

"I will tell you all about that later, my love." Kess scratched his thick beard. "Where are you all going in such haste?" Kess asked.

Ralyn stroked her shiny black hair and kissed her again on the side of her head. "We're going to have a little talk with Alshin's men that we captured."

"Why would we want to do that?" Lisha firmly asked. "I do not have anything to say to them." The rage in her voice was clear.

"That is why I will do all the talking," Sanch said as he released Bethany's face and turned to address Lisha.

"He has an idea that may be a good one for the situation we find ourselves in," Deem added, backing Sanch.

"Thank you, Deem." As he started back on course, Sanch tried his best to explain himself to Lisha and the others. "Some of Alshin's men seemed far too willing to lie down their swords and give up. Their fight was too quickly taken from them. They did not mourn him, nor did they want revenge for his death. They seemed almost relieved that he was dead. I think some of them may want to join in bringing Sillack's reign to an end. I feel that the easiest way to find out if any of what I think is true is to ask them."

"What if they do not all feel that way, my friend?" Menis asked, concerned.

Not slowing his pace, Sanch asked, "Lisha, did you bring your sword?"

She had a sound of glee in her voice. "That I did, my friend."

On their way, they went close by the blacksmith. The smell of a weapon being forged filled their noses. The sound of hammer meeting steel rang out.

In the distance, they heard a faint voice. "Lackshin's boy, Lackshin's boy!" the blacksmith shouted. "Your friend's sword is coming along nicely. It shall be ready on time. That I promise, my lord."

"Thank you, blacksmith!" Lisha shouted back. "What you are doing means a lot to me and my family. We appreciate what you do for us. You honor us."

As they continued, Ralyn took the lead. Being the lord and leader of the village, he would have to okay anyone that wished to speak to the prisoners or to go into where they were being held.

As they approached the gates to the prison, one of the young fresh sentinels leaped to his feet.

"Relax, boy. We want these gates open and we want access to the men," Ralyn commanded.

"But, my lord, there are at least a hundred of them in there," the boy said.

"I think we will be fine." Silma said, fluttering back onto Hush's shoulder.

"Just open it," Ralyn commanded as he pointed to the heavy steel ring that held the keys to the huge lock that kept the gate secured.

As the guard removed the key from his waist and went to the gate, Menis and Lisha took their place at Sanch's side. The position they had taken and kept since first they met. Menis towered over Sanch. Lisha stood half a head shorter than him. Close behind looking down at all of them stood Hush hovering at the ready to protect Sanch if, and when needed. The gate was a thick wood door framed all the way around by dark steel. Its hinges were as thick around as a man's forearm. It had the same carvings as the ones on the doors of the war hall. The loud sound that the gate made echoed through the village as the guards pushed it open letting them into a large courtyard filled with their enemies.

There were not enough manacles to chain every prisoner by themselves, so they shackled one man to another by the wrist. Menis saw the number of prisoners, and turned to look at Sanch. "I do hope you are right, brother."

"So do I, brother," Sanch replied as he led them into the courtyard. First surveying over the yard, Sanch cleared his throat and walked closer to make sure they could hear what it is he had to say.

"I do not know if anyone here knows how or why it is we stand here as enemies, or how this war we fight even began. For me, I was given a sword. I was also given a task that I was told I was born for. I am fighting a war that chose me—a war that has been passed down like some kind of birthright. Your master Sillack would rather not see me fight. If I was given the choice to fight a war that started before my time, I would gladly choose not to fight, but that was never a choice given to me. I know why I fight—I know why I pick up my sword and engage in battle with you who follow Sillack. I fight to protect those who cannot fight for themselves. I fight to give others who will come after me the choice I did not have myself. The thing I do not understand is this: Why do you all fight? What makes you want to pick up weapons and lay down your lives for such an evil man? I hear Sillack would give you all up to die if it meant killing me and stopping any chance I have at stopping him and his reign over the lands he holds and everyone on it."

A voice came from the middle of the crowd. "No one is safe. Not us nor our families. That's why we fight. Not for Sillack but to keep them safe. We fight and he shows them what little mercy he has." A man stood still wearing his breastplate. All that was left of the armor he wore into battle that morning.

Another voice joined in and saw things differently than the first man.

"Lord Sillack is the rightful ruler of these lands. He took it all with the edge of his sword like every great man before him. We all should bow at his feet and be thankful for what he does for us all." After that was said, a great number of the other men erupted in cheers. A large man, dragging a smaller man chained to him, walked over to Sanch. He was clad in a black leather breastplate that had a hole in it where the shoulder met the left arm. One of the archers barely missed their mark. A few inches to the right and he would have not been here to have this conversation. He looked down at Sanch with hate in his eyes and growled. "How does a boy like yourself with nothing but his father's sword think you have the slightest chance of defeating the great Sillack?"

An all too familiar smile found itself on to Sanch's face. "You get twenty of your best men and the six of us will show you just how we plan on doing away with your great Sillack. In my short time out here I have found that you animals understand nothing more than a sharp sword at your throat, and I am more than happy to speak to you in the language you best understand. But know this, those of you that chose to face us will not be given the chance to change your minds." Sanch then walked past the wall of a man that stood in front of him. He pushed through, parting the crowd of his enemies—men, who this morning, wanted nothing more than to see him dead.

Close behind him was Hush watching every move of the men around Sanch. Sanch walked over to the first man who spoke. He put his hand on the man's shoulder and leaned in close and whispered something in the his ear. A look of relief came over the man's face. Whatever it was that Sanch said to him reassured him in some way. The man looked at Sanch, nodded his head and said, "Thank you."

Sanch turned to Hush. "Let us go. We have a point to make." Then he added, "In case any of you disagreed with what this man had to say, that is your right. However, if any harm comes to him, if he feels one of you breathe heavily in his direction, please understand I will ask no questions. I will kill everyone in this yard. I will burn this building down around you all with these gates open. If you try to leave, one of us will be waiting to end your lives quicker than the flames will. And if you heard nothing else I have said, do hear that." Sanch and Hush rejoined the others. Sanch made quick eye contact with Bethany, but not quick enough to where Kess did not notice. As Sanch walked past Lisha it gave her the perfect opportunity to speak her mind.

"Really, Sanch, did you say six? You do know my cousin brought her sword with her as well," Lisha informed him.

Silma felt a bit left out. "I also have my sword, Sanch. You're going to want me out there. I have saved your butt once already today, remember, Hush?" Silma stomped her little feet on Hush's shoulder trying to get him to back her up.

"Not now Silma," Sanch said as he turned to walk away.

Now flying next to Sanch, Silma did not let up. "I know I am small, but ..." Shouting back to Kess, Silma made a request. "Kess I am going to need the good stuff."

Kess quickly replied. "I have you covered, Blue."

They walked back through the open gates. The guards standing there heard the whole thing. One of them asked, "Sanch, did you say that the six of you were going to take on twenty of their best men? You will be largely outnumbered. Let me fight with you."

Lisha quickly responded to the guard's request. "First, there are seven of us, eight if you count the blue fly. The eight of us is more than enough for twenty of their men."

"She is right, but we thank you for your noble gesture," Sanch added. "We need to show the other men that we can go up against a greater force and win because that is just what we are going to have to do when we face Sillack's army along with the vicious Xyles. If they are going to put their family at risk to follow us in battle, they are going to need reassurance that we can win against the man who holds the lives of their loved ones in the palm of his hands. They are going to need to believe I can … *we* can indeed finish what my father started long ago." He looked to Ralyn and Kess. "You all kept us safe this long, and now it is our turn. We need to bring this to an end. If that means making an example of those who don't believe in our ability to end this fight, so be it." Looking at Lisha, he added, "I am sure we all agree on this."

"That we do, Sanch," Lisha assured him.

"As do I," Menis added. "I see good reason to do this, for if they think us weak, they will not stand with us, and might even try to overtake us. If they see we are willing and capable to lay waste to some of their best, they will think twice about challenging us."

Stepping forward from between her mother and father, Bethany offered her sword in Sanch's fight. "I, too, wish to fight. Like my cousin pointed out, I brought my sword as well."

"Bethany!" Ralyn shouted.

Kess grabbed his hand, pulled him down to her level, and whispered in his ear, "We should stay out of this." She showed him the rose that Bethany had turned to the color of Sanch's eyes, now known to the girls as the "Sanch flower."

Ralyn took a closer look at Sanch's eyes, seeing them to be the same. "What is going on here? I do not think I like what I am seeing," Ralyn whispered back to his spouse. "Does this mean she has picked him?"

"The rose never lies, my love. It shows what is in our hearts," Kess replied.

"But he is not a very big guy like her father, and he has so much going on right now. What happens if he does not notice her?"

"Ralyn, does it look like he has not noticed her? He is a good boy that is good with a sword," Kess said, sticking up for Sanch.

"Yes, that is what I am afraid of … a boy and his sword around my little girl."

Still pleading her case, Bethany went on. "You have seen me fight, and I am just as good as the rest of you. Do remember that this is my village they invaded looking for you and that sword. Besides that, you like having me around, so why not have me fight alongside you as well?"

"She has you there," Menis interjected. "You do like having her around. We can all see that."

"That is true," Lisha added.

Sanch looked at Bethany and realized he had no choice but to admit what she and the others were saying was true. With a big sigh, Sanch gave in to her request. But first looked to Kess for her approval before the young warrior said yes. "I would be very honored if you would once again fight alongside us." Sanch leaned in close and whispered, "Please stay close." He then turned and walked away.

Everyone followed Sanch out of the large guard shack. As Kess passed her little girl, she uttered, "It looks like he already can't say no to you, and trust me, that is a good thing."

Before they were too far from the guard shack, Sanch stopped one last time to give out some instructions for things he needed done. He and the others needed to prepare for the fight they were to have.

"Ralyn, Kess, can I ask you both something?"

"Oh boy, here it comes," Ralyn said.

"Father!" Bethany shouted.

A confused Sanch continued to speak. "Ralyn, can you check in with the blacksmith and see to the completion of Thrant's Sword? The eight of us have some things we need to go over before facing Alshin's men. Kess, can you go back and have the guards move those men to a secure location? Also, have the guards inform them they have until we burn our dead to pick their fighters and prepare themselves to face us. I also would like you to get your best archers to help keep watch over the captives. We need to let them know a wrong move of any kind will be their last."

"So, what do you intend to do with these twenty men, Sanch?" Kess asked.

Sanch looked at the other seven and in their face's they knew. "We intend to kill them, Lady Kess. All of them. And may even take pleasure in it."

CHAPTER EIGHTEEN

As Kess walked alone to where the guard kept watch, she could not help but wonder if she wanted Bethany to be a part of this fight. She had seen Sanch and the others fight, as well as Bethany. She held her own in her first battle, yet Kess could not help but to think that this may be different. She knew Sanch would not let any harm come to the others and would especially go out of his way to protect her little girl. Kess looked back to see the eight of them as they walked and talked off in the distance. Even then she saw Sanch kept Bethany close to him, which made Kess feel a little better about things. She could not help but to ask herself if the Son of Lackshin started a fight he couldn't win? Getting closer, she could hear strident talk coming from the prisoners.

"What is going on here?" Kess asked as she entered the guard's area. The room had stairs that led up to where you could look down on the courtyard where the prisoners were. "What is that noise?" Kess asked.

"That has been going on since you and the other's left. I take it they are trying to decide who of them is the best, and who of them will fight Sanch and the others," the guard said. "They sound eager. I think a few fights have broken out from them challenging one another for the right to fight in the name of Sillack. Kess, do you think Sanch and the others can take on twenty of them, with it only being six of them."

"Yes, and it's eight now," Kess corrected the boy. He looked like he was nothing over sixteen if a day. "There is not a doubt in my mind that Sanch is going to kill that big one. Sanch has a point to make, and he intends to do so with that man hanging from the end of his sword." Kess put her hand on the boy's shoulder. "At ease, young man."

From the lack of doubt in Kess's voice, the guard looked reassured.

"So why have you returned, Lady Kess?" another guard asked.

"Is there a way to see in there as well as speak to them all at once?" Kess asked.

"Yes," he replied as he led her to a poorly light hallway leading to steps. At the top of the steps, it opened to the sky. It was a guard tower that overlooked the holding area. Kess had forgotten about all of this, for it had been so long since they had prisoners of war. The war was never over, but their village had stayed out of the fighting. Sillack had left them alone, remembering from the past the kinds of warriors that came from this village. He fought alongside Thrant, his brother, and even Ralyn when the evil they fought was the Xyles.

Kess walked up the stairs and to a wall that overlooked the yard. Before she spoke, she stood there for a while and observed, looking on as these animals fought among themselves. She watched as the large man Sanch challenged all but ripped a man's arm from his body. By the looks of things, Sanch had one thing right; It did not seem like every man there felt like that animal did. Some men steered clear of the fight and off to one side. Other men were not as lucky and were dragged into the commotion.

"You, there!" the large man shouted. "Coward, what did that boy say to you?" He moved closer to the man. "I will see to it that you die right after I kill that boy with his father's sword." He threw the man several feet. "You dare speak against the great Sillack? Your family will burn for treason." He walked over toward the man. Just as he was about to reach down to grab the battered chap, an arrow flew down, cutting his sleeve open.

"That could have gone through your arm, but I want you in good shape for when that boy lets you hold his sword in the center of your chest!" Kess shouted, holding a bow in one hand, the string still vibrating. She grabbed another arrow and readied it. "I am here to inform you that you have until we put our dead to rest to pick your twenty. And for the twenty you pick, take time to make peace with whatever gods you pray to, for you will soon be able to pray to them face to face. To make sure you do not somehow get hurt before it comes time for you to die, my archers will be up here keeping an eye on you all." Kess then pulled the other arrow back and put it right next to the other one. "See you all soon."

As she walked past the guards, she ordered them to get her archers on the walls immediately. "That man needs to be moved to a safer place," Kess said. "Put him in one of our cells by himself, just in case they do not take his threat seriously. Also, he wants the others to see that we will protect those who chose to join us. I suppose that we will need swords or other weapons for those men. Weapons of their choosing."

"Kess?" a guard said. "We are going to give those men weapons?"

Kess placed her hand on the man's shoulder. "Would it be a fair fight if we did not give them weapons? How else would they be able to defend themselves against Sanch and the others? Sanch is trying to show them there is hope, that he brings hope, and that he is the one that can defeat Sillack and free us all. So yes, weapons they will need, and weapons they will get." Kess turned and left in the direction of the blacksmith's.

As she walked, wind blew her long black hair into her face. With her left hand resting on the shiny handle of her sword, she raised her right hand to sweep it out of the way. She thought back to her time training with her sisters and the extra work her father made her put in with her sword. He always told her that her work with a bow was unmatched, but when there were no more arrows left, her skills with a sword would decide her fate. Her father also told her it was great to have sons, but a well-placed daughter was just as good if not better. He also said he would not be happy until she could match her older brother's skills as well as the other boys in their village. As she got closer to the blacksmith's, she could see the silhouette of her husband through the smoke-filled room.

The sparks of the hammer hitting Thrant's sword danced in sync with the music of their kiss. It was as if the blacksmith was breathing life into metal with every strike he delivered. She slowed her pace and watched as the blacksmith put everything into every strike, then took it off the hard anvil and pushed it back into the inferno's arms and embrace of the white cowls. Then he pulled out a white-hot blade ready and calling out for life.

Ralyn felt familiar eyes on him and turned to find his love standing saddened by just the need for swords to once again be worn by peace-loving people.

The sword she watched being made was to take the journey to the gods with an old friend. As their eyes met, it was clear to them both that they shared the same sadness. He noticed their similar pose—his hand also on the handle of his sword. With a jerk of his head, he signaled for her to come over and join them. She replied with a nod with her hair once again veiling her face. The sight of her as she fought off her hair made Ralyn reveal a small smile, for that reminded him of better times—times of peace, and times of love.

The first time that Ralyn laid his eyes on Kess, she was fighting the same losing battle with her hair. It was a problem he saw his sister, Vaness, have all too often. Their villages, along with others, would have tournaments that would give their young warriors the chance to test their skill against other upcoming warriors, but all in fun. Most of the young boys and girls took it a bit more serious than others. Kess was one of those girls that took it very serious, but it was the opposite for Ralyn. His future had already been set, for he was the son of the village's leader.

In a way, Ralyn was looked at as a king in his own right. That meant he was next in line to lead. He was expected to be the fastest, the strongest, the bravest, and the best fighter. Ralyn was all of those things, and he added one more to that list. He made sure to be the smartest as well. When his peers had finished practicing their skill with their weapons, he would practice into the night. His father told him the strongest weapon any warrior had was his or her mind. Ralyn also read books and studied battle tactics with his father. He learned to use other weapons, not just a sword. He learned to wield a staff. It could be mistaken for a common stick and was said to be a woman's weapon, but that did not stop him from learning the skills from his mother. A skill he then later passed on to his daughter when she was a little girl.

At a tournament where the archery challenge was being held is where he took notice of Kess's serious gaze as she pulled back her tight bowstring that gave no sound when pulled. It was like there was nothing between her hand and that arrow. He also noticed that this beautiful girl with a warrior's eye did not use a girl's bow, but a bow belt for a man that could give or take away from that shot she made. As he looked on and she took her aim, a slight breeze came in from the east blowing her hair into her face. Kess did not move, nor did she attempt to fix it, nor did she loosen her pull on her bow. It was as if she was waiting for another breeze to blow in to assist her.

Ralyn saw all this and decided to be that breeze that she needed. He rushed over quickly and quietly as to not disturb her concentration. He gently brushed her hair from her face allowing her to hit the bulls eye, winning her first place over his own village. As quickly as he was there to help her, he was gone before she could turn around to thank him.

Ralyn managed to accomplish two things that day: He made his father proud and showed him that his village would be left in good hands if Ralyn was left to lead, and he had brought up a boy into a man that looked more to the right thing to do than victory. The village may have lost the archery part of the competition, but Ralyn won the heart of Kess. She spent the remainder of the tournament looking for Ralyn, her hero. When she found him, she walked up to him and put her hand in his.

"How is Thrant's sword coming, my love?" Kess asked as she squeezed the hand of her hero.

Pulling her close, Ralyn leaned down and kissed her on the side of the head. "This sword will see the sun, draw its first breath, and be put to rest alongside its master and never take life. That is not a proper life for a sword," Ralyn said solemnly.

Kess stood there and thought for a moment. "I think I may have an idea to give that sword a good sending off. It will live a full life."

"Well, whatever that idea is, I am sure it is a good one that would please Thrant. Anyway, how did it go at the prison? Did the guards understand their orders?" Ralyn asked.

"That they did, Ralyn. At first, they did not understand why we would want to arm the prisoners, so I explained to them that Sanch wanted to give them a fighting chance so the others could see they could trust him to lead and defeat Sillack." Kess looked up at Ralyn. "Do you think he can do as he says?"

"I fought alongside his father in the Xyles war, and I have seen Sanch fight and what he can do and I am impressed. The boy is faster and stronger than a boy his size should be. With a sword in his hand, I feel he is unstoppable and determined like no one I have ever seen. It is almost like his father himself was watching him and he has something to prove. Above all that, I would not entrust my daughter's life with him if I did not think he could do as he said. I feel neither would you, my love, so do not have any doubt. I feel that boy can do what he claims because he has no other options. He has been left a war that no one other than he can fight, much less win. I hate to say it, but it is all on him and the ones that choose to follow him."

"Ralyn, that is what scares me. I will follow you into the fires of Hell. I would give my life if it meant saving yours." Kess scratched his thick beard.

"And I would do the same for you, Kess, and more. But what does that have to do with what I am saying?" Ralyn asked.

"Have you seen how she looks at him?" Kess put the Sanch flower on Ralyn's face. "Look at this rose. It is the same color as his eyes in every way. This rose will not die until one of them does. Watch." Kess walked over to the blacksmith's fire and held the rose directly into the flames. Even with the flames consuming the "Sanch Flower," it remained untouched. "Do you see this? She has picked him, and she plans to follow him just as I follow you, Ralyn."

"Do not forget, for that rose to be as strong as it is, he has to have the same love for her. He must be equally willing to give his life for her. Bethany has fallen in love with The Son of Lackshin, the would-be king of all the lands." Ralyn walked over and gently placed his hands over his wife's, and pulled the rose out of the fire. "By the look of this flower, Sanch feels the same for her. The way I see it, she may just be the safest of them all. Let us leave the blacksmith to his work and get back to the others to see what their plans are for this fight Sanch has picked." Ralyn put his arms around Kess, and they took their leave. "Good day, blacksmith!" Ralyn shouted back as they walked away.

"We shall see you soon," Kess added. "Bring the completed sword to our home when it is done, and we will have payment there for you."

"It shouldn't be long!" the blacksmith shouted back. "It takes breath, won't be long now before it opens its eyes!"

The two lovers walked hand in hand through the village that was just starting to see life again. Kess and Ralyn stopped to talk to the people they saw on their way and answered questions and tried to reassure the people of the village. The older people were worried that they would be faced with another long war like the one they had seen with the fight against the Xyles. The younger of them did not know what to expect of war and wanted to know what they could do to help. Those of them that were old enough to learn to fight were encouraged to report to some of the men and women in charge to learn to defend themselves and their family. They may be the last line of defense if the walls do not hold.

Neither Kess nor Ralyn mentioned the release of the Xyles and the fact that they would be with any army Sillack would send now. They kept that from them in fear, for that information would take away what little hope Sanch and Shallin brought with them. This victory against a greater force is just what the village needed to put their heart in the fight. An old ally thought to have been extinguished from the lands, now joined in this war alongside them. The Elarguns played a big part in assuring the day's victory as in battles past. Once again, kids started playing outside like in days past.

As Kess and Ralyn continued on, they ran into Evian's mother who was on her way to pick up some supplies for Evian and Evian's Father to eat. It was coming close to midday and it was time to start lunch.

"How is Evian doing?" Ralyn asked. "He fought bravely. He reminded me of his father, the way he handled his sword. He is a skilled swordsman and a great leader. Tell him when he's rested, his men await their leader's return and will follow him anywhere."

"Thank you. We are very proud of him. I will tell him what you said. He will be happy to hear that come from you. You and his father are the kind of man he would like to be." She came in close, as if she had something to say. "Tell me, Ralyn, what is the story of the boy called Sanch? Is he the son of the great Lackshin and does he have Shallin with him?"

Kess smiled and whispered, "Yes, he is, and yes, he does, and your Evian was there to help him win his first battle this morning. Evian is a natural leader and will play a big part in things yet to come." Kess stepped back and put her arms around Evian's mother. "I know how you feel and what you worry about, for I have the same fears and the same worries. My Bethany saw her first battle this morning as well. She too was in the thick of things fighting for her life. They both took lives today in defense of their own. Those are things that will change a person. I pray to the gods that it does not change our babies. I still remember the first man brought to his end by my sword. It is a thing you never forget. It makes you look at life with new eyes. You see your mortality in every life you take, and in the eyes of the ones you kill. I wish this to be over soon for the sake of both our children and their mortality."

"I hope so as well," Ralyn agreed as he put his muscular arms around the women, giving them a big hug, trying to lighten the mode. "Have Evian join us and his men later when we put our fallen to rest. He will be expected to be there. We must be on our way, but we all look forward to peace and a quick end to this."

"As do I," replied Evian's mother.

Kess and Ralyn walked back to the young warriors. Kess let out a sigh. "Did you notice that Sanch is the only one without a bow?"

"Yes, I saw that," Ralyn replied. "Maybe he lost it, or maybe he forgot it back at his home."

"Do you think we should get him a new one, Ralyn? We cannot have him going into battle without one."

Ralyn reached down and grabbed his wife's hand. "Yes, my love. Let us get this boy a new bow."

With one more stop to make, they hurried to the bowmaker's shop with the hope that he had one that would fit the young king. When they arrived at the shop, they found the bowman in the middle of making a bow. They looked on as he worked at his art before they made themselves known to him. They watched the precision he took as he curved the wood that would come to be a bow. He weaved the string slowly and meticulously with amazing care. He was a man who took pride in his work.

"How long do you two plan to stand there before speaking? It is always a pleasure to see you both. Did you not bring little Bethany with you this time?"

"Not so little anymore," Ralyn answered. "That bow you made her gave her many reasons to shoot apples from my hand. How have you been, my friend?" Ralyn and Kess moved closer to get a better look at the bow.

"Much better now that you and Sanch stopped Sillack's men from entering our village," the bowmaker said.

"The Son of Lackshin is the reason we are here," Kess added. "We need you to make him a bow, something fit for Lackshin's boy."

"Yes, something fit for a would-be king. Tell me, is he anything like his father? Does he have any idea who he truly is?"

"He is much smaller than his father," Ralyn said. "Yet, he is somehow just as strong as his father was. I trust his story is safe with you, Sir Archer?"

"His secrets are mine as well, Lord Ralyn, do not forget. What, beside his strange strength for his size, should I know about him before I start making his bow?"

Kess smiled and stepped forward. "Bethany has found him very intriguing and has shown a liking for the Boy King."

The bowmaker laughed. "My Lord must not like this Son of Lackshin very much. Do you plan on giving this boy the bow or using it on him?"

Both Kess and the bowmaker laughed.

"When will you have this bow made?" Ralyn asked, smiling.

"By the end of the day, or at first light. I have something started that would fit him just fine. I will work through the night to finish it. A warrior of his standing should not go another day without a great bow. I will supply Bethany and her young man with new arrows as well. I will deliver it to him myself. I would like to see him all grown up. I will show him how to quickly string a bow when in the heat of battle. A skill I was to show him when he came of age."

"Thank you, my friend," Ralyn said as he placed a stack of gold coins in his hands.

"This is more than you would pay for ten bows, my lord!"

As Kess and Ralyn walked away, Kess shouted back, "That is for your troubles, my friend, and a good laugh."

CHAPTER NINETEEN

The sound of swords as they kissed rang out. The closer Kess and Ralyn got to their home, the louder it became. Now running with swords drawn, Kess and Ralyn quickly descended on their home where they found Sanch, Bethany, and others practicing for the battle to come.

"Does Sanch think holding back on Bethany is going to help her in a fight when her life is on the line?" Ralyn asked as he sheathed his great long sword.

"Yes, this coming from a man who was worried about putting a dent in my sword," Kess replied to her husband. "He, like us, wants her safe, but like you, it will take him some time to learn that making us strong and not holding back is the best way to keep us safe and give us what we need to protect ourselves in battle."

"You are right as always, my love," Ralyn said as he mockingly bowed.

"Do not forget, my big strong protector," Kess answered with a curtsy.

"I will not forget, my wife." Ralyn leaned down and kissed her softly on the lips. Such a large man with such a gentle touch.

"Can we go play with the kids now?" Ralyn asked.

With a smile on her face, Kess nodded. "Yes, but I get the boy."

With swords drawn, Ralyn and Kess quietly moved in on the kids as to catch them by surprise. When they were close enough to make their move, they launched their assault. Battle cries followed with a full-speed attack. The young warrior caught off guard tried to defend himself, but was no match. Kess meant what she said and went straight for Bethany and Sanch. The other six tried to stop her, but barely slowed her down. Ralyn then closed the path behind his wife and made it impossible for them to follow Kess or help Sanch.

Sanch, not sure what was going on, looked as Kess got closer. Standing in front of him was Bethany, ready to greet her mother. Kess closed in fast and hard.

"Sanch, Sanch!" Bethany shouted. "I think she is for real!"

Sanch picked up his sword and gently pushed Bethany out of the way in time to greet Kess's blade. Her blade came down with more strength than a woman her size should have.

"Don't go far, little girl. When I am done with your man, I will teach you some new moves."

"Mother!" Bethany shouted. "What are you and father doing?"

"We saw you two playing and wanted to play too." Kess got in close and slammed her body against Sanch, shoving him to the ground. "See. We're just having fun."

Kess leaped over Sanch and made her way over to Bethany. Sanch sat on the ground for a moment processing what just took place.

"Mother, what are you doing?" Bethany asked as their swords met.

"Stop talking, cousin, and save your little man. I think my aunt is for real!" Lisha sounded as if she was having the time of her life fighting her uncle.

"To your feet, Sanch!" Ralyn shouted. "She's mean!"

"Shut up, Ralyn!" Kess shouted back.

"See, boy. What did I tell you?"

"Ralyn!" Kess shouted again.

"Yes, my love," Ralyn replied with a smile.

Sanch gathered himself and got back to his feet. With Kess still in full on attack mode with Bethany, she turned to Sanch. "This is how you prepare her for a fight against men who wish to kill her? She has to be ready to fight for her life. You two will have the chance to dance at your wedding."

"Mother!" Bethany shouted.

"She is right," Sanch replied.

"She is?" Lisha shouted as she laughed.

"Yes, I was taking it easy on her, but those men we will be fighting will not do the same," Sanch added.

"For now, you must prepare her to fight and kill, cause even if you want to, you won't always be there to kill for her. Those men wish to see you all dead and you need to make sure that does not happen, Sanch," Kess told the would-be king.

Sanch walked over to where Kess had been laying crushing blows on Bethany. "My Lady!' Sanch shouted. "It is my turn."

When Kess heard that, a smile crept across her face. She maneuvered in close to her little girl and before pushing her to the ground, whispered, "We are going to see what your man can do."

Sword in hand, Kess turned and ran at Sanch, yelling her people's battle cry. Sanch gripped his sword and thrust it above his head in time to deflect Kess's attack, which slid him back, causing dirt to kick up behind him. The sounds of the two swords kissing stopped everyone from what they were doing.

Deem, Dagger, and Hush looked on. Silma powered down, and even Lisha and her uncle stopped their scrimmage. During the battle for the village, Kess's skill with her bow had been shown from the wall, but this was the first time they witnessed her skills with a sword. She moved like water, yet her strikes were like steel and her form was flawless and beautiful. She moved with the elegance of a woman and swung her short sword with the strength of a man twice her size.

At one point, the sun saw its way in through a break in the clouds and shined on the two. Sanch found himself a chance to advance, but that did not last long. Kess managed to capture a ray of sun on her blade and with perfect timing landed that ray of light right into Sanch's eyes, blinding him momentarily. To Kess's surprise, even being without sight, Sanch was able to defend himself. They all looked in amazement as Sanch continued to fight with his eyes closed.

Kess saw this and watched what else he could do. Sanch started to blink trying to regain his sight from the glare. Kess wanted to keep the upper hand and saw her next weapon. She started to maneuver him toward a tree stump. Bethany was unable to take any more of Sanch clearly not putting his all into it. She walked over to where the battle was taking place.

Ralyn noticed his little girl and smiled. "Look, your cousin is going to save her man."

"Someone needs to," Lisha replied. "She is good, but I have seen him fight to win, and this is not him fighting to win."

"I agree," Menis chimed in.

Sanch's left foot hit the stump and just as he was about to lose his balance, he felt a back against his and heard a familiar voice.

"Duck," the voice whispered.

To Kess's surprise, Bethany's sword met hers. "Let me know if I get this right, mother," Bethany said, then planted her right foot and pushed her mother off balance with a firm shove with her shoulder.

"Oh boy," Ralyn said.

From that moment on, it looked like Kess had been fighting her shadow. It was like two streams of water beating against rock.

As Sanch regained his focus, he saw what was unfolding in front of him. The intensity of the fight increased, and even with the upper hand, Kess was still met with strong counters from Bethany.

Ralyn walked over to join Sanch and placed his hand on the young man's shoulder. "Are we going to put an end to this?"

Sanch looked at Ralyn and smiled. "Maybe we should, but I get the prettiest one."

Ralyn laughed and asked, "Which one is the prettiest?"

"Really?" Lisha shouted as she laughed, then added, "That would be me, but you two should really stop them before they make a mess."

Ralyn and Sanch rushed in just in time to deflect their next attempt at each other. Smoothly, and with similar technique, both mother and daughter used the momentum of Ralyn and Sanch's interference to return to their assault on one another.

"Good one, cousin!" Lisha shouted.

"Really, Lisha?" Sanch turned and tried to get back into the fight. "We try again?" Sanch asked Ralyn.

"Yes, we try again," Ralyn agreed.

They put themselves between the two, but their efforts were deflected. Sanch was able to keep Bethany's attention momentarily, but she went back after her mother with a point to make. The two tried to keep their attention long enough to fight them back putting distance between mother and daughter.

"Hold her back as long as you can!" Ralyn commanded Sanch.

"I'm trying, but your wife has made your little girl angry!"

Bethany's hair looked like it had taken on a life of its own. The wind blew it almost straight behind her, soft strands laid soft across her left eye. Fully focused on Sanch, she stepped back and lowered her sword. "So, I am a little girl? Is that how you see me … as just their little girl?" Her knuckles were white from the death grip on the practice sword she held.

Sanch looked at the others. "What now?"

"She is your problem now, boy."

Sanch turned to see Kess and Ralyn standing there with their swords over their shoulders.

"Looks like the mean witch has plans for you," Silma said, perched on Hush's knife handle.

"Show him what momma taught you, baby girl," Kess said as she put her sword back in its sheath.

Sanch turned in time to see Bethany tighten her stance and give her mother a nod.

"Are you kidding me?" Sanch muttered.

"I told you to look out for the women in this village," Ralyn scowled the boy.

Sanch planted his feet and moved side to side, kicking up a small puff of dust around his feet. As he looked at this small but strong girl in front of him ready to take his head off, he could not help but feel an overwhelming need to protect her. "Okay, whenever you are ready, Lady Bethany."

"Make me ready," Bethany whispered as she moved so fast that Sanch almost missed it.

"What was that?" Sanch asked as he stepped back giving up ground to Bethany. "Make you ready for what?" Sanch countered and gently repelled her.

"That is what my mother is talking about," Bethany said.

"What are you talking about? If you have not noticed your mother is a bit off. I did not want to say anything, but that arrow she put in that man's chest out of nowhere forced me to think."

Bethany became more aggressive with her next attacks. "That is what she is talking about! Do you want me ready to fight alongside you and the others, or are you trying to kiss me?"

"Sanch put your sword up!" shouted Menis noticing Sanch dropped his guard.

Sanch threw his head back just enough to avoid Bethany's blade.

"Are you trying to lose your head, Sanch?" Menis asked.

"You're saying that kissing you is an option? I would rather do that than to fight with you. Bethany, those men are killers and will kill you if given a chance. I would much rather you stay out of harm's way."

"That is the thing," she said as she spun catching him off step landing a backhand on his left cheek. Sanch stumbled back, shocked at how hard she hit him.

"Should we stop this, Kess? He is barely fighting back."

"No, Ralyn. He has to learn how to lead, and she needs to understand that Sanch and the others came here fighting for their lives. She needs to know that sword she holds is for killing those trying to kill her and the people she loves. Before I let her fight alongside Sanch and Lisha again, I need to see him put her on her ass like we all know he can."

"Ok, I am taking that kiss. But after I show you I am not just a pretty face." Sanch straightened his back, and with his hand at his waist, he took a bow and outstretched his sword. "Are you ready?" he asked Bethany.

Bethany's next advance would be met with real opposition. With little effort, Sanch disarmed her sending her sword flying into the air. He placed his shoulder in the center of her chest and pushed her back just as her sword landed blade down right in front of her.

"Lesson one, hold on to your weapon. Now pick up your sword, it will soon be time to kill more of Alshin's men and you need to get that pretty sword of yours dirty again."

"Is that better, wife?" Ralyn asked Kess.

"Yes, Ralyn. Let us give them some time to themselves. She is in good hands now."

"I want to see this," Lisha said as she took a seat on a large rock.

"We should be getting Thrant ready. The blacksmith could be done any time now and we should have him ready before that." Kess rested her hand on Lisha's cheek. "It has to be you, and no one else. I will help you."

"Come on, we will build a glorious pile. My friend will be sent off like the great warrior he was." Ralyn led the men away. Deem and Dagger were not quite sure of the customs of man, but they were curious to see what the wood pile was going to be used for. They followed closely behind Ralyn and Menis trying to decipher what was being said.

Ralyn looked back over his shoulder and motioned. "Deem, come closer. It is Deem, is it not? I heard them call you Dagger." He waved for them to walk at his other side.

"Yes, My Lord. I am Deem and this is my brother, Dagger. He is the one who led our small force here just in time to give us the advantage."

"I thought the Elarguns were all but extinct, or at the very least, there had not been many of you left." Ralyn rested his hand on the young prince's shoulder.

"We were just a few, and if not for Lackshin and his quick thinking to relocate our people back to one of our old kingdoms thought lost to us, we would have been hunted into extinction by Sillack and the men that followed him. My father did not want to leave the fight, but Lackshin insisted that he go into hiding with his people. Lackshin told him he would better serve the world by leading his people and rebuilding his army. I guess he knew one day his son would need that same army to finish what you all before us had started." Deem sounded humbled when speaking of Lackshin's sacrifice.

"Is that why you were so willing to join us when you found out who Sanch was?" Menis asked.

"Yes, and this guy's hand around my throat very much helped me to jump on board." Dagger laughed and looked over at Hush. Deem and Menis laughed as they remembered their first meeting.

"Sounds like you all had an eventful meeting," Ralyn said. "You will have to tell me of that meeting someday."

They walked for not much longer. They passed what looked like a church in the distance behind a small field of gravestones. Deem and Dagger's nose flared up. The overwhelming smell of flowers consumed the air around them. It looked as if a lot of attention was paid to the graves. Beautiful white flowers covered the ground as the wind blew them all in the same direction like a well-choreographed dance. The most amazingly red roses were set in bushels that resembled pillows right at the headstones.

"That is beautiful," Deem whispered as he slowed down and took it all in.

"It is the least we can do for those who have lived and died for this village. It is something Lisha's mother started a long time ago before she was taken from us. We kept it going well after her death." Ralyn increased his pace. This was somewhere he did not wish to spend a great deal of time.

"How did her mother die?" Dagger asked.

"That, my boy, is a story that Thrant may have died with. Only he knew that whole story. It's best that way. I would not want to have to relive it every day as Thrant must have had to. Enough about that." He pointed to a large log with axes embedded in it. "Grab one and start chopping," Ralyn instructed the boys.

Menis smiled. "This is just my style. Axe work."

Deem and Dagger walked over, looked at them, then tilted their heads and looked at one another. They turned around and whipped the ends of their tails as they pulled two axes free from the log. They made their way over to the trees, but before cutting any down, they first looked to Ralyn for consent. He gave them a slight nod showing his approval. With a single swing from his powerful tail, Dagger took down a small tree. The loud crash of the tree meeting the ground broke the silence. Menis quickly turned to see what was going on in time to see Dagger and Deem standing inches from this tree still bouncing.

Ralyn saw this and laughed. "That was amazing. A couple more like that one and we will have what we need.

"Save one for me, guys," Menis said as he started on one of the trees.

Hush patted down the light brown fur on his head and took a seat on the log. The two Elarguns were very attentive to all that Ralyn had to teach about building a funeral pile. On some occasions, he pulled the boys in close to show the detail of a cut and how to ensure it will hold the wait and burn properly. Sadly, this was not the first pile Menis had seen, but the first he had to build for a man he fought alongside. That made it very different for him. It was surreal.

The clearing had patches of scorched earth where grass no longer grew. The faint smell of burnt wood still lingered as a reminder of war and who was brought here to finally find peace. It was an altogether different graveyard than they had seen earlier. It was not as beautiful, but equally well kept.

CHAPTER TWENTY

Sitting on the ground, Sanch focused on Bethany's hand. He did not see her as her eyes stared at the parts of his face she could see from high on the rock she sat. He ran his index finger from her wrist to the tip of her middle finger.

"Are you ok? Did I hurt you?" he asked, looking up at her.

"Really?" She quickly looked away. "You hardly touched my hand. You keep this up and I will tell my mother you are taking it easy on me again."

A smirk crept across his face. "You're going to tell your mommy on me?"

Bethany pulled her hand away, placed her foot on his chest, and pushed him to the ground.

"What? I was just repeating what you just said. But really, you are not going to tell her, are you? Your mother scares me."

"Really, but you are Sanch, Son of Lackshin. Are you not fearless? We were told you were seven feet tall and unstoppable. That is the story we heard as children"

"Oh no, I can be stopped like any other man, and I am far from being seven-foot anything." Sanch raised his right eyebrow.

"But you are not like other men I have met. The stories I have heard of you make you out to be a god."

"No, I am just a boy trying to live up to the stories told about my father. I am trying to be my father's son. I am a little harder to stop than most men. That is all. Besides, being stopped is not what worries me most. What worries me is how many people I care about will be hurt or killed to make sure I am not stopped. This fight that I picked with Alshin's men is a fight I did not want you involved in. I cannot assure your safety, and I will fight stronger if I am not worrying about you."

Bethany got up on her knees and leaned in close. She placed her right hand on his chest, her long hair draped over his face. She could feel the thumping of his heart. His eyes fixed on her as she moved closer. She moistened her lips. He could feel her breath on his face. She whispered, "But you will fight harder if you have me to protect." She lowered her lips to his cheek. "Let's go before I tell my mother that you tried to talk me out of the fight." She smiled and pushed him back to the ground, and grabbed the blunted sword they practiced with.

A petal flew free from a nearby field filled with the most beautiful pink flowers. It made its way down onto Sanch's chest, and he could not help but smile. It is not that he saw hope—or even the chance of victory—he saw a glimpse of what he could have when this was all over and done. Killing Sillack was now only a means to an end. The end is what he could give to everyone—the end of living in fear. He was no longer fighting for a dead father. He saw now that he needed to fight for the living. He lay there for a moment, watching Bethany walk away. He let out a sigh. "That is indeed a reason to bring this all to an end," Sanch uttered out loud.

"Are you coming, Sanch, or are you going to lie around gathering dirt?"

"But of course," he replied. He climbed to his feet, reached down, and grabbed the blunted sword that rested next to him. As he hurried to catch up, he dusted off his pants.

"We really are not saying anything to your mother about me taking it easy on you, right?" Sanch asked nervously.

Bethany laughed. "Why are you so afraid of my mother? The only man I have seen work so hard to keep that woman happy is my father. What about her holds you at bay in such a way? You do not even jump to my father's commands the way you jump to hers. What does she have on you, boy?" Bethany stopped to let him catch up.

Sanch fixed himself and tried to dust off some of the dirt still on his back. Bethany shook her head and pushed him in front of her so she could better assist him.

"So, tell me, Sanch, what is it?" she asked once more.

He looked at her. His eyes always welcomed her. "It is not fear that keeps your mother at such high standings with me. It is respect. What she gives you is what I received from my own mother. Yes, I am my father's son, but I am what my mother made me. Then there is everything that is in between..." He turned away.

She stepped in front of him and brought their walk to an end. She tilted her head back just a bit to receive his eyes once more. "What do you mean? What is this part of you that you do not understand?" She gently placed her hands on his chest.

"What I tell you must stay to us and only us." Sanch placed his hands on her hips.

Bethany gave him a nod. "Your words are mine and only mine," she replied.

"Till about a few months ago, I had never killed a man, or as much as pulled my sword in a real battle of any kind. As a boy, I knew what was going to be asked of me one day. My mother tried her best to keep it from me. That allowed me as much of a childhood as possible. I had to be very skilled with a sword, and that could not wait. When other boys were out playing between lessons, my lessons went on." Sanch took a deep breath.

"I do not know how my mother knew what she did or how a sword seems so natural in her hand. She would teach me what the other boys were being taught, and then she would show me how to take all they knew apart and leave them with nothing. When I walked through the town, I would hear the whispers of those who thought they knew who I was. They would call me young prince and would say I will have to kill many men to claim my kingdom."

Bethany listened intently, as he revealed intimate parts of his life to her.

"The other boy's parents told them to stay away from me when they did not have reason to be around me. They told their sons that men died for my father, and they did not want their sons dying for his son. Needless to say, I did not have many friends. I am still thankful for them, for they kept the secret of who I was from others that passed through. I had one friend. A brother. It still pains me to have left him behind without a word. I would secretly teach him some of what I had learned. I knew he would give his life for mine. I did not want to give him the chance to prove that to me. My mother also taught me languages of lands that many had never heard of and for reasons I still do not know. Knowing all that waited for me, and how many people were probably going to have to die for me to reclaim a kingdom I knew nothing about or had any desire to obtain … I wanted none of it." He clenched his jaw. "I craved nothing other than to kill the man who took so much from me."

"Your kingdom?" Bethany asked.

"No, my father's. Sillack took from me all that I still hear about to this day. The stories of this great man I truly know nothing about. In these stories I was supposed to live alongside him, not hear of them from everyone I come to meet. That is what was taken from me. When I killed my first man on my way to get to Sillack, something new came over me. That is everything in between."

"What is this between?" asked Bethany

The life in Sanch's eyes dimmed. "I was good at it and I thought nothing of it. I felt nothing other than they died far too quickly. That, Bethany, is the between. There is the man my mother made me to be. Sanch with the warm red of life on his hands?"

She cradled his face in her hands. "That Sanch is needed in the battles yet to come. We will take him, point him at Sillack and his men, and unleash him with me close behind. You are the man my mother wants out there, keeping me safe. That part of you is what may keep you on her good side." Bethany firmly slapped him with her left hand. Bringing back the look in his eyes that motivated the color of her rose. "Come on, we must join the others. There is a lot to do before we send Alshin's men to meet him in whatever hell he's in."

A smile crept onto Sanch's lips. The thought of ending that large man in the prison camp brought a strange joy over him.

The walk from the training grounds took Bethany and Sanch past the stables, where they could hear the hands shoeing the horses. They passed Bethany's family granary, where everyone was back to work, and things were getting back to some kind of normality.

Bethany was more comfortable with Sanch after he entrusted her with his story of Sillack's men. He killed them on his way to the town, where he met the innkeeper who told him how to find Lisha.

His traveling companion asked question after question.

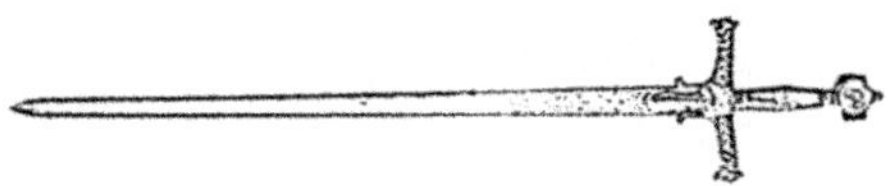

NOT A WORD HAD BEEN SPOKEN FOR SOME TIME. MANY stood over Thrant reverently. The somber silence was broken by the sound of a hand grazing the water's surface. Steam bellowed off the white cloth Lisha pulled from the ceramic bowl that dawned similar markings as the great doors of the war hall. The steam made its way up to her face, moistening her cheeks. Standing on the other side of the table, Kess was ready to lend assistance to her niece. Over on a nearby shelf, Silma sat, not quite sure how to help with such a task. Thrant, finally at peace, lay still with a calm look on his face.

"He and my father both have the same ears," Lisha said as she gently cleaned some dirt from her uncle's cheek.

"The same ears you hid under that beautiful dark hair of yours," Kess lovingly added. "He loved your father and mother, but nothing compared to the love he was filled with when you were born. He was such a proud uncle. He threw a party the night you came into this world. We all drank our fill that night." Kess reached into the bowl and pulled out another rag and started wiping down the wounds on Thrant's chest.

"Did he have any children of his own?" Lisha asked.

"There was talk about him fathering a son, but that was never confirmed by him or your father. Those two kept many secrets between themselves. There are things that only your father or Thrant can give answers to. Who knows the secrets they obtained over the years when this world was being torn apart and set ablaze. Sanch will once again find himself seeking out your father to ask him some questions about all of this. He sent Sanch to find you knowing that the safest place for you in these times would be at that boy's side when that sword was pulled from that volcano. All hell opened up the day Sanch closed his hand around the hilt of it."

"Where did that sword even come from?" Silma asked. "I feel a magic coming from it that I do not yet understand. It's neither good nor evil. Not only that, but I feel an echo of the sword's magic, but cannot figure out where it is coming from." Silma fluttered over to join Lisha and Kess.

"It is probably that dragon that's never far from that sword," Lisha pointed out.

Silma sat on Lisha's shoulder and replied, "You are probably right. There is something else, Lady Kess. As we moved through the village, I heard people refer to Sanch as the young prince. What do they mean by that? Like the Elarguns, I thought all nations peacefully had their king that ruled their people. Last I checked, Sanch's father was not of royalty, so how could Sanch be called prince?"

"No, his father was not," Kess replied. "The kingdom of man is a complicated story filled with secrets men worked hard to keep. Sanch has a future waiting for him that he may not be ready for at this time. Right now, all he needs to do is stay alive because he and that sword are the only things that are going to keep Sillack from truly having all the power he craves. That is part of what made Sillack grow to hate Lackshin as much as he did."

"Why is that?" Lisha put the rag back into the bowl. "What of his mother? I have never heard much about her or where she is from, or what people she belongs to. There is less said about his mother than there is about Sanch himself."

"After seeing how Lackshin led them through the threat of the Xyles, they were going to fall behind him and make him king above all the nations until his son, who was of royal background, could take his place as king. I know this is hard to understand. Your father can make this clearer to you all. He was very close to Lackshin, and in turn, Lackshin trusted Thrant and your father with the story of Sanch. As for Sanch's mother, not much had ever been said about her. Her beauty and skills with a sword were all that had been talked about, but no one has seen her so there is no way to confirm any of it. I have yet to meet anyone that could speak to that."

Silma still had questions. "Are you telling me he is the one they have been speaking about all this time?"

"Who?" Kess replied. "Whom do you speak of?"

"The lost one. When I was a child, my father would tell me stories about a future we all could have if the lost kin of Allen could be found and made ready to end a great evil. The lost son of a king that would know how to kill Sillack."

"Where is the real king? Was he killed?" Lisha asked as she kept on preparing Thrant.

Kess looked up at them. Her eyebrows dipped down, making her eyes look smaller than they were. The lines in her forehead deepened. "Last I heard, he was still alive, hiding safely behind his big walls as his people suffer in places where Sillack and his men control. We all looked to him to join the fight, but he never did. The king had a great army of his own he could have dispatched to help Lackshin stop the power-hungry wizard with his army of Xyles and men that were willing to kill everyone to get what they wanted. Ralyn said the alliance between Sillack and the wizard came about soon after talks of Lackshin replaced what everyone started to refer to as the "Cowardly King." That must have been the last of what his jealousy could take. Sillack knew if this war ended under the leadership of Sanch's father, he would spend the rest of his life in his best friend's shadow. His ambition would not allow him to stand by and let that come to be. Sillack saw no other way to stop that but to make sure there was no victory under Lackshin. He took the men that were loyal to him and joined the wizard called Daren and stood against his childhood friend. He could not stand to see Lackshin called king when he would still be seen as Lackshin's second. He was even willing to put Sanch to sword to make sure that Shallin would not put another man above him."

A blue flash lit up the room. "How much of this does Sanch even know? Could it all point to Sanch? My people are going to want to know about this. Here I was, thinking I was paying back a debt to a boy and his witches. Do you all know what this means? We can once again fill the skies and fly free!"

"Yes," Kess replied. "I know what this means. Before Sanch can sit on any thrown, many more will have to die. That's if he has any desire to sit there."

"Why would he not?" Silma asked.

"Revenge," Lisha whispered.

"What was that?" Silma still did not understand.

Kess nodded her head. "Yes, Lisha, you recognize the look in his eyes now, do you not? When I look at him, he is a man that is driven. We need to ask ourselves by what. His desire may only be to kill this man and leave this world to itself along with the rest of us." Kess wrung out the water from her freshly dipped rag. She shivered as some of the water ran down her forearm.

"I have spent more time with him than the rest of you, and from what I have seen, he is a boy with revenge in his eyes. Many times he had the chance to walk away from a fight that was not his to fight, yet every time he drew his sword. Even on our way here, when the rest of us slept, he kept his eyes fixed on getting here before Alshin and his men. When he had Thrant, we could have left everyone Alshin had caged behind and slipped away without anyone knowing we were even in the camp. He refused to leave and even put his self on the line to save a man of no consequences to his quest. Does he have revenge in mind? Yes, we all do," Lisha said as she slammed her hand in the bowl of water. "But does he want to sit on a thrown? Probably not, but for us, for Bethany, he will sit where we need him if for no other reason but to keep us safe. In fact, when he and Bethany return, I need to speak to him about our forces. We won this battle but the war to come will take more than this little village offers."

Kess nodded to show that she understood what Lisha had to say. "Yes, but too much talk of war. Let us get my friend ready to be put to rest. No more war for him, just peace. Eventually, we will have to turn him over to the Obeah-man to mark him with the words that will allow him passage to the other side." She wiped more dirt off Thrant's face.

"What words?" Lisha asked. "What do these words say?" She used one of the dry rags they had nearby to wipe up water that splashed on her from the bowl.

"You have a lot to learn of the customs of your people and your history. As for the words that are written on his body, only the Obeah-man knows what they say. Only the dead need worry to read those words," Kess said.

"Do you think he will take his place on the throne?" Silma asked one last time, desperate for an answer.

"Little one, I think he will not let us down, and he will sit wherever we need him to sit," Kess said.

The room returned to its somber, quiet state. Only the sound of the breeze blowing in from a window remained. The water dripping back in the basin rang out like bells ripping through the silence.

Lisha brushed Thrant's hair while Kess added rose petals to a fresh bowl of hot water before leaving to go prepare Thrant's armor.

"Silma, can you help me with something? I need your small hands." Kess motioned to Silma to follow her. Silma quickly flew over to Kess as instructed. They left the room, giving Lisha well-needed time. Maybe she was not paying attention because Lisha didn't even notice they had left the room. She looked to Thrant's left hand and saw he still had the cloth she ripped from her vest to wrap his hand when he cut it on Shallin's scales.

"I am so sorry. It was my turn, and I did not make it in time." Lisha slowly unwrapped the stained cloth from his hand. "Rest well knowing that Alshin was not allowed to draw breath long after he fell. I sent him to Hell soon after he took you from me. Know this, uncle; I have many more to kill before I feel my debt to you is paid. I plan on leaving a lot of them praying for death before I am done." She tied the strap around the handle of her sword, then leaned down and placed her forehead to his. "I will bring death to all of them," she whispered. As she stood back up, she saw two figures standing outside her peripheral. Lisha turned to see Bethany and Sanch standing there. Sanch pressed his lips together and nodded as to say that he too planned on putting many men to his sword as well.

"Bethany, when did you get back?" Kess walked past Sanch and Bethany with Thrant's armor in hand. The heavy steel brought life to the room when Kess placed it on a nearby table in the corner.

Silma hurried over to Sanch and perched herself on the shoulder closest to Bethany. She glared down at Bethany. "How old are you anyway?"

"Excuse me?" Bethany said.

"What?" Sanch overhearing looked over at them.

"What took you two so long to make it back?" Silma added to her interrogation.

"I am sure Sanch was hard at work showing Bethany his sword technique," Lisha chimed in as she gave her cousin a slow nod.

"Wait, what?" Sanch quickly looked over at Kess, who was very interested in what was being said. "Whatever is going on here, I no longer want to be a part of. I am going to find Menis and the others." Sanch slowly backed out of the room, then quickly turned and walked down the long hallway.

As he approached the large door, he heard a soft knock. The ever-ready warrior slowly and gently closed his hand around the handle of his unique dagger in his belt. Using his other hand, he slowly unlaced the door and quickly pulled it open. There he found a young boy that could not be more than ten. He looked like he had been rolling around in black soot.

Sanch stared at him for a moment. The young boy looked up at Sanch.

"Can I help you, lord?" Sanch asked as he released his blade.

"Are you him?" the boy asked as he wiped some of the dirt from his face.

"Am I who?" Sanch replied.

"Are you the Son of Lackshin?" The boy looked at Sanch's sword. "Is that her? Is that Shallin?" The boy pointed at Shallin. He was almost close enough to touch it.

Sanch placed his hand on the pommel. "No, my lord, this is not my father's sword, it is mine. Shallin is put away for now until I need her."

"You *are* him!" The boy shouted. His voice squeaked awkwardly. He stepped back and looked Sanch up and down.

"What is it, boy? Speak," Sanch commanded.

"Well," the soot-stained boy hesitated.

"Go on with it." Now curious, Sanch encouraged him to speak.

"I just thought you would be bigger." The boy looked to his feet. A heavy breeze blew in, sending a puff of dust in through the door.

Sanch laughed. "You know I get that a lot." He got down on one knee so that he could be face to face with the lad. "What brings you here, young lord?"

"I am no lord. I am just the blacksmith's grandson. He sent me here to tell you that the sword is ready, and you can pick it up."

A sad look came over Sanch's face. He knew this sword was all they were waiting for so that they could send his friend off to be with past warriors.

"Tell me, is it a sword fit for a great warrior?" Sanch asked.

"Yes, it is. One he would have been proud to have held in life and will be proud to take with him to the afterlife. My grandfather said this sword was for a great man that spent his life defending this village. He gave his life for us all." The boy looked into Sanch's eyes, searching for the truth about this man whose sword he watched as it came to life. "Is what my grandfather said true? Was Thrant a great man?"

Sanch placed his hand on the boy's left shoulder. "Remember that name you just spoke, for that is the name of a very great man. It will be up to men like you and me to make sure that name is never forgotten. Tell everyone that will listen that the great hero Thrant saved the life of the Son of Lackshin several times over. Tell them if it were not for him, the great sword, Shallin, would have been forever lost along with the chance to defeat Sillack. We have him to thank for any chance we have at winning this war. Remember this and help me honor this great warrior, Thrant."

The boy became distracted by something over Sanch's right shoulder. Sanch turned to see Lisha, Kess, Bethany, and Silma standing there. He returned to his feet. "Come, my young lord. Lead the way. Take me to this great sword so my friend can finally be at rest." Sanch and the boy left without a word to the women. The last sound was the sound of the door behind them.

CHAPTER TWENTY-ONE

The sun cast a long shadow as the two walked toward the billowing smoke. It had been a long day for everyone, and the smell of battle still lingered in the air.

"Look, now you are taller than I am." Sanch pointed to the boy's shadow next to his. "You were right. I should be bigger."

The boy stopped and looked. He squared his shoulders and puffed out his chest. "Yes, I guess I am pretty big, aren't I?"

"You are, young lord. You are as big as your heart will let you be," Sanch replied as he jostled black dust from the boy's hair.

Still admiring his shadow, he asked, "Why do you call me that? I am no lord. I am just the son of a blacksmith who is also just the son of a blacksmith. I will never be more than I am or more than they are."

Sanch laughed. "You looked at me not too long ago and told me my friend's sword was one he would have been proud to have held in life and will be proud to take with him to the afterlife. That is something that I will never forget. At your young age, you say words that would enlighten the minds of men well older than yourself. You are much more than a son of a blacksmith. I hope to be lucky enough to be around to see the man you become. Look at me. I keep hearing about the man my father was and how much he did to save the lives of so many. Now, here I am with everyone looking to me to finish what he started. Want to know a secret?"

The boy hung on Sanch's words waiting to hear what would come next.

"Even though I am Lackshin's son, I am not him. I am just a boy with a sword trying to make his father proud as the world looks on to see me succeed or fail. Just like you, I am my own man, and we will win or lose on our own. Our fathers do not dictate the men we will become. Always remember that you are a blacksmith's son. Forge your own future with fire and steel and never be ashamed of who you come from cause without them there would be no you. Now, where is that sword?"

"This way."

This boy and his outlook on his little world reminded Sanch how little his world used to be before the rest of the world knew he was still alive. Now everything he does or does not do would be measured against the deeds of his father. The young boy walked proudly through the village as everyone watched him with Sanch.

"Look how they stare at us. You must be more than the son of a blacksmith. I must be walking with someone of importance. Seems to me that you are already someone big around here."

As they came closer to his grandfather's shop, Sanch could feel the heat from the forge. It reminded him of when he and Unghell went to pick up Unghell's sword when they had come of age. Unlike him, Unghell's father was there to commission Unghell's sword. Sanch's sword had been made for him years before, but not letting him feel left out, Unghell's father commissioned a dagger made for Sanch. The dagger resembled the sword that was made for Unghell who also had the sister to Sanch's dagger. It still pulled at him having to leave his best friend and brother behind.

The blacksmith's house had two doors. The door that the boy led Sanch to opened out to a yard where the blacksmith brought steel to life. A good blacksmith saw his work as his own religion and was said to pray to his own gods. They chose to do their work in private. Only a small trusted few were allowed to watch.

"Let me get the door for you. We can't have the people of the village seeing you opening the door for a commoner like myself. Show me the way to Thrant's sword."

They entered an open yard and were instantly greeted with heat and the smell of molten steel and hot coal. The young man ran in shouting for his grandfather.

"This way." The young boy waved his hand to his new friend. "My granddad keeps them back here." The boy led Sanch to another door that led across the courtyard into a room that separated the yard from the main part of the house. The room was almost holy in nature. The flames glowed a beautiful orange, and when the bellows went down and breathed more life into it, a hint of blue showed itself and gave the room a new color and soul.

As he moved through the room, he passed what looked like an altar. The great black slab of stone was almost shiny, but when examined closer, you could tell this was no altar; this was where the blacksmith gave shape to his blades. Sanch was drawn to the stone and did not understand how it was so cold sitting so close to such a flame.

"Who is this that you have brought to our humble place?" the blacksmith asked as he pulled his grandson close to embrace him.

"This is the great Sanch, his father was Lackshin. He is here to pick up the sword." The boy could barely stay still as he talked.

"Yes, he is right. I am the Son of Lackshin, and I am humbled by this place. How is it hot where it needs to be and so cool elsewhere?" Sanch looked like an excited boy himself.

The old man smiled. "Just some tricks I have picked up over the years. Some would say it is magic."

"Your grandson has told me you have a great sword here for my fallen friend." Sanch moved closer trying to get a better look at the sword that lay close to where the blacksmith stood.

"I am sorry. Here I am, I know your name, but did not tell you mine. I am Edwin Sting, and little Edwin here is my grandson." The old man gave Sanch his hand. "Looks to me like you know about swords yourself, my boy," the blacksmith said as he looked over the sword Sanch wore. "That's some blade you got there. May I see it?" The smith reached out his hands reverently.

Sanch pulled his sword hilt first. The blacksmith looked on as he examined the blade. When he got to what Sanch's mother referred to as a birthmark on the blade, his eyes lit up. He walked over to the black altar stone and placed the sword on it. "If I may, who made such a blade?"

"I do not know. My mother herself did not know either. All she was told by my father was to make sure when I could hold a sword that this was the sword I held. Why do you ask?"

"Because this sword was forged without heat, and the black stain here always remains ice cold." He beckoned Sanch and his grandson over to where he was. The two raced over jokingly pushing one another

"Look at this." The blacksmith put heat to the black part of the blade. The air around it was so cold that water formed on it.

"Why is that happening, granddad? Where is the water coming from?" Little Edwin pushed in closer.

"It is because of the heat meeting such intense cold. It seems there is more to your sword than you know," Edwin said.

"What is it? What does it mean?" Sanch wiped the water from his sword.

"I do not know but be true to your sword. Shallin is your father's sword, and this one was made specifically for your hand. Moreover, I am not sure you know the entire story behind your father's sword. You did not come here for the words of an old man, so let's get to what you did come here for. I do say this is some of my best work. The reason I was able to finish so quickly was because I was already working on its blade before this battle came to us. I thought this sword would come into this world with no hands to hold it. It was a great honor to have been tasked to do such a job. To make a sword for a great son of this village humbled me. I fear that I will be making many more swords for the battles to come. Tell me, Son of Lackshin, do you think this war with Sillack is one you can win?" The old man placed Thrant's sword in Sanch's hands.

Sanch looked at the sword. He knew that Thrant's death was only the first of many to come before Sillack was made to answer for all he had done. As he reverently wrapped the sword in white linen provided by the smith, he winked at the boy.

"When will my lord be starting his hand at sword making? I am excited to see what steel you will pull from the forge for men who can wield them to better the world we live in and the world yet to come. I see you having a hand in bringing this all to pass. But do not think that is all you are to be." Sanch's gaze became intense.

"Your hands around the handle of one of these swords will be expected of you." Sanch looked at Edwin Sting. "If I were you, I would put some steel in the fire with Little Edwin's hands in mind. If he has not already, he should start practicing with a blade."

The blacksmith pressed his lips together and gave Sanch a nod.

"Ralyn told me that they would be off building the pile that shall take my friend to the other side. Where shall I find this holy place?" Sanch secured linen to the sword with three green cords.

The old man rubbed his lips. "It should be easy to find. Walk toward the church until you see beauty, then keep walking till you see scorched earth and the air becomes heavy. It does not stop being beautiful ... it will just be a different kind of beauty. You will see what I mean right away."

The boy ran behind Sanch as he was about to clear the threshold. "I hope one day to be like you, Sanch."

Facing away from the boy, Sanch lowered his head. "To be like me I would not wish a upon you, my young lord. Who I am is a man's son carrying around the weight of his sword, hoping to have better luck with it than he did. Please hope for something more than what I have." The door closed softly behind Sanch as he added another sword to the weight he already bore.

Quietly, he moved through the unfamiliar village. His responsibility for, and the safety of everyone that lived there, weighed heavily on his shoulders. With the Sun no longer high in the sky, it was starting to grow dim. A hush came over the village. The people were trying to come to terms with what they had lived through this day, and lay to rest those who did not live to see the sun set. With a war certain to come, they knew they had to be prepared. Sanch questioned if he should have left from his own small village. At least there he was kept hidden from the world. He thought maybe these people would have been better off had he not.

"Would they have been?" He heard a voice ask. The voice came from everywhere and nowhere simultaneously.

"What was that?" Sanch looked around trying to see who it was that spoke to him.

"Would they have?" the voice repeated. "Would they have really been better off if you had remained hidden? Do you think Sillack would not turn his gaze on these people sooner or later?"

"Maybe not," Sanch said, still looking around and getting a bit frustrated.

The voice laughed. "He would have certainly turned his attention on these villages. Do you know what the difference would have been?"

A frustrated Sanch commanded, "Show yourself!"

"I am right here."

Sanch turned to see a cloaked figure standing there holding his sword. Sanch tried to make out the face but saw nothing but darkness where a face should have been. He could make out lips and haunting eyes looking back at him, but nothing more.

"Who are you? What are you doing with my sword?" Sanch asked as he walked toward the figure that never got any closer no matter how many steps he took.

"Is this it?"

Sanch assumed it was speaking of Shallin. "No, that is not my father's. That sword is mine, not Shallin. Can I have it back now?"

"So, this is the one?" the figure whispered. "Your father's sword was much colder."

"Colder?".

"Do you know what the difference would have been?" the figure asked.

"No. I do not know what the difference would have been." Sanch tried to stay calm. "What would have been different?"

"You," the voice echoed. "They would not have had you to fight off Alshin and his men. The Elarguns followed you into battle because of who you are, otherwise they would not have been here to even the odds to win the day. If you would have stayed hidden not one of these poor people would have died."

"Yes, that is why I should have stayed where I was," Sanch said.

"If you would have stayed safe and sound with your mother, they all would have been killed. They all would have been put to the sword." The figure placed his sword back in Sanch's hand hilt first. "Your sword, young prince." The sword was now ice cold.

As sudden as the figure appeared it was gone, leaving Sanch once again alone in the world.

CHAPTER TWENTY-TWO

The room was lively with movement and conversation, and smelled of ale and bad decisions. With all that was going on, it was easy to go unnoticed from questioning eyes. The establishment served all types of characters: men of good standing who meant others no harm and were there for a hot meal and a mug or two of ale; and men with a bit more wealth that would chase their hot meal down with wines brought in from faraway lands. All would engage in a bit of gambling, and not always for the reward of coin. At the end of some wagers, someone could leave fingerless when he didn't arrive that way. Some games were that of life and death, but those were played more by the harder men that frequented the inn.

Men that called themselves "assassins for hire" wanted to show off their skills with a dagger, sword, or a small throwing knife. Then there were the men that held loyalty to the lord or king that offered gold or the promise of land and the chance to be brought up to more than what they were born to. This man would challenge the worst of all the men that would occupy tables in this town and its inns and establishments. Every man that wanted to show their worth would openly challenge one of Sillack's men. Now with so many of Sillack's men finding themselves being put into the ground, there was an urgent need to recruit men willing to kill without question.

Doing just as he was told, he sat quietly at a table in a dark corner listening as men talked about all that had been going on for the last couple months. Talks of dragons and a boy thought dead— all the conversations were interesting and filled with mixed accounts of what was really taking place. One large man dawned a thick brown beard and armor that showed Sillack's mark. His armor was dark blue and encrusted with the silver head of a fanged snake. The long sword he proudly wore was clearly one that would take a man of his size to wield. Sitting down, he was still bigger than some of the men that stood around him listening to his account of what was unfolding outside this humble town. This man spoke of a great force sent a month ago by Sillack to hunt down a runt of a boy that claimed himself the Son of Lackshin. "They were said to have been closing in on this boy and his companions. One of which was said to be that coward, Thrant. He was once a high-ranking officer in Sillack's army, but now rides with his master's enemies. A man like him belonged at the end of my sword."

"I heard they were held up at a village over three week's ride from here," a man at a nearby table said. "Riders came in last week saying that the boy calling himself Sanch, the Son of Lackshin was making his way to the village of Quiet Waters." The farmer brought another spoon of meat stew to his mouth.

In his dark corner, he could see the mention of Quiet Waters spark the attention of his host.

The innkeeper paused and listened. He stopped one of the serving girls, whispered something to her, and sent her along with a bottle of his strongest red to the table Sillack's man occupied. The young traveler saw the exchange and remembered when his father told him and his brother that a man with the taste of wine on his lips will tell you all you wish to know. The innkeeper seemed to also know these words.

The large, bearded man happily accepted the bottle of red and showed his gratitude by giving the young girl an unwelcome pat on the behind. He poured himself a cup of wine, guzzled it down, and started back at his story. "That is true, little man." He pointed to the farmer with a half-eaten turkey leg. "Lord Alshin leads the men that probably already swooped down on that poor little village before they knew what hit them. Alshin is probably already on his way back to Sillack with that boy's head and Quiet Waters village burning behind him. I can hear the screams of the people from here." The bearded soldier put up a toast with the other soldiers around his table. All of Sillack's men in the room lifted their cups to the assumed victory of Alshin.

With all the talk and activity going on, nearly no one noticed the man clad in black walk in and make his way to the far corner of the bar. The stranger pulled up a stool and ordered a cup of ale and a bowl of the day's special. After downing his first cup, he ordered another and some bread to eat until his stew arrived.

The soldier's account made the innkeeper glare at him with unpleasant eyes. He looked at his guest in the corner and shook his head to show his doubt of the man's account of the result of the so-called battle. As he poured the stranger his second cup of ale, unknown words were shared between the innkeeper and the man. The innkeeper gave a nod and grinned as relief crept across his face.

"That village is not as helpless as most may think."

"What was that?" said another of Sillack's men that stood close to a young stable boy.

The boy was trying to be part of the conversation. "That village is not as helpless as most may think." Then he added, "My father and I have bred warhorses for that village less than two years ago. When we went to deliver their horses, they were peaceful enough people, but far from incapable of defending themselves. The leader of Quiet Waters is well known for fighting at Lackshin's side many years ago. He still carried a sword from what I saw." The boy nervously looked at a tall, slim man who had his hand fixed on the handle of his dagger.

"Quiet!" the slim man shouted, but went unheard. "Quiet!" he shouted once more. This time the bearded man slammed his mug on the table and sprung to his feet. The slim man must have been of some rank because when he made it known he required their attention, he received it. Soldiers in attendance fixed their eyes on Maurice. Thick, curly red hair rested on his collar. Unlike the others, his face was shaved smooth, and his uniform was well kept. The sword that hung from his hip was not one of just a foot soldier and his armor bore no fanged serpent.

"This boy has something to say that may be of some interest to us." Maurice rested his gloved hand on the stable boy's bony shoulder, applying just enough weight. "Tell them what you just told me, and anything else you can remember about this village," Maurice commanded him.

The boy meant to sound older than he was, but when he opened his mouth, the squeaky voice of a boy leaped from his lips. "If it is Quiet Waters you speak of, your man, Alshin, may find more of a fight than he was looking for."

"What are you talking about, boy? Many of us have fought alongside Alshin, and I do not see how a village can stand against him and the men he leads." The big, bearded beast pushed his chair over.

"Shut up, and let the boy finish," Maurice calmly commanded. "Is there more, boy?"

"I heard you say Thrant, and if he is taking Sanch to that village. He is returning home and is taking Sanch with him. Unknowing to most, that village is filled with well-trained fighters that gave up war but did not give up the skills of fighting in one. When I was in that village two years ago, I witnessed kids at play, and their play was with swords and bows." All that talk must have made the boy's throat dry because when he finished speaking, he drank heartily, spilling ale down the front of his garb.

"Sounds to me that old Alshin may have taken on more than he had expected this time," a self-proclaimed assassin said under his breath, only to find eyes glaring at him from Sillack's men.

"What was that?" Maurice spun around to see who spoke ill of his fellow soldier. "Speak again and you will find your tongue pinned to the wall." His red hair bounced with his every step. Although his voice was strong, his face remanded calm. Maurice fingered the hilt of his short sword that sat just above his great, long sword. A short sword was good for fighting in a small environment such as this one.

The assassin took Maurice's advice and said nothing more about Alshin's situation. Everyone at the assassin's table kept their heads down and fixed on their cups in front of them. After Maurice found no one had anything more to say, he walked over and took a seat with the large, bearded brute, and finely discarded the assassin's words.

"I want wings in the air first thing," Maurice uttered to his men before pouring himself a cup of the strong red.

The stranger at the bar and the innkeeper spoke off and on for some time before the stranger started taking short glances at the boy. Now it appeared that the stranger and the innkeeper were looking at him and talking. It was apparent the boy was the topic of the conversation, and this cloaked man seemed to be very interested in him. For what reason he was enquiring, and to what existent the boy did not know. After telling him to stay quiet and out of sight, why would he be bringing attention to him now? This just did not seem to make sense.

The innkeeper sent one of the serving girls into the wine cellar. She came back shortly carrying a fine bottle of sweet wine. He thanked the girl and sent the stranger over to the boy's table. Under his cloak, you could make out strange curved, twin swords. He had a small but firm frame. He walked in a smooth, silk-like motion. It was as if no one in the entire room could see him. Just as he walked in unnoticed, he somehow managed to stay that way. As he passed one of the tables, a man sprung to his feet and knocked a cup from the table. Without missing a stride, he snatched the cup from the air and placed it back onto the table. Even then, he went unnoticed. He placed the bottle of wine on the table. His strong, ebony hand gripped the gray bottle by the neck.

"May I?" he asked, pulling a chair from the table.

The boy gave the stranger a nod of approval, but only after he looked to the innkeeper for a sign.

"Very nice dagger you've got there, boy. It is quite unique." Natluc eyeballed the blade that called the boy's right hip home. "I have seen another of the same likeness." After saying that, he now had the boy's attention.

"Where have you seen a dagger such as mine?" The boy sat forwarded and leaned into the conversation. "Because I doubt that you have seen another such as this one," he said as he pulled the dagger out just enough the show the shine of the blade. The fire that glowed in the center of the large room showed brightly in the blade.

Natluc smiled as he worked the cork from the mouth of the bottle. He poured himself a cup of the wine, and filled his mouth with it. After holding it for a moment, as if to savor it for just a time, he swallowed, then whispered, "I saw him about three days ride from here. He was making paltry work of two men; one large man that did not look too smart, and another smaller man that did not look any smarter. They must have seen him as easy prey and found that not to be the case. The boy was not alone. There was a girl with him that shared a face with our host over there." Natluc motioned toward the innkeeper that had his eyes locked on the table.

"Well, what is it that you want from me? Are you here to compliment me on my dagger over a bottle of wine?" The boy wondered if he was wrong about trusting the innkeeper. It was as if he already knew what he was doing here, and whom he was searching for. The innkeeper also recognized his dagger. "Do you mean to steal my blade from my hip?" the boy asked, gripping the hilt of his dagger.

Natluc laughed and poured the boy a fresh cup of wine. "I see you misunderstand our intentions. I, like the keeper of this establishment, mean to help you and your brother."

Unghell's eyes widened. This man knew what he even kept from the innkeeper, or did the innkeeper say less than he knew? Unghell picked up his cup and drank. Sanch was always the one that thought well on his feet. Unghell tried to think of his next move. He decided to do as his brother would. "Should I consider you a friend, or someone I will have to pull my dagger from one day?" he asked as he motioned to Natluc to pour him another cup of wine. "I am not here seeking trouble. I just wish to find my brother and draw as little attention to myself as possible."

Natluc did as he had been instructed and poured the boy more wine. "Well, then you are in luck because our friend over there and I have the same plans for you. We both wish that you go unnoticed and draw as little attention as possible. I am here to help you with that." Natluc took another sip of the sweet wine.

"But if I went so unseen, how did you know where to find me? I said nothing to anyone in this town. I came straight here when I arrived here." Unghell was concerned. If this stranger noticed him, then who else had?

Natluc gave him a crooked smile. "Why straight to this place? What was it about this place that brought you here?"

Unghell licked some wine from his lips and thought. "I always heard my father speak of this place and how the innkeeper was a good man and could be trusted."

"Your father was correct," Natluc replied. "The innkeeper is only following orders left to him by your brother's father."

"How is that possible?" Unghell asked. "Lackshin is long dead. How is he still giving orders to anyone?"

Natluc laughed. "These are orders that were left some time ago. That man is not as he seems. He is not just an innkeeper here to fill our cups and keep the rooms we sleep in clean. There is much more to him, and he is no friend to Sillack nor his men."

The boy looked to their host that still stood behind the bar giving one of the serving girl's instructions. "Who is he, and what orders did Lackshin leave him with?" Unghell started to understand the depth of what his brother and himself were a part of.

"He was to notify us of when Sanch passed through this town and his establishment, and that's what he did, and here I am," Natluc said. "I am one of many that laid dormant waiting for the day when your brother was ready to show himself. When he came here months ago, words were sent up and out to us. Now I sit here in front of you with my sword at your service." Natluc rested his forehand on the hilt of his sword.

"Why is that? Why have you been sent to be at my service?"

"Me and one other returned here to stay close to your village and keep an eye on Sillack's men. In case any useful information was slipped, we could get it to the powers that be right away. To keep your brother safe, we had to stay ahead of Sillack and his next move. However, Sillack learned from Lackshin how to keep his enemy's always guessing. When you showed up with that dagger swinging from your belt, our friend knew who you were and sent for me. Now here we are sharing a bottle of excellent wine." Natluc took another drink and once again held a mouth full to savor the flavor.

"You are one of the good guys?" Unghell asked, his voice filled with hope.

"Oh, God no," Natluc said with a hint of laughter in his words. "I am not at all what someone would call a good man, nor am I a bad one.

"Then what in hell kind of man are you?"

Natluc twisted his mouth and thought for a moment as if he had never been asked such a question before. He bit his lip, and then said, "I would have to say I am the kind of man that does what needs to be done. I am the man you will want around when those hard decisions show themselves. When a child soldier is charging at you with a blade in hand, you will find yourself with the moral dilemma of killing him or not. That is where I come in. I will cut him open without hesitation. I don't care if he deserves to die or if his mother has his body to burn. When a man promises friendship, you find him false, and you think to just let him go from your sight and swear that you will kill him next time you see him. For me, there will be no next, I will open his throat at the first sign I find him untrue." Natluc's words left his mouth void of any emotions.

Unghell could see in Natluc eyes that the words he spoke described who he truly was. The young boy sat and took it all in over more cups of wine.

The serving girl brought over food for Natluc. A bowl of mannish water and bread. The dish was made with the parts of the goat that you would rather not know you were eating. Yet, if you had it once, you would look forward to the next time you could partake of it.

The smell of the mannish water was good. Unghell had Natluc order him a bowl; even after Natluc refused to tell him what was in it. After his first spoonful, the boy no longer cared what was floating in his bowl. A pitcher of ale came with the stew over to the table.

Wine was not a drink to pair with mannish water. Natluc and Unghell went on speaking into the evening and into the night. The boy had many questions about his bothers past, and Lackshin. Sanch and Unghell only heard the stories their parents chose to tell them. Many were kept from them. It was as if they thought the two boys would run off in search of some kind of adventure before they were truly ready. Natluc answered as much as he could, however, there were parts to the stories he also wasn't aware of. Now it was Natluc's turn to find out a little about the boy he was to protect. He asked questions about him and Sanch.

"What do you know about that dagger you and your brother carry on your hips?" Natluc asked as he filled their cups once again with more of the brown ale.

"Not much," Unghell replied. "A boy's first sword is a big thing for a father. His sword was made well before he could lift one. Therefore, he never had the chance to be a part of what a father and a son shared during this time. When our father was having my first sword forged, he insisted that my brother be a part of it. Since he already had a sword, he and our mother came up with these daggers."

"Was there anything peculiar about the forging of the blades?" Natluc asked what Unghell found to be another strange question.

Unghell drank down some more of the bitter ale and tried to think back to that time. A look came on Unghell's face. One of recollection and confusion.

"What is it, boy?" Natluc demanded an answer. "What have you remembered?"

"It may be nothing, but it is the only thing that stands out to me about that time." Unghell took another drink.

"Well, speak of it," Natluc again demanded.

"It was earlier that day before we went to the blacksmith. My brother and our mother were practicing with swords, which was normal for them, for they would stay at it well after everyone else was taking water and rest. This time, she did not let up on him at all. He did something that day that he's never done again." A partial smile crossed Unghell's face.

"What was that?" Natluc pressed.

"He never dropped his guard when he was facing our mother again, or anyone else. She took the opening, and with a blunted practice sword, she cut him on his left shoulder." Unghell stopped and started chewing on his bottom lip.

"Nothing about that sounds strange to me," Natluc said. "The boy had to learn. In a real fight that lapse could cost a man his life."

"That is not what was strange about it. When he and I went with our father to the blacksmith, both of us were made to carry two boxes of metal that our mother kept under the bricks of our home. When we arrived at the forge, we gave the blacksmith our boxes and our father removed the rag used to bind my brother's wound. He gave it to the blacksmith and asked if that would be enough for two. The man looked at the skinny little boy next to me, nodded, and started at his craft. A week later, the blacksmith delivered two identical daggers to our home along with my sword. Only he and I could tell the difference between the two blades. We could not carry our swords, because we were still just boys and still too small to have the weight of swords on our hips. They instructed us to never be without our daggers, and we did as we were told. Even to this day, as you could see." Unghell patted the hilt of his dagger.

"Now that makes sense and clears up much." Natluc nodded. "Your brother is truly who he claims to be. And you can truly call yourself his brother." Natluc held up his cup to have it met by Unghell's.

Unghell asked, "Will you be taking me to him?"

"No, no, I will not be taking you to him, boy," Natluc replied, placing his cup onto the table.

"Why not?" Unghell asked.

"Your brother is safe and in good hands, but there are things he will need if he is to have a chance against the Sillack's forces. What I will be doing is taking you to where you can do more for your brother than just fighting at his side." Natluc tried to reassure him that he would not be letting his brother down by not running to be at his side. "Trust me, boy, when this is all done you will stand shoulder to shoulder with your brother to end this all. But, for now, you should get a good night's rest. We move out in the morning at first light."

As they sat there eating and drinking, they became more aware of one another's intentions. Sillack's men also drank and spoke loudly, revealing much of what was going on outside the gates of the town. Maurice left not too long after the assassin spoke about Alshin and his possible defeat at the hands of Sanch. Maurice's close guards followed him out, leaving the enormous man and his rowdy band of men behind. With Maurice gone, they became even more unruly, and the games of chance became more intense.

More and more men left because of this increase in excitement. Some men stumbled out under the assistance of women intending to lighten his load of the coin he carried for an evening's worth of work. They were the lucky ones. There were others carried out to find the Obeah-Man in town to patch him up from a lost gamble. When a drunken man tries to catch his knife as it spins, it only ends in two ways. Most of the time, it ends with a trip to an Obeah-Man. With the crowd thinned, it was safe for Unghell to move about the room.

"I am sure you've noticed most of Sillack's men have left, or are too drunk to notice you," Natluc pointed out. "That is a good thing, since your brother has every village and town from here to Quiet Waters looking out for strangers and queer behavior. Some even look to the sky, hoping to catch a glimpse of a dragon carrying a boy and a magic sword," Natluc said mockingly.

"There is a dragon—" Unghell's eyes lit up.

"Not you too, boy," Natluc interrupted. "Make your way up to your room and get that rest that you will need for what is coming. Who knows when you will have a bed to sleep in or a roof over your head." Natluc rose to his feet. He was not a very tall man, but he could still command a room. He ordered Unghell to bed and made his way back to the bar where he and the innkeeper spoke more.

Unghell did as instructed, and once satisfied in the security of his room, he walked over to the window that overlooked the hill that separated his home from the rest of the world. He watched as the moon hung in the sky so far away; farther still from where he was to journey come dawn.

Before he closed the shutters, he closed his eyes, and let the wind caress his cheeks. He walked to the bed, sat down, and placed his face in his hands. Unghell put the thoughts of home behind him and thought only of his brother and Natluc's promise of having him at Sanch's side when the real fight takes place. He lay back on the bed not knowing that Sanch had also slept there months ago. With his stomach full and his head still swimming from all he had drunk, he let his eyes close and allowed sleep to take him.

CHAPTER TWENTY-THREE

The sound of the wood crackling as the fire flickered gave the shadows life. The whispers of men around the flames eating, drinking ale, and telling stories filled the night air. There were stories of women in taverns back in the big city that they couldn't wait to get back to. The sound of wet stones scraping against metal joined the fire in song.

"If it were not for that stray arrow that landed perfectly in reach for me to grab and plunge into that man's head, he would have had the better of me. I am sure of that."

One man drank to life and the death of others. Just as much as he got in his mouth, the same ran down his wiry beard.

There was talk of what they were doing out there and what they were expected to achieve and who they were looking for by direct orders of Sillack, and why such a young soldier was put to lead? But above it all, there was one thing that had every man in the camp keeping their swords close and very much afraid, but no one spoke of it. The horses felt the same way and were not shy about making it known that they did not like the company that they had to keep. You could hear the nays and snorts of the horses reacting to every sound they heard.

The fire made her already red hair look like it was ablaze. It was hard to make out the color of her eyes through the rapid movement of the fires when the wind blew through the flames.

Taddayuse did not hide his knowledge of the wondering stares he received from all around him, but he ate and drank as if he were alone. Not dressed like the rest of Sillack's men, he always stood out. Instead of armor, he dawned traditional wear. He wore lightweight leather. On his chest was a crown of thorns with what looked like teardrops dripping from them. His arms were covered with leather girds with steel spicks coming from every inch of it. The shiny, black glimmered from the light of the night.

His was the only fire that was without conversation until the silence was broken like glass by the words of Ros.

"Are you who they think can bring back this miracle boy and his father's magic sword? We have all heard the rumors that every year or two finds itself on the lips of someone wanting to give hope to otherwise hopeless people. The word is that Lackshin's heir has truly shown himself and now everyone is up in a frenzy." Ros leaned closer to the flames. "Some are looking to him to right all the wrongs, and to kill the one all you wankers blindly follow like the stupid men you are." She sloppily cut a chunk of meat off the goose cooking over their fire.

Taddayuse looked annoyed by this sudden invasion of privacy.

"Then there are the ones that know if this is for real and all the power that had been obtained in this world made under that want to be king will soon come to a violent end for all of them. That is if it is true that the Son of Lackshin somehow lived and has come to put a stop to all of this." Ros chewed violently on a piece of goose and smiled as her green eyes lit up. "There will be armies and kings that have not been heard from for years. They will be looking to either join the fight to stop him or join the fight to see your prick king killed by this boy. I think there will be no boy for us to find, because he is either dead or still suckling at his mother's breast, not wanting to face the real world waiting for him out here."

"The sword," Taddayuse whispered as he brought his cup of wine to his lips.

"What sword?" Ros asked, tempted to knock the cup from Taddayuse's hand.

He placed the cup down and wiped drops of wine from his scruffy face. Coarse black stubble grew from his light brown skin.

"If you do not speak soon, it will be my sword you will need to worry about." Ros placed her hand on the hilt of her blade.

Taddayuse gave her a crooked smile. "The sword is no longer in the volcano. It has been gone for weeks now. There have been a lot of men killed by a boy fitting the description of this suckling child you speak of. If this is someone's way of getting a wank by telling stories, then this has been the best I've heard yet." Shaking his head, he added, "Because it was a good enough story to have Sillack so worried he had that skinny-faced wizard to unearth those unholy creatures. I think maybe we will find a boy this time, but the question is will we be able to bring him and that sword back with us even with help from the five of you?" Taddayuse poured the redhead a cup of wine and handed the girl next to her the bottle.

"How do you know this to be true?" Jess asked as her braided hair fell over her shoulder. "We have all heard the stories of the sword gone missing just to find out that it was rubbish. What's to say it is not so again?"

Fillip walked into the light, picking up the abandoned wine at Jess's feet. He uttered one word, "Dragon," then sat next to Jess.

"What was that?" Ro fixed her eyes on Fillip.

"Over the years, there have been several rumors of the boy warrior freeing the sword from the volcano and leading a march on the black city to put an end to Sillack. The small revolts that came about from these rumors were quickly and violently brought to an end every time. But this time is different. What has gotten my attention is the talk of the volcano erupting, but not before a dragon was seen flying free from its mouth. There is also talk of Thrant being taken from Alshin's prison camp. All these things happening leads me to believe this time it may be true." Fillip scratched his balding head.

"A dragon?" Jess turned to face Fillip. "Dragons disappeared centuries ago, except for the ones that were captured and turned into mindless beasts. The men who did this and their dragons are worlds away. How was a dragon seen?"

Before Fillip could answer, a soft voice echoed in the darkness. "The last time a dragon was said to have been seen is when one flew into that same volcano you speak of on the same day Sillack had that sword thrown into it to be destroyed. Lackshin, his sword, and that dragon were somehow connected. Hundreds of years before that, the dragons and the men and women that lived side by side with them left when this world felt that dragons should be pets and weapons of war, and not seen as equals. That is when dragons no longer saw their place to be next to man. Man's fears got the best of them." A woman walked out of the shadows. "If a dragon was seen, the dragons and their men have returned after hundreds of years. This is proof Sanch has reclaimed his father's sword."

Taddayuse sat on his log. "I guess we will soon see." He threw a bone into the fire, disturbing the ashes and causing them to fly into the night.

Reaching for her sword, the smallest of the five, Viv, stood up and pushed her chin toward the darkness. The four grabbed their weapons and fell in beside her. Fillip and their young leader rose to their feet, staring out into the darkness like the others.

"Can you hear that?" she whispered.

"Yes, and I can also smell it, too," Taddayuse replied. He was in front putting him closest to whatever was out there . Suddenly, something jumped out of the dark and grabbed one of the soldiers.

"Everyone at the ready!" ordered Fillip.

Drunk and sober men alike jumped to their feet. Fillip grabbed a torch and lit it with the fire behind him.

"What are you doing?" Taddayuse asked, placing his hand on Fillip's shoulder as he walked past him into the night.

"Get the rum ready," Fillip whispered.

Ros picked up the rum and handed it to Taddayuse. She and two of the others grabbed their bows and took aim at the darkness while the smallest of the five pulled their weapons. In the quiet of it all, you could hear the cracking of the strings as the bows were being pulled back into their ready positions. The two daggers, almost sword-like weapons with its curved single-edged blades that the little cherub held, glimmered in the fire's light. The sword the other cherub held was both beautiful and threatening, especially in her hands.

Fillip threw the torch high into the dark, reached back, and took the rum from Taddayuse. They all waited for his next move. Right as the torch was to meet the ground, he shouted, "Now!" He threw the bottle of rum onto the flames, igniting the night, revealing the beast closing in on them.

The once quiet night now played the song of battle. The first sounds to break the silence were of bowstrings singing their harmony as arrows released into the air. The breeze of the arrows passing Fillip was so close you could see the hairs it cut from his head falling to the ground before it made it to the thick hide of these gorilla-like creatures covered in knotted human hair. They were being attacked by Forest Men. One ran through the camp carrying a man into a tent where spine-chilling screams came from it.

"I have to stop that thing!" Taddayuse shouted as he left Fillip's side.

"Taddayuse!" Fillip was in the middle of his own fight. He could not leave to join him.

"I got him." Viv followed close behind Taddayuse with her two swords in hand, still wet from the last Forest Man she put down.

Taddayuse grabbed a flaming log from a nearby fire pit and ran into the large tent where the creature had dragged the soldier.

"What the hell are you doing? Boy, get out of there!" Viv shouted, standing at the opening of the tent. "Great, this one is brave." Using the sword in her right hand, she moved the tent's flap out of the way as she slowly entered. See saw Taddayuse had set the room ablaze and was holding the beast back with his sword and a flaming log. With its attention fixed on him, she saw this as an opportunity to make a move. She ran up and over what little furniture was there to avoid the ground that was engulfed in flames.

Just as there was nothing more to run on, she found herself on the back of the angry beast. As she landed, her two blades sunk deep into its shoulders, causing its arms to go limp, but did nothing to stop his mouth from snapping at Taddayuse. With its legs still working, it pushed past and ran out of the tent and towards the forest with the small cherub in tow. A loud howl sang out into the night. The sound of the air being cut was undeniable.

As the arrow hit the beast, you could hear its skull break from the impact, throwing its rider and her swords loose and onto the ground. Chasing the runaway Forest Man, Taddayuse, looked to see Viv standing there with the string on her bow still vibrating from that powerful shot she had just landed. To hit a target moving at that speed with such poor light was an amazing thing to see. He hurried to help her to her feet and to retrieve her weapons.

"Get off me! What were you thinking? You almost got us both killed! That soldier was already dead. There was nothing you could have done for him. And if you really had to go in, have a plan, not just a candle and a sword!." Viv stood there, looking at Taddayuse. "You just going to stand there with that stupid look on your face? Do all the brave ones have to be stupid as well?"

"You think I am brave?" he asked with a smile on his smoke-stained face.

"Stupid. I think you're stupid." She turned and walked away to rejoin the others.

"We almost died together, and I don't even know your name. What is your name? I want to thank you properly," he asked as he followed closely behind her.

She quickly turned with one of her swords outstretched. "Viv."

A startled Taddayuse came to a full stop. "What?" He took a step back.

"My name is Viv. The five of us have been with you for almost a week now and you have said little to nothing to us, much less ask our names. Here I stand, lucky to be alive because I ran into a tent after you. And now you ask me my name because you want to thank me? You are welcome, but the next time I am to save your life, you will have to call for me by name. From what I've seen from the way you do things, you will need me to do that a lot."

With two fingers, he lowered her sword. "Yes, Viv. Your name is not one I will forget."

They reached the others in time to help them fight off the last of the Forest Men.

"Fillip, what were those things?" Taddayuse asked, still a little out of breath.

"Are you okay, boy?" Fillip looked him over for injuries.

"Yes, I am fine, thanks to Viv literally running into fire to save me. What were those things, and where did they come from?"

"Did your mother or father ever tell you the story of the Forest Men?" Ros joined the conversation.

"Ros is right boy. Have you never heard of the Forest Men and how they were made to be what they are now?"

Taddayuse stood there with a confused look on his face. "Fillip you know their names?"

"You must be joking. The one that looks like her hair is on fire is Ros. The one with the black hair that made that amazing shot to save the little one there is called Neile. As for the one that pulled you out of the fire, her name is…"

"I know," Taddayuse interrupted. "Her name is Viv."

"The one over there with the white hair is Jess, and the one that seems to know a lot about Sanch and his father's sword is Lo. They have been with us for almost a week now. How do you not know their names?"

"That's what I said, Fillip," Viv said, giving Taddayuse a dirty look, pushing him out of her way as she walked by.

"You really don't know what Forest Men are?" Ros asked.

"No, I've never heard of them. I am not from here. I was born in Tegra, a long way from here."

Now he really had Lo's attention. "You are from Tegra?"

"Yes, why?" Taddayuse replied.

"I haven't met many people from Tegra. I mean, why would anyone from a place safe from all of this come here, much less find himself fighting in a war that's not his when he could be safe with his own people."

"I have my reasons."

Lo walked over to Taddayuse. "I would surely love to hear what those reasons are, my friend. Did you say you volunteered to hunt this boy with his father's sword?"

"We can all talk about why we are here later. We need to see how many men we lost and how many are fit to still go on," Fillip said, bringing whatever was going on between Lo and Taddayuse to a stop. "Lo and I will check on the south side of the camp, and you and Viv can check the north side with Taddayuse. You three can walk the perimeter and make sure we are not in for any more surprises tonight."

"Yes, Fillip," Ros replied as she cleaned her blade and gave Jess and Neile an awkward look.

Lo started walking away, but suddenly stopped. "Viv."

"Yes, Lo."

"Watch yourself with that boy from Tegra. We all know what kind of people the Tegs are."

"Everyone be on guard. We don't know if that was just a first wave," Fillip said as he hurried to catch up with Lo.

Viv and Taddayuse were the last two to start their task. Viv turned and looked at Taddayuse. "She dislikes you more than I do, it seems." Viv walked away, leaving him standing there. "Keep up. We both know you are not safe by yourself out here."

"Lo, wait up." Fillip rushed to catch her. "What is your problem with the boy? Has he wronged you somehow? If so, I am sure he did not mean to."

"My problem is not just with him," Lo replied. "It is with him and his people and their sneaky ways of doing things. When you swear loyalty, that is supposed to mean something and when it mattered most, it meant nothing to them."

"Very true, but do you understand what you are speaking about happened before that boy even took his first breath? I am not even sure he knows what happened." Fillip looked curious. "Why is it a problem for you, anyway?"

Lo stopped, allowing him to reach her. "It means nothing to me other than I do not like fighting alongside someone with betrayal in their bones. If a boy from Tegra did decide to fight in a war that is not his, why would he choose Sillack to fight for? If anything, he would owe his sword to Sanch, but yet here he is hunting him instead of Sillack."

"Do you not also fight for Sillack? Are you not helping this boy on his hunt for the Son of Lackshin?" Fillip said

"First of all, I do not fight for Sillack. I am a cherub and I only fight for my sisters. As for us being here to help you hunt down Sanch, you have made a very wrong assumption there." Lo returned to assess how badly the camp was hit by the Forest Men.

"Then what are you five doing with us?"

"That has yet to be decided at this point. For now, we are helping you and your men stay alive."

As they walked through the camp, the carnage they saw was that of men pulled apart as if they were children's toys. There were men alive but so badly chewed on that they would be better off dead and were loudly asking for that to be so. Lo and Fillip would make it quick and as painless as possible. Some of the Xyles were still fighting over the Forest Men they killed in the attack. It could have been much worse if the Xyles were not there. This was one time where it was good to have these beasts there and not dead or locked away behind a spell.

Neither Lo nor Fillip trusted the Xyles, and along with the other men, still felt uneasy with them moving freely among them. Not far from where two of these creatures were, there laid a man with more of him on the outside than the inside. The other men stood around him. Lo pushed her way through them to the man who was begging to be ended.

"Get those things out of here!" Lo pointed to the Xyles. "He should not meet his gods with them being the last thing he sees. Move them."

"Who is this woman, Fillip? Why does she feel like she can give us orders?" one of the men boldly asked.

Lo rested her hand on her short blade and ran towards the soldier. The wind blowing in from the north pushed her hair forward, causing it to cover her face. The flickering of the surrounding fires bounced off her eyes as she focused on this man.

"She is the woman that will likely open your throat if you don't do what she says. Please get those things out of here. We cannot afford to lose any more men tonight." Fillip quickly put himself between the two.

"But how?" one man asked. "They kind of do what they want, short of eating us."

"Just move." Lo pushed Fillip out of the way and walked over to the Xyles and pulled out her sword. "Take what you have and move away from here." They looked at her as if they knew what she was saying to them. They did just as she commanded. They grabbed up their meat and hurried off. She rushed back to the dying man and kneeled over him.

"Look at me," she whispered. "They wait for you." She plunged her dagger into his heart, bringing his pain to an end. She rose to her feet and walked over to the man who questioned her orders and cleaned her blade on his chest as a crooked smile crept across her face. "Now bury him, would you?"

Fillip was a little unsure of what he was seeing. Who is this woman? Why would Xyles obey her?

As they continued around camp, Fillip broke the silence. "Why is it that the Xyles seem to be afraid of you?"

With no emotion in her voice, she replied, "They fear anything eviler than themselves. If you are finished asking your questions, we need to continue and see how many bodies we will burn tonight." The camp was still alive with movement.

"Have you ever seen Forest Men before tonight, Lo?"

"No, Fillip, but I have heard the story of them and what made them what they are. Have you seen many of them before tonight?

Fillip, a strong-looking man for his age, stood a good six feet tall. His hair was almost all white with a little black peeking through—the color it was when he was a younger man. He scratched his thickening beard. "Yes, in my younger days, I put a great many of them into the ground."

"The story of how they became this?" Lo kicked one that lay lifeless. "Is all that true? Were they really men that asked for and agreed to something they did not quite understand?"

Fillip stood there, nodding his head. "Yes, they were at one time men and women, just like us. Magic is not always the best way to fix people's problem."

"No," Lo replied. "It is not always the best way. Magic takes away as good or even better than it gives. I and my family know that all too well."

"Where is it that your family is from?" Fillip, now curious, asked Lo.

"When we become cherubs, we give up who we were. The answer to that question is irrelevant to where we are at this point."

"Fair enough, Lo. Fair enough. Let's go see what the others have found on their side."

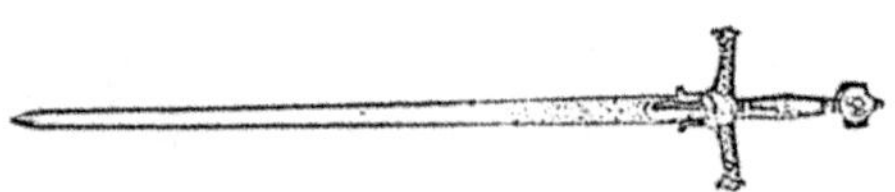

MOVING QUIETLY, THE THREE CHERUBS WERE ON full alert. The attack by the Forest Men had them and everyone else uneasy. Swords and daggers were drawn and ready for whatever may be out in the darkness. The smell of death still filled the air. The closer they got to where the horses were tied, the more they could hear the horses pulling at the stacks they were hitched to. Some had even broken away and were running off into the night or into the camp. The girls hurried to secure the remaining horses before they were all lost to the night.

"I'll hold them. You two secure the stacks and hammer the others into the ground."

"Yes, Ros," Jess replied as she used the back of her dagger to pound the stacks farther into the ground.

Neile grabbed the rope and pulled it tight.

"We need to get these animals under control before we lose them all." Ros ordered, still trying to keep her voice down. The rope cut her hand as she pulled back against the weight of the horses.

"I got it, Ros. Just try to get them calm so they don't pull free and drag us all along with them," Neile barked.

It took some effort and a lot of rope burn, but they were able to get the horses calm and secured. Even some of the others made their way back.

"See, Ros. No problem. All is well"

Ros turned and glared at Neile. "What is wrong with you, Neile? You seem to have a problem, so spit it out."

"Now we're taking orders from you?" Neile replied. "I thought we were taking orders from the men."

"Neile, did you know better than Fillip how to defend against those things? Cause I know I did not, and our mission here isn't to end up dead," Ros said.

"What is our objective here? Because I am still not clear on that myself. What did Deadra say we were to do here? I've always said I am glad to have Lo around when there is a fight, but why is she here with us and not leading her own girls? I do not get why Deadra sent her with us. We all know Lo and her girls are not truly one of us. I've never been sure about them." Jess made her concerns known.

"All I know is when it got out that we were going with the men that were tasked with bringing this boy with his father's sword back to Sillack, Lo told Deadra she would come with us. I do not fully understand what is going on, but I am following my orders. Come the time we may have to kill Taddayuse or the old man, so be it. Let's just hope Lo understands what we are here to do," Ros said, trying to put the other's minds to rest "Let's get back to the others. We still need to try and get some rest tonight. I feel that we are going to have a long day tomorrow when we can truly see the damage done by these things."

"Were they not once human?" Jess asked as she put her dagger away. "How does something like that even happen to an entire race of people?"

"Maybe you can ask the old man when we get back. He seems to know something about these creatures. To tell you the truth, I would like to find out more about them myself. Especially how better to kill them," Neile said, turning to make her way back to where there was more light.

They were all uneasy from what they had just seen. Men being pulled apart, and some ripped out of their armor only to make it easier for the Forest Men to consume them. It was a sight that none of them will soon forget. On heightened alert, they finish walking the perimeter, making their way back to the others. Every sound had their heads turning. Their grip on their swords stayed tight. As far as they knew, those things were still out there trying to make a meal of any one of them. The night was cold and windy, and they could still smile the stench of the Forest Men. It was clear they were still out there, maybe done for the night or planning to stop in once more for another quick snack. It was going to be a long night waiting for sunrise.

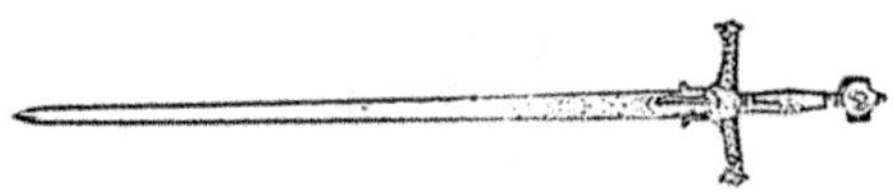

"SO, WHY YOU?" VIV ASKED AS SHE MOVED THE FLAP OF another tent with one of her short swords. Taddayuse slowly moved in to make sure it was empty.

"Why me what?" he replied. "I do not understand what you are asking."

"Why were you picked to lead these men to find this boy? It sounds to me like he is very important to Sillack, and it does not look to me like you have led many men. I would have expected him to send a more experienced warrior to lead such a quest."

"Thank you for pointing that out," Taddayuse said. He waved the torch around the tent. "It looks to me like this one is empty. As for your question, I have asked myself the same thing. Why me? Before a week ago, he didn't know I existed much less said two words to me. My plan was to say little, do what was asked of me, and hopefully go unnoticed."

"So, what happened? That sounds like a good plan, especially when you are dealing with an animal like Sillack and the men that follow him," Viv said.

Around them were the same men she spoke of. Most of the men that fought for Sillack were men that had no honor and no other army would have them. His army was filled with men exiled from their own country and pledged their sword to him to feel like they served a purpose, or simply had to do something in order to feed themselves. Others see it as an opportunity to terrorize those weaker than them and take what they could not otherwise earn. Then there were those with different intentions altogether.

"For some reason, Haygen picked me to accompany Sillack and his creepy wizard on an expedition. I did not know we were going to the cave where the Xyles were locked away behind a ruby claw entwined with water and fire. I know it sounds crazy, but it was the most amazing thing I have ever seen. But beyond all that beauty, Xyles were all around us trying to kill us. That is where I met Fillip. His words and guidance are what I feel kept me alive through all of it. I have gone up against men before, but these were not men. Xyles were things nightmares are made of. There I was with a few of them on the other side of my sword wanting to kill me. As far as I knew, that was going to be my last night on earth and if I died, I was going to meet my end with their insides on the blade of my sword."

Taddayuse paused and looked at Viv.

"After they killed those of us they could, they saw that the rest of us were not that willing to leave this earth. That's when they backed off into the darkness. The Forest Men were animals in the way they attacked, but human-like in the way they came at us. Xyles attack without any humanity. They are evil. They do not just want you dead. They want to see you suffer. The screams of the men that were dragged off into the woods went on for some time after they pulled back the attack. It's as if the pain they were causing brought them pleasure. I can only guess that Sillack took notice of how I fought and felt I could bring Sanch to him. Or he has sent me out to test the strength of my forces and couldn't care less if I live through this or not. Either way, I am here and am very grateful that Fillip was willing to join me." For the first time, he had Viv's undivided attention.

"But what I still do not understand," Taddayuse said as he looked down at her, "is why a team of cherub are here with us. You ladies are known to be called upon when there is someone or something needed to be killed. My question is why did Deadra dispatch the five of you to join us on our little quest to find Sanch?"

As if she had just been given the answer to a great question, her face came alive. "That is a question that I did not ask. I just follow the orders that are passed down to me. I thought that Ros would keep us abreast of what we were doing here among you men, but at this time, I cannot say I know why we are here."

"Was it an order to follow me into a tent that was on fire?" Taddayuse smiled.

"No, it was not an order. In fact, we are not supposed to leave the side of our fellow cherubs in battle."

"Then why did you follow me?" He stepped closer to her.

"Because Fillip couldn't. He was fighting with my sisters, so I felt it right to follow you. I am sure I will hear about it from the others as soon as we are all alone. Maybe Lo will tell me all about why she hates people from Tegra, or would you like to enlighten me as to why?"

Taddayuse stepped back, looking ashamed. "What she knows of my people has nothing to do with me. I was but a child when the betrayal took place. I learned of it, but I was not a part of it. What Lo speaks of is about what happened between the people of Tegra and their betrayal of the Allens. She seems to know an awful lot about Lackshin, Sanch, Shallin, and his pet dragon. What do you know of her?"

"To tell you the truth, none of us know very much about her. All we know is that she and Deadra have known each other before Deadra even started with the cherubs. Lo only showed up eight years ago from what I have been told."

"She was in the cherubs before you became one of them?" he asked, hoping to understand why she had so much hate for people from Tegra.

"Yes," Viv replied. "I only recently became one of them, which is lucky for you."

"Why is that?"

She smiled. A thing she rarely does. "Because none of the others would have followed you into that tent and jumped on the back of that thing in order to save your sorry life. More than likely, they would've bet on how you would die. Burned to death or eaten by that beast. As fun as that would have been to watch, I don't think Fillip would have been okay with that. He reminds me of one of my uncles."

"So, you saved me for Fillip?"

"Why else would I bother? It is not like you even knew my name as he did."

The smile left his face. "I said I was sorry, didn't I, Viv?"

"Yes, you did, but why do you keep saying my name now? It is almost like you are trying not to forget it." Viv turned. The answer to her question was written on his face. "You really find it hard to remember a three-letter name? I swear to the gods. Come on let me take you back to Fillip before one of my swords finds its way into your chest."

He thought she was joking, but he still didn't want to risk if she wasn't. "You are right. We should get back to the others. After you." He stepped out of her way, allowing her to walk ahead of him. He was not looking forward to seeing Lo again tonight, knowing how she felt about him now that she knew where he was from.

As they walked, he tried to put together what reason Lo would have to feel that way about him and his people. What little he knew about his people's fall from grace didn't amount to much. He was told that when time came for the Tegra army to reinforce the Allens and the Archers, the royal family shifted their alliance and sent the army to fight with the enemy of the Archers. In that great battle, the oldest Allen son was taken captive and never seen again. He was said to have died in a Tegra prison camp or dungeon. With the loss of the oldest Allen son, their army was weakened and so were the Archers. Even after losing him, they still beat the army of the Croyanites. They then cut off the outside world and along with the help of the Skeritts, they rebuilt their forces. Even when the Xyles appeared out of nowhere, they only sent a force large enough to hold them back from their lands.

Why his people had to betray the Archers and the Allens was still a mystery to him. He thought maybe she could educate him more on this, or she could just as well try to kill him for asking. Taddayuse had no choice but to see himself as a man with no country and no people. He had spent more time away for his people and his lands and saw himself as a Teg more now by name than much else. Yet here he was wearing the dishonor that being a Teg brings, paying for a sin he did not commit.

"What of your people?" Taddayuse asked. "Where do you call home?"

"The cherubs are my people, and wherever I feel safe for the night is where I call home," Viv replied.

"But before the cherubs, who were you?" He kept pressing.

She took a deep breath. "I have always been Viv, but no one before I became a cherub."

"Is that really how you feel?"

"I cannot take liberties and speak for the others, but that is simply my reality."

"Fair enough, Viv. I understand," Taddayuse said in a low voice.

"I doubt you do, but thank you," Viv whispered.

As they neared where they were to meet the others, Taddayuse could not help but to be a little concerned about having to see Lo once again. He wanted nothing more than to apologize for a betrayal he had nothing to do with.

"Is there anything you can tell me that could help me?" he asked.

Viv stopped and turned to face him. "What are you talking about now?"

"I need help with Lo. How do I stay off her bad side?" He stood there with apology in his eyes.

The cold-hearted Viv could feel herself softening to the look of genuine pain.

"We don't know much about Lo. She was a cherub before any of us, but she holds no rank. She comes and goes as she pleases and answers to no one. One thing we do know is how fierce she is in battle and how important her family is to her."

"Who is her family?" Taddayuse asked.

"That is the thing," Viv said, with a confused look on her face. "None of us have any idea where she is from, or who her people are. As for this family of hers that she holds so dear, we do not know who they are or if any of them are still alive. She is with us because she chose to join us, not because she was sent. She is of us, but not with us. As for help, if you ever find yourself on the wrong end of her blade, make peace with whatever god you pray to. The smile she wears while ending you is there because she can already see your dead body and the thought of that is one of the few things that makes her happy."

"A smile?" Taddayuse asked.

"Yes." Viv replied. "It is very disturbing when you see it."

"If she starts smiling at me I should get the hell out of there. Is that what you are saying?"

"Yes, Taddayuse, that would be a great plan." Tapping him on the chest, she added, "When we get back, try to keep me or someone between the two of you. Because I have never seen her react to anyone as she did to you. I have seen her cut limbs off of men in battle that she did not look at the way she looked at you. Watch yourself with her the best you can."

Taddayuse nodded.

CHAPTER TWENTY-FOUR

As they approached the burning fire, there stood all the others. Lo was the first to see Viv and the boy from Tegra. She looked relieved to see Viv, but she was not happy that Taddayuse was with her.

"Looks like he brought Viv back in one piece. I was sure he would run and leave us to fight alone," Lo said. She turned to Fillip. "Why do you follow him? You seem to be a man with honor, yet you follow a man who comes from honorless people."

Fillip scratched his beard. "I follow him because he showed me his honor before I knew who his people were. That is what I see when I look at him."

"What is it you see?" Lo asked.

"I see what he is and not who his people were," Fillip replied. "We all know the story of what the Tegra people did to the Croyanites and what it cost us all."

"Yes!" Lo interrupted. "A weakened Croyanite nation allowed the checked to become unchecked. It allowed the wrong people to become powerful. The time the Allens and Archers took to regroup allowed the powerful to become even more powerful and greedy." Lo glared at Taddayuse.

Trying to better understand what Lo had invested in all of this, Ros and the others listened as Lo and Fillip spoke about why she had such hatred for this boy and his people. Still not clear what she was doing there, they now knew why she did not trust Taddayuse. Ros knew of the Tegran's dishonor, and how it did not just stop there.

Viv laughed and shook her head.

"What?" Taddayuse asked.

"She looks very happy to see you. Does she not?" Viv picked up the pace.

"What's the rush?" he asked, trying to keep up. "At least Fillip looks happy to see me."

Everyone was so tired, but alert. The men were trying to settle down to get ready for some well-needed rest. None wanted to take the risk of being asleep and not ready for a second attack.

"Excuse me, ladies," Fillip said as he made his way to Viv and Taddayuse.

"Good to see you well, Viv. May I borrow him for a moment?"

"You can take him and not give him back if you like," Viv replied as she kept walking.

Fillip smiled. "I think that one likes you, boy."

"I am just happy one of them doesn't want me dead. How about Lo? Have you learned anything about her?"

"Yes." Fillip smiled. "She most definitely wants you dead. And probably plans on doing you in herself the second I'm not looking."

Taddayuse laughed. "You are kidding, right?"

Fillip looked at him, confused. "No. No I am not kidding. She will kill you and will have that look on her face the entire time." They both looked over at Lo. She had an eerie stare on her face. "If you are not careful, that will be the last face you will see before you die." They both quickly looked away when she noticed them looking at her. "But for now, you need to address your men. They need to hear from their leader."

Taddayuse stepped back from Fillip. "We both know I should not be leading anyone. I still don't know why that evil man had me lead. As far as I know, he sent me out here to evaluate Sanch's forces, or just to keep him busy enough so he can come up with a real plan. Did Alshin ever come back with any of his forces?"

Fillip put his hand on the boy's shoulder. "None of that matters. You are here now, whether you want to lead or not. Most of these men that you partly handpicked are just like you. They've never seen real battle, much less anything like the Forest Men. The strong live tonight, and the unlucky will burn tomorrow. But for now, deserving or not, you are what they have in the shape of a leader.”

Taddayuse looked off into the darkness.

“Taddayuse!”

Taddayuse turned and gave a nod and walked past Fillip to the center of the camp where most of the men were congregating. They were trying to build the fire so to keep away anything else that may be out in the dark.

“This is not where we need the fire,” Taddayuse announced.

“What was that, sir?” one of the men asked.

“This is not where we need that fire to be.” Taddayuse now had all of their attention. “We need to set fires around the perimeter of the camp if we are to keep them from attempting another attack. They only entered the camps where there were no campfires. They are not afraid of fire, but they avoid it when they can. After we do this, we will take shifts in teams of three on either side of the camp. Those who are dead we will burn tomorrow. Those of us that are still alive will stay that way if we stay alert and ready. Get the fires set, that way, if they decide to return, we will see them coming.”

The cherubs looked on as he addressed his men. Lo looked disgusted. Taddayuse reached in and pulled out a burning log and made his way past the cherubs and Fillip to the outer perimeter to set his fire. The men followed suit.

Fillip looked to Lo. “Do you still think him garbage of Tegra?”

“I have seen nothing that makes him any less Tegra waste than he was a moment ago. He comes from dishonorable people and now he follows a dishonorable man. We all know the story of Lackshin and Sillack.” She slowly turned to look at Fillip.

At a loss for words, he turned to Taddayuse.

“Fillip?”

“Yes, Lo,” Fillip replied.

“Help him not to give me a reason to open him up, would you please?”

Fillip nodded and continued on after the boy from Tegra.

Everyone, including the cherubs, helped prepare the camp and set the perimeter fires. Fillip remained with Taddayuse and helped to keep him as far from Lo as possible. Viv also remained with Taddayuse. It was like she did not trust him to keep himself safe. Or maybe she was instructed to keep an eye on them two. From what Fillip could tell, Viv did as she wanted and looked up to Lo, and not the leader, Ros. Their small force followed whatever Lo would suggest.

Viv would disappear and reappear without notice. She was a perfect scout if ever they needed one. She was small and light on her feet and most of all, deadly. As Taddayuse walked through the camp, the men who first questioned his ability to lead, now nodded and went from calling him "boy" to calling him "Captain".

"Looks to me that the boy has earned their respect," Viv said as she pushed past Taddayuse to walk next to Fillip.

Fillip laughed. "That is Captain to you, little one."

"Captain?" Viv replied. "They only call him that because they were not in that tent to see their captain's face when I jumped on that thing's back. I was sure he was going to wet his britches. In fact, I think he may have." Viv grabbed Taddayuse by his britches.

"Hey!" Taddayuse jumped back from Viv's grip. "I had a plan," he said. "You ran in before I implemented it."

"Really?" both Viv and Fillip replied.

"What plan was that?" Viv enquired. "Because it looked to me you were only helping him build up a healthy appetite for Tegran meat."

Fillip laughed so loud that he would have woken everyone up if any were asleep. With a heavy blow on Taddayuse's shoulder, Fillip said, "I like this one. We should recruit her."

"Yes, we should," Taddayuse agreed. "It is always good to keep someone around to keep me humble." He looked down at Viv and gave an affectionate half-smile.

They continued their walk. Fillip filled the silence with stories of the past. He told tales of Sanch's father, and his great deeds and bravery. If Sanch were anything like his father, facing him and winning would not be a simple task. Fillip told of battles where Lord Sillack and Lackshin fought in lockstep together. "They were something to behold," Fillip said. "If he indeed has his father's sword, gods help us." Fillip fingered the hilt of his sword.

Viv seemed extra interested in the story of Lackshin. As a child, tales of him were told but never a firsthand account from someone who saw him fight with Shallin. She had questions about Sanch and why he scared Sillack the way that he did. Especially since Sanch was still a boy untested at the ways of war. After Fillip answered both Viv and Taddayuse's questions, the attention was turned to Lo. Both Fillip and his captain had their own questions about the one cherub more mysterious than Viv herself.

"Where is Lo truly from, Viv?" Taddayuse asked. "Why does she hold such hatred for people from Tegra? I left Tegra at such a young age. I have no memory of it."

It may have been that Viv truly knew little Lo's background, or she said just enough, making sure not to give away too much of what she really knew. Fillip questioned why, with the way Lo felt about dishonorable people, would she be in service of a man such as Sillack? Taddayuse could see that question was one Viv had no answer to.

"All that I really know for sure is that she normally would take no part in anything that has to do with the wishes of Sillack. Imagine our surprise when she was saddled and ready to move out with us. I have been training with her, so the others assumed she came along because of me." Viv paused with a look on her face.

"What is it?" Fillip asked.

"Well, I've been on several deployments before," Viv said. "Some much more dangerous than this one. Yet this is the one she joins me on?"

"What is her motive?" Taddayuse asked.

"I do not know, but I do feel that there is more to her reason than just me and my well-being," Viv replied.

"What do you know of the sword she wields?" Fillip asked. He wondered about it when he first saw her draw it.

"I do not know," Viv answered. "It is not like any sword I have ever seen before."

"What about this sword?" Taddayuse asked.

Fillip scratched his salt and pepper beard for a moment before he spoke. "Well, you two are still very young and would not know it by first glance, but Lo's sword is not made by the same metal that your swords and mine are made from." Fillip pulled his sword partly out to reveal naked steel. "See how the steel is shiny?" Fillip twisted the blade to reflect the little light their torches made. "When she draws her sword, it only reflects a small amount of light it encounters. So, her swords movements go almost unnoticed."

As Fillip spoke, Viv rested her hand on the dagger that Lo had given her.

"If not steel, what is her sword made of?" Taddayuse asked.

"Croyanite," Fillip replied.

"What?" Viv was unsure of what she heard.

Fillip repeated, "Croyanite. It is a metal that few have access to. The question is, did she take it off someone she killed, or was this blade specifically made for her?" Fillip scratched his beard again.

"I don't understand," Taddayuse said, not any more enlightened than before.

"Let us make our way back to the others and see what is left to be done before we finally put this night behind us." Fillip walked away in the direction they came from.

They walked all the way back in silence. Fillip looked to be deep in thought. Taddayuse still tried to put all that he learned together to have it make sense. Viv realized she did indeed know more than she had first thought but kept that to herself. When they made it back to the others, they put together the rest of the night's plans and went their separate ways.

The perimeters had been set and Fillip took charge of assigning the men to watch. The cherubs returned to tents that were set up almost like a separate camp all its own. Taddayuse returned to his tent where he washed off what was left of the Forest-Men. When he was done, he laid down to try and get some rest.

"Did you know Fillip put guards at your tent?" a small voice announced. "I guess he wishes to keep his captain safe as he sleeps," she said mockingly.

Taddayuse sprung up to see Viv standing there dressed in a robe being held together by nothing but her sword belt.

"How did you get past them?" Taddayuse asked.

"I think they may just be a little more afraid of Lo than Fillip." She came closer to where he lay, holding a candle that dimly lit the tent.

"To what do I owe this visit?" he asked, unsure of what she was doing there. He even thought for a moment that she was sent by Lo to dispatch of him.

"'Owe' is a good choice of words." She smiled. "I saved your life the way I remember things going tonight. I am here for payment for my serves."

A speechless Taddayuse looked on as Viv unbuckled her sword belt and placed her twin short swords with his next to the bed.

"What about Lo?" he whispered.

"She said as long as I leave you alive for her to kill, she did not care what I did with you."

CHAPTER TWENTY-FIVE

Helen awoke with the smell of hay from her father's barn strong in her nose. It was like every other morning, but this morning somehow felt peculiar. She sat up in her bed and peered around into the darkness of her room. Helen did not know what she would see, but she continued her search. Finally, she turned to climb down from her bed.

Through an open window, a cold breeze blew in, sending goosebumps across her bare shoulders, causing her to shiver and pull a blanket over her. The cold of the smooth wood sent a chill up her legs that caused her to put her bare feet back onto her bed. It took a few minutes of rubbing her feet to build back up the courage to try that again. She started with just her toes and eventually made it to her feet. Every step she took towards the window became less and less a struggle as she became used to the cold.

Covered by only her blanket, Helen stood there and looked out the window, still not sure what she would see looking back in at her. She saw dawn peeking through the cloud-filled sky. Months had gone by since that day, but she kept him fresh in her thoughts. Helen looked off in the distance. She took in a deep breath trying to recollect the smell of him. Helen found that she never felt alone after she met Sanch. When he threw his cloak over her nakedness it was as if he covered her with his promise of protection.

Days after Sanch left, she insisted to learn to defend herself. Helen wanted to be strong for him and not someone for him to save. Instead, she wanted him to see her as a strong woman that could confidently stand at his side.

Her mother saw no problem with Helen learning to defend herself in the war they knew was coming. However, her father told them once you pick up a sword and start living by it, it will be hard to ever come back from the feeling of cold steel in your hand. "In some way, it will change you greatly," he told them. "Your brothers and I carry swords to keep you both safe. A sword is a burden to carry and a burden I wish not to put on my daughter." Helen heard her father tell her mother.

"If he had not come when he did, then what of your daughter?" Her mother's words stopped his advance to the door. "They would have raped her, and then killed her so she could not speak of what they did to her. Then what good would you or the boy's swords have been? Only thing you three would have needed then were your skills with a spade, and even your daughter and I are skilled in that art." Her mother's words became more aggressive.

"You both meet us in the yard in the morrow," her father muttered under his breath. "Your point is well made, wife." He left their room.

From then on, Helen and her mother expected to join her father and brothers in the practice yard where they trained with blunted swords. It took days before anyone was willing to strike her mother with a practice sword. However, Helen spent the evenings nursing her own bruises. They all were surprised how well Helen took to close-counter weapons, like the short sword and daggers. She quickly learned all the vital strike points and started delivering bruises to others.

After a month or so, as Helen honed her technique with a blade, her father told them that she and her mother were to join him on a two or three day ride to a town south of them. Helen was instructed by her father to say nothing of Sanch. In addition, the boys would remain home to keep an eye on things while they were gone.

When they arrived at this humble town, they found temporary lodging where they settled in and had a small meal. Helen's father then inquired where he could find the blacksmith, for he wished to have some tools made. He was advised that if he wished a strong sword made for him, he would seek out Tris and try to buy some steel from him to mix with what metal the blacksmith would use to make the tools Helen's father desired. Tris's wife took an instant interest when she heard that one of the tools would be for Helen.

The men worked out their agreement without interruptions. Vera brewed them some tea and offered Helen some sweet bread. Vera only had sons and always desired a daughter, so she took a liking to Helen. When asked where her sons were, Helen noticed a familiar look of sadness in Vera's eyes that took her thoughts back to Sanch.

Helen watched the ripples in the water as the droplets fell from her face back into the basin. She wished it were his face that looked back at her when the water smoothed out. As she scooped up more water, she thought back to his hand in hers and how she could see nothing but that moment. The thought caused her to smile.

Helen dressed by candlelight as all others in her home slept. Now fully dressed, she made her way over to where her sword hung on a wooden peg next to the dagger she cherished. She always delighted in seeing the little sprinkle of black in the blade of her dagger. No matter how much Helen begged, Vera would not translate the three words on the weapon's hilt written in an ancient script Vera herself wrote when the steel was still hot.

Helen's sword came free from its sheath with ease. One swift pull is all it took for her to expose the blade that still shined like new and unstained. She remembered what Vera told her when she brought her sword for Tris and her to examine. "This sword you carry was made for you. Remember to always be true to your blade and always keep it as close as a trusted friend." Vera's words always resonated with Helen when she dawned her sword on her hip.

Helen buckled on her sword as she now did every morning. Another thing that was said by Vera stood out to Helen. It was when Vera examined the blade of Helen's dagger fresh from the forge. Vera got in close and whispered, "If my boy was here, I would have made this dagger even more special for you, my sweet child. It will serve your will. It will open doors for you if the time ever shows itself."

Helen found it strange that even as Tris and Vera spoke of their sons, they never once mentioned their names. When she brought it to her father's attention, he excused it away like he did not like the subject of their boys and told her she need not worry about it. Helen could not help but to think her father knew more about that than he let on.

Despite her suspicions, she quickly let it go. She then turned her attention to the relevance of the steel they obtained to mix with the blacksmith's normal blend of metal. Her father had her hold his sword in one hand and hers in the other. It was almost identical in length and blade thickness as her father's, but there was an obvious difference in weight. They blended the two metals together in order to give her and her mother the same length swords as him and her brothers, but at the same time kept them lighter and twice as sharp. Even the blunted swords they practiced with were heavier than the swords they now carried.

The door to Helen's room lightly scraped across the smooth wood floor, making only the slightest sound. She pulled it slow as to not wake anyone else. She crept through the torch-lit hallway. First, she passed her parent's room. Its heavy door was closed, as always. It was kept like that even when not occupied. The snoring coming from her oldest brother's room masked any sounds she made. When she told them about what happened the day she met Sanch, it took everything Helen's parents could do to keep her brother from getting his friends together and marching into town and killing every one of Sillack's men they could find. Even though he and her other brother returned home well after Sanch had left, they both felt that they owed a great debt to him. Whereas for the other brother, he just settled into bed after sneaking in from whatever mischief he and his friends were into the night before.

They both increased their time with their swords the day their sister came home bruised and almost raped. Their father spent a great deal of time speaking to the other men in the nearby homes as if to get them prepared for what was to come. All the men worked on subtle parameters to better protect the humble village they called home.

Sillack and his men had always left them alone to live in peace, except for the occasional rape and bad dealings. Two soldiers had gone missing without a trace some months ago, which brought some unwanted questions to the village. It was weeks before Sillack's men stopped popping in asking around about their missing men before they dismissed it as desertion. It was good that it was almost a day and a half ride to get to their village from town. That gave Helen's father and brothers enough time to retrieve the bodies and dispose of them where they would never be located.

Helen stood out in front of her family home, looking up at the orange and blue sky. She could not help but to wonder what sky Sanch was looking at. Rarely did Helen go a day where the thought of Sanch did not fill her mind. Where was he? What was he doing? Was she on his mind, and most of all, was he safe? Would she ever see him again? That last question weighed heavy on her mind and motivated every swing of her sword. For if he could not make it back to her, she wanted to be ready to go to him if ever he needed her.

A soft breeze blew in from the north, sending a chill over her, causing a shiver. She thought she could almost smell him. She closed her eyes, shutting the world out, and tried to take in as much of him as she could.

"You are going to catch cold if you keep this up," Helen's father whispered as he lowered a familiar cloak over her shoulders. Sanch's smell now became even stronger.

Helen sheltered her face in the cloak and breathed deep. "Father, where did you get this cloak? It smells like..."

"I know," her father interrupted. "With all that went on that day, your mother could not find his cloak, so she gave him one of mine and sent the boy on his way. She knew the longer he stayed, the more danger we were all in. I found it shortly after he left and gave it to your mother to put away in case he ever came back for it. However, I saw you out her cold and alone, so I thought just maybe you would find comfort with it again keeping you warm. He did leave it with you, after all." Her father kissed her softly on the top of the head. "Don't stay out here too long, your mother will be up soon, and she will be looking for you to help wake your brothers for breakfast."

Helen remained in the yard, covered in the memory of Sanch until she could feel the warmth of the morning sun on her face. When she heard her mother calling her brother's names, she knew it was time for her to go back into the house. She hurried to make sure the swordplay waited for the yard and did not start before breakfast. Her older brother woke fast enough, where her other brother had gone to bed only hours ago and was in no hurry to get up.

With everyone now seated for the morning meal, there was only talk of better times and funny stories. In addition, her mother questioned her sleepy brother. She wanted to know if she should expect any visits from some mother of any girls in their village today. She then turned her attention to Helen, asking her if she slept with her sword on. That made her father smile.

"When I was her age, I slept with my first sword," he said and turned to look at Helen. "Your grandmother would throw my blankets back to find my sword tucked in with me. She would always tell me the day she caught me taking my baths with that thing she would throw it out."

"So, what did you do, father?" Helen asked.

"Knowing this man, he made sure not to be caught with it in his bath," her mother said before her father answered. That sent the table into a laughing frenzy.

"I will remember that in the practice yard later, woman," he joked. "Now eat up boys, you will clean up after breakfast."

"Again?" the middle child whined.

"Yes, again," his father replied as he smiled at his little girl. "When you two make it to the table before your sister, then you won't be cleaning plates."

Her oldest brother laughed and messed up her hair with a hard rub. "I am not sure this one sleeps anymore. You should do as I did and accept your new life as a kitchen wench." He stabbed a half-eaten sausage off his sister's plate and shoved it in his mouth. "Quick with a sword, little sister, you could use some work with your fork play." He gave her a big greasy kiss on the side of her head.

They sat for a short time longer, talking and enjoying the quiet of the morning. Their father served Helen two more eggs like he always did. Even as a grown woman, she did not stop him, and would always say, "Thank you, daddy."

With breakfast over, the sounds of swords kissing in the yard rang out as her two brothers showed her techniques on how to take on two foes at once. They wanted her ready for anything a man could bring her way. They would often scare their mother with how hard they were on their sister. Their father had to reassure their mother that they only pushed her that hard to assure she would not require a man to save her next time her innocence was threatened. They even had a blunted dagger made for her to practice with. More times than not, she would use it to even the odds when her brothers stopped holding back.

Their parents looked on with heavy hearts as their children played war, unaware of how likely they would need those skills sooner than not. It would only be a matter of time that the war the Son of Lackshin had started would come through the village. At that time, no sword would remain dry and innocent.

"Yes, he saved our daughter, but now he puts the world to the torch," Helen's father said as he watched her swing her sword.

"That does appear to be so." Her mother paused and hovered in thought for a moment. She put her hand on the hilt of her sword and rested her head on her husband's chest. "Maybe the world need burn my love."

CHAPTER TWENTY-SIX

Sanch stood in a forest cloaked in fog. Just beyond the tree line, he saw two red eyes glaring at him through the mist. He turned to run. Behind him, he heard a horse galloping.

Closer. Closer.

After running a few yards, the young man's courage returned to him. He stopped, turned, and drew his sword. The creature broke through the fog with the sound of shattering glass. Its eyes were bright red, thick crimson flowed from its mouth. The creature reared up and tried to kick the boy's sword from his hands. This time, Sanch saw it coming and leaped back to avoid the beast's hooves. This creature still advanced fearlessly at the boy, causing him to fall to one knee. The beast now hovered right above him, snarling and breathing his foul breath onto Sanch.

Sanch awoke with the smell of rust still strong in his nose. No longer in a forest, he found himself warmer and safer than he had been in some time. Deem and the small Elargun force insisted on keeping watch at the village gates, so the people made space for them to set up camp.

Those who had never seen an Elargun were standoffish at first, but soon they warmed up to them when they saw how eager the prince was to learn their ways. Deem and his men even allowed the children to take rides on their horse-like animals. Kess kept torches lit on the walls along with archers patrolling day and night with their eyes set looking for anything that approached.

The lady of Quiet Waters was not going to allow it to be caught off guard. Through an open window, a faint smell of ash from the night before streamed through the entry. The cold of the smooth stones sent a chill up his legs. Every step he took towards the window became less and less a struggle as he became used to the cold. Bare-chested, he stood there and peered out in thought. Dawn was not long from the sky above a village that still mourned its fallen friends, brothers, fathers, and uncles. Sanch looked off in the distance, at everything, and at nothing. He took in a deep breath through his nose, attempting to rid the smell of rust that still lingered from his dream.

As a boy, he found it hard to tell if his dreams were a thing of his past or things yet to come. Whatever the dream was, he always felt that he brought something back with him every time he awoke from one.

Never able to dream anything other than visions of things that brought pain and fear, Sanch learned to go with less sleep than most boys did at his age. Vera would always find her little Sanch awake when all else slept. It would break her heart to know whatever haunted his mind was nothing like what he would have to face. Now, even less sleep was required for him as a man. These were the times he felt the loneliest. When the world slept, he looked into the darkness. Torches burned bright in the distance. Archers cast their shadows as they walked the walls cloaked in black to blend with the night.

Elarguns steered outside the walls. Their ability to see in the dark made them best equipped to patrol the perimeter at night. The rest of the village was unable to fully be at ease so soon after the battle that took place right outside its gates. Ember from the funeral piles still gave off heat. When the wind blew just right, an orange glow showed in the distance.

Days later, he would find Lisha still trying to put a shine back on her uncle's sword. Ralyn would catch her and knowing he had not the words to make anything better, he would just walk over and kiss his niece on top of her head.

Sanch and Lisha would not allow Alshin's body to be buried or burnt in spite of all that tried to reason with them. Menis stood silent, but they all knew where his allegiance lied. Therefore, Alshin's remains stayed to the elements and animals that roamed wild outside the walls. What seemed cruel to some, was justice to those who were changed that morning.

Sanch watched the ripples in the water as the droplets fell from his face back into the basin. He no longer knew the boy that looked back at him. He found that he no longer woke in fear of his nightmares, but he woke with purpose. Dressed, he sat and pulled on his boots, tied them, and strapped on his unique dagger. His mind returned to his home and to his brother. He wondered if Unghell would stay mad at him for leaving him behind? Not sure why he had not mentioned Unghell to the others, he pondered which sword he should carry when he heard the words of his mother saying, "The sword you seek is your father's, but the sword your carry is made for you. Use his sword for what you require it, but remember to always be true to your blade and always keep it as close as a trusted friend." Her words always resonated with him.

Today her words rested on deaf ears as Vera's boy buckled on Shallin. Sanch wanted to feel her weight on his hip in the sheath that the blacksmith sent little Edwin over to present to Sanch an evening ago. Shallin came free from it with ease; one swift pull is all it took. A blade black without stain shown in the night. The blade consumed the darkness like a thirsty man in a desert. Sanch ran the back of his hand down the her as you would the cheek of a lover.

The cold of the room paled in comparison to the coldness of Shallin's skin. She stopped her soft song when her blade was once again covered. Sanch found it peculiar how the sheath fit perfectly without the blacksmith ever laying eyes on Shallin. It even had a cut in it to accommodate the strange way the pommel attached to the black blade making what looked like the tail of a dragon.

The door to Sanch's room lightly scraped across the smooth stones. Making only the slightest sound, he pulled it slow as to not wake anyone else. Quietly, he walked through the torch-lit corridors trying his best not to make a sound. Tris would always tell Sanch how light he was on his feet. Sanch's mother said had things gone differently, her boy would have most likely been trained in the way of a assassin.

In the courtyard, Sanch took in the night. Slowly, he unlatched the door that led out to the front courtyard. He walked for a short time to put some distance between him and the small castle he found himself sleeping in. It was a big change from the humble town and home he grew up in. Furthermore, to have his name used without fear of the wrong person hearing was a change for him. He became thankful for his bad dreams the older he became.

Every time he woke from one of his many nightmares, he had no doubt in his mind that his future was meant to be filled with violence, death, and loss before any peace was to come to him. Sanch looked around taking in as much of the world around him as it slept. The soft orange-blue sky favored the eyes of some exotic animal. The loneliness he once dreaded he now desired.

When the world joined him, it asked much of him. He longed for the times when he could wonder off and not have to worry about anyone other than Unghell venturing out to find him. His big brother would always get so angry when he returned home to find Sanch already there halfway through a hot meal. The thought of his brother brought a longing for home over him accompanied with a smile. For the life of him, Sanch did not understand why Unghell would come after him even though he knew it was unlikely he would find him. Yet, every time his big brother would buckle up his sword belt, saddle up his horse, and come after him. That thought suddenly made Sanch uneasy. Sanch now found he questioned if Unghell would truly be extreme enough to follow him with no knowledge of where he was traveling.

The answer to that question brought a fear over Sanch that the faint smell of rust could not. He asked himself, what could stop him from following Unghell through one of the many gates of Hell if that were where his brother meant to venture?

Sanch stood there for some time watching the slow rising sun change the color of the morning sky until he felt a familiar presence looming not too far away. Sanch's grip loosened on Shallin's handle.

"How long have you been standing there?" Sanch spoke. "I must have been truly distracted to not have noticed you sooner. Come, stand with me. I've had my solitude for the day. I suppose. The sun will soon betray me to the rest of the world."

Out of the darkness, Guardian slowly revealed himself to the faint light of the new day. A creature his size should make more noise when he moved.

"Had trouble sleeping as well, did you?" Sanch asked, glancing to his right. The sight of Hush still set the boy back a bit. "I speak to you, but I do not know if you understand me. I must thank you several times over for pulling my skin out of the fire. I left my brother behind. He was my first ever friend and I could not stand the thought of laying my burden on his shoulders. It is mine and mine alone to bear, and I know if I gave him the opportunity, he would happily share the weight of it with me. I could not do that to him." Sanch pressed his lips together and stood silently for several moments. "I find you to be a true friend. In addition, I strangely feel as if we have been friends for some time before you dropped me from that tree."

Sanch thought back to that day with affection. He looked up and caught Hush looking at his hip where Shallin rested. His orange eyes narrowed in disapproval.

"Oh, this?" Sanch patted the pommel of his father's sword. "I just wanted to feel her weight at my side. I have only bore her on my back, and if I am to take her into battle against Sillack, I should know how well she wears at my side."

Hush diverted his gaze from Shallin and looked forward.

"My quiet friend, whatever could you be thinking of?" Sanch asked, expecting that question to go unanswered.

"You've never mentioned anything about a brother before," a soft voice came from Guardian's right shoulder.

"What the?" Sanch jumped back, startled. He and Guardian stood in silence.

"How is it you speak, and your lips do not move?" Sanch examined the creature's face.

"Because he is not the one speaking, you foolish boy." A soft blue glow slowly emerged from behind his shaggy hair that fell down onto his shoulders.

"Silma?" Her name passed his lips as a question. "Is that you in there?" Sanch asked, now able to see the silhouette of a little woman.

"Do you know of anyone else that can fit on our friend's shoulder?" Silma parted Hush's hair like a curtain. "Would you believe this was his plan? He understands you. In fact, he understands all of us, but there's a strange bond between you two that I sense. Being what you humans would call a magical being, there is a different spectrum of the world that we see. There is something about you and him that mirror one another ever so faintly. It became more visible in battle but went away when the fighting ended. The subject of it, for some reason, he will not expand on."

"You are able to communicate with him?" Sanch asked. "What have you learned from him? What have you asked him, and have you asked him what he is? Where are his people from?" Sanch pelted Silma with questions.

"It is not like that," she replied. "He has said nothing."

"Then how do you know he understands a word we say if he has not said a word to you?" Sanch asked.

"It is simple. Did you not notice him responding to your every command? I have even seen him smile when I had a go at the two young witches. Remember in that cave when you told him to look over me as if I were you? Well, as you can see, he is still about your business. There is far more to him than we know. He seems to know more about you than he lets on."

Sanch looked at him as he tried to make sense of it all. This creature's person was familiar to him, but until months ago, Sanch had never laid eyes on him. Never once did he feel the need to question his quiet friend's intentions.

When Sanch felt air beneath him and looked up to find his life in the hands of Hush, he somehow knew he was safe. It was like the nights where he woke from one of his nightmares to find his mother's face over him. Sanch turned to face the sun, and closed his eyes, trying to shut out the world for a moment and to picture his mother's face. To his surprise, he found another face looking back at him.

"Who is Helen?" Silma asked.

"What?" Sanch slowly opened his eyes. "Who is what?"

"You just whispered that name," Silma pressed. "Is that someone you've left behind?"

"You could say that. I have left a lot behind," Sanch said, dismissing Silma's question.

"What is that?" Silma's sharp eyes saw something or someone traveling fast towards them in the distance.

Hush placed his left forearm on Sanch's chest and pushed him back. He drew his bone-handled sword and readied himself. Sanch, surprised by the impact, stumbled back. As he reached for Shallin, Hush covered Sanch's hands with his own, and forced Shallin back into her sheath.

"There is no time for that," Sanch said, looking up into his friend's worried orange eyes. "It is fine. I need to familiar myself with this here. She and I need to fight as one when the time comes."

A blue light shot over both their heads. Silma hovered there, trying to get a better look at what approached. "It looks like two riders moving quickly this way. It's that one guard that was there when we stopped in two days ago, and one other with him." Silma slowly descended back onto Guardian's shoulder.

As the two clouds of dust got closer, swords returned to their place of rest.

"What brings you two in such haste?" Sanch shouted when the two riders were close enough to hear him. "And at such an early hour. We have not yet broken bread this morning."

"Lord Sanch," the rider spoke. "They killed him."

Sanch stepped forward, clenching his jaw. "Who did they kill?"

The boy swallowed. "The prisoner that you wanted separated from the others for speaking up against Sillack. We found him dead this morning. He was still chained to another prisoner. I questioned the man, but all he would say is they got impatient waiting on the son of a coward, and they will kill him too if he says any more than that."

Sanch felt his body go cold as rational thought left his eyes.

"What would you have us do, Sanch?' the guard asked, awaiting orders.

Sanch pointed to the guard that did all the talking first. "I need you to pull some of the archers from the wall and bring them to where the prisoners are kept." Sanch turned to Silma. "I need you to go to the Elarguns and have Deem and Dagger meet me there."

"But Sanch—"

"Deem and Dagger! Now, Silma!" Sanch cut her off. He walked up to the other guard and calmed his horse down.

"What would you have me do, lord?" the quiet boy asked nervously.

"I need your horse," Sanch said, now calmer and without emotion. "Can you keep up?" Sanch asked Hush as the guard quickly dismounted, making his horse available to him. Hush nodded.

Now mounted, Sanch ordered the boy to wake Ralyn and the others and make them aware of what was going on. Sanch rode off to the makeshift prison. Hush kept up the best he could, but Sanch rode hard, putting some distance between them. As Sanch rode, the world quietly passed him. All he heard was the galloping of hooves and the beating of his heart.

By the time they arrived to where the prisoners were being kept, he had only traveled a mile or two, but he felt like he had been riding for days. Sanch dismounted the mare before she came to a full stop.

"Whatever your plan, wait till the others are here before you do anything," Silma said as she flew in as fast as she could, afraid of what Sanch might do if left on his own.

"Well, they should hurry," Sanch replied as he moved in on the large gates with purpose. Light on his feet, Hush arrived and fell in at his side.

"Open it," Sanch demanded.

The soldier shook his head nervously. "I cannot open these gates without Lord Ralyn's orders," he told Sanch as he squared his chest and stood lofty.

Sanch dawned a smile that looked borderline evil. "Move him." As soon as the words made it past Sanch's lips, Hush pushed the man halfway across the room where he landed on the ground and stayed there not moving. Hush grabbed the lever and pulled the latches open. Sanch started to push the gate open as soon as the last latch was free. The other four guards stood back after what they saw happen to the other man. One of the archers that were on the wall overlooking the prisoners rushed down to see what all the commotion was about.

"What is going on down here?" She stepped out from the dark hallway that led up to the wall with an arrow notched and ready. When the ebony archer saw Sanch, she lowered her arrow. "What are you doing here, Sanch? Where is Lord Ralyn?"

"He should be with us shortly. For now, did anyone see what happened to the man I ordered to be protected?" Sanch looked around as if he misplaced something.

"All I know is we found him dead this morning. It looked like he was strangled to death with the other prisoner's chains."

"Oh, there we go," Sanch said as he picked up a bottle of oil that guards used to refill the lanterns. "I remember you," Sanch said as he glanced at the archer.

She stood there clad in garbs that would fit a man. A quiver of arrows was strapped to her back, and a short sword hung at her side. "Yes, Sanch, I was here last you spoke to the men we keep here."

"Good. Do you remember my words?" Sanch asked. The archer followed him around the room.

"Yes. You said if any harm came to that man, you would..." The archer paused and looked at Sanch's hand where he held the bottle of oil.

Sanch nodded. "Get back up top and ready your archers. More are on their way." He pulled a torch free from a notch in the wall. "Are those the weapons you gathered for the twenty men that were to fight me and the others?" Sanch asked the guards that still stood speechless.

One guard slowly turned to look at the table where swords, axes, spears, morning stars, and other weapons were. "Yes, those are they."

"Good," Sanch replied. "Make them available to them. I do not find it honorable to fight unarmed men. First, let me have a word with the man chained to the dead man." As Sanch and Hush passed through the gates, Sanch broke the bottle of oil on the ground after a few paces. Hush watched Sanch as he walked over to the man still chained to the body. He kneeled down in front him.

"I know you have been asked this before, but this time is going to be a little different," Sanch said, trying to help the man understand the severity of the situation. Sanch bit his lip, designing his words just right for this man. "You need to tell me who did this to this man that lay chained to you." Sanch placed his hand on the man's dirty face. "And please make these words mean something."

The man stared into Sanch's dead eyes for a moment, then looked past Sanch to the large man that stood in the distance, hanging on every word. "I do not know who killed the coward. If I knew and told you anything I would end up like him." The man smirked at Sanch.

"Now what, Sanch, son of a coward?" a large man shouted from across the yard.

Sanch stood up and handed Hush the torch he held, then kicked the man that sat there in his face, pushing him onto his back. Sanch drew his dagger and fell onto the man like an animal. Placing his right hand behind the man's head, Sanch pulled him up onto the dagger he held in his left. Sanch stopped just as the blade touched the skin on the man's throat and leaned in and whispered," If you told me they may have killed you, but you didn't tell me. And for that, I will kill you." Sanch slowly pulled him onto his dagger as everyone looked in silence. Only the gurgling sound of this man drowning in his own fluids could be heard. Silma flew overhead as she watched in horror.

After cleaning his dagger off on the man's tattered shirt, Sanch stood up and reclaimed his torch. "No more questions. Give them their weapons," Sanch demanded.

With the Elargun camp being at the village wall, Deem and Dagger were the first to arrive in time to see Sanch standing over two dead men. With no questions asked, the two Elargun princes fell in next to Hush. "We are here, Sanch," Deem announced.

"What is going on here, Silma?" Dagger asked.

"You both heard me warn them, did you not?" Sanch asked the princes.

Deem looked around. He noticed that the man that lay dead was the man that spoke of his family and that it was for them he fought for Sillack. "Oh, no. They killed him."

"What now?" Dagger asked his brother.

Weapons were thrown over the walls to the prisoners that wished to fight, along with keys to their shackles. Sanch walked over to where the broken bottle and oil were and lowered the torch into it.

"Now, brother," Deem said. "They burn."

As they approached, the smell of burning flesh was undeniable, and the song of battle was once again being played.

When Menis and Lisha saw the fire separating them from the fight, they looked at each other and to the barrel of water that was used to give the prisoners their daily ration. They rushed over to the barrel. Lisha wrapped her arms around Menis's waist as he picked it up. Right as he went to pour the water over them, Bethany fell in under the shower that left the three of them drenched. As they jumped through the flames with swords drawn, Kess looked on as her daughter disappeared behind a wall of fire.

"Get me a bow," Kess shouted as she ran to the stairs that led up to where they could get a better view.

"You men put out this fire," Ralyn ordered as the heat from the flames kept him from following the others in. "I need more men in there with them," Ralyn demanded. "NOW." He followed Kess to look over the battle that was going on without him. He got up top in time to see his wife launch an arrow into the yard below. "What is going on down there?" Ralyn looked into the yard to see his little girl wrenching her sword free from a man's chest. Half of the men stayed to one side, not wanting to have anything to do with Sanch and the others. The men loyal to Sillack found killing Sanch and the others harder than they thought. Silma held her larger size by emptying the life force from the first man that thought a spirit would be an easy kill. She left him looking like an ancient corpse.

Sanch and a giant of a man fought fiercely. Every strike of the man's axe came down on Shallin with no mercy. If Shallin had been less than what she was, she may have given under those blows. The brute pushed Sanch back twice the distance. Sanch dug into the wet sand and held his ground. He took all the brute had to give and when opportunity showed itself, he gave back. Sanch's mother had always told him no matter how strong a man was, his sword would eventually get heavy. From what Vera's boy could tell, this man's axe started to show its weight. Sanch, smaller and lighter on his feet, started his offensive. Staying under the strikes, he started cutting away at the big man. First Sanch opened a deep gash in the man's right thigh that caused him to take a knee. As the man tried to get back to his feet, Sanch landed a thin line across his lower back, dropping him back to that knee.

Using the axe as a crutch, the man pushed himself to his feet, only to have the back of his left knee cut almost to the bone, causing him to cry out and return to his knees. With the torch in one hand and Shallin in the other, Sanch circled the beaten man.

"What is he doing?" Kess asked as she notched another arrow to her string. "Why is he not finishing him?" She turned to Ralyn.

Ralyn stood there with his eyes fixed on Bethany. Two men had their attention focused on Menis. They were no match for him until a third man came in his blind spot and landed a cut on Menis's left side, catching him off guard. Menis spun around and planted one of his axes in the center of the man's head, splitting it down to his chin.

"To Menis, Lisha!" Ralyn shouted down to her. "To Menis!"

Lisha turned to see Menis holding his side. Not moving without Bethany, Lisha ordered her cousin to follow her. "Bethany, come with me," Lisha ordered. The two ladies moved in quickly and made little of the men that threatened Menis in his weakened state.

"Sanch, end this!" Lisha shouted as she and Bethany struggled to hold Menis as they moved him to the exit, still engulfed by flames. "End it now!" One man came at her with his sword over his head, and with half of Menis's weight on her, she raised her sword and braced for impact. Bethany was helpless to do anything. From her position, she could do nothing but watch Lisha barely keep both her sword and Menis up. To Lisha, all else stopped. All that she heard was herself breathing and the heavy sound of the man's steps as he came for her. "One, two, three …" Lisha counted step by step .

As the warm droplets slowly ran down her face, she now heard nothing but the beating of her heart and two thumps hitting the damp sand. When she opened her eyes, she saw Deem with his foot on the back of a man cleaved almost in half. Deem pulled his sword free from the gyrating body.

"Get him out of here!" Deem instructed. Silma and Dagger were behind him, cutting a path to the fiery gate.

"Put that fire out," Ralyn commanded the men below when he saw Menis's injury. "Summon the Obeah-Man."

Kess notched another arrow, took a deep breath, pulled her string, and let loose. The arrow met with Shallin's blade. The song she sang when kissed by Kess's arrow brought Sanch back from whatever dark place he stepped into. What sounded like a shout to everyone else sounded like a whisper to Sanch. He turned and looked to where the arrow came from. There he saw Kess and saw her mumble, "Finish this."

With his enemy still struggling to his feet and shouting curses, Sanch put his head back and let the heat from the sun wash over his face. He spun Shallin loosely in his hand, and with every eye focused on Sanch, he brought his father's sword down on the man's neck. Sanch took three steps before the head came free from the body. He dropped the torch on the still rolling head, catching it on fire, and walked away, leaving a headless body on one knee leaning on an axe.

"If we are not careful, this boy will set this world ablaze," Kess said as she looked up at Ralyn and handed her bow off to one of the other archers.

"Well, maybe the world need burn, my love," Ralyn said, putting his arms around Kess and kissing her on top of her head.

CHAPTER TWENTY-SEVEN

The night's air was cold and filled with hard decisions. This night, shadows breathing the breath of death walked among men going unnoticed. Sounds of men and women filled the air. Songs of stories passed escaped from open windows of the taverns that lined the busy streets. Women tried to convince men to spend all they made that day on an evening of sinful pleasure and piss poor wine. A rich man stumbled out of a high-end establishment where the wine is of quality, the room's smell of flowers and incense, and the serving girls are exotic from faraway lands. His men walked with him as he struggled into his small carriage.

"Come, master." One of the men grabbed the rich man under his arm helping him from nearly falling on his face.

Torchlight glimmered off their armor as they tried to keep hold of him and his silk tunic. When a man heavy with coins like him moved through the city, they felt the world was there to serve and pleasure them. In their minds, nothing should be unobtainable with their money. That is how they looked onto others. Everyone and everything comes with a price. Moreover, with his money, he can have it all. The women he left behind were just things to him. Nothing more than a cup or a spoon to him, merely objects for him to use.

The carriage made its way down the coble stone streets accompanied with those of his escorts that rode large mares alongside him. His large home sat apart from others, surrounded by walls to keep out the undesirables. However, shadows move in the dark and are capable of slinking over tall walls with ease. Men with gold to pay men to protect them do not walk with a healthy fear of what lives in the dark. Now behind the safety of his walls, he moved around unconcerned. His men remained close so as to keep him from taking another tumble. Draped in expensive silks, he was the picture of wealth.

From a glance you could not know he was a man who had done many wrongs. He had left people in his wake desperate and without choice. Others he had taken everything from, leaving them desolate and equally desperate. Men like him should never find it easy to sleep, but they do, and very soundly. Large feather beds comfort them like the soft arms of a loving mother. Sweet smells of lilac lull him to sleep when some of his victims can barely keep a roof over their family's heads.

Once established men could be found sleeping on the streets without any idea how or when they would get their next meal. They hadn't been noble by any means, but successful men in their own right. Those of them who were able to hold on to what they built usually owed the Royal Bank. For to owe the Royal Bank was to owe a pirate, and those with daughters now could never enjoy a good night's rest.

In a large home, there are so many rooms, corners, and places for shadows to hide. As he moved, so did the shadows. Men without fear take no time to look into the dark, even when the dark holds eyes that look at them.

As he approached his chamber, he untied the strings of his tunic and dropped silks behind him as he walked. The doors to his chamber stood tall and cast a long, deep shadow.

"That is far enough," he instructed. "Close the door and take your leave. Send your replacements to stand guard." Now naked, he swayed as he bellowed, "And get my garbs to the washerwomen before morning." Those words escaped through the last crack before the door slammed shut.

Drunk, naked, and covered in the smell of unwilling affection, he climbed into that feather bed next to his wife. Cold air blew in from a window across the room that sent a chill over the nobleman that caused him to break free from sleep in time to open his eye to greet the shadow called death as he breathed his breath on him and to a slumber, he shant wake from.

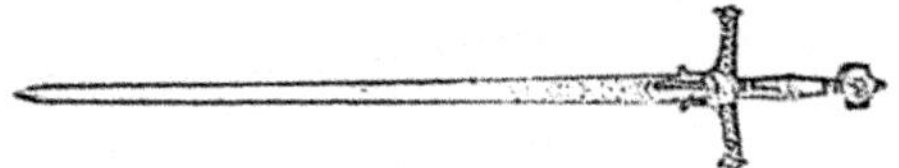

"MAY I SIT WITH YOU?" THE KNIGHT ASKED AS HE rested his hand on the back of the empty chair.

"Please," the seated man said as he raised his cup of wine to the night. "If a man of your station wishes to join a lowly sword like myself, who am I to deny him a chair to rest his heavy armor?"

"How have you been, my friend?" the knight inquired as he called over for a cup of wine for himself.

"Get yourself some of the egg and sausages. They are exceptionable this morning, friend." He bit a chunk out of one of the greasy sausages on his plate. Sitting there across from the knight, he was dressed in hard leather instead of heavy armor, like the man that sat opposite of him. "How do you move in that thing?"

"Quite well, if you do not remember." the knight replied.

"Yes, I suppose I recall a time or two where you moved well on your feet dressed in that mobile cage," he mumbled out between chewing. Washing it all down with what was left of his wine, he signaled for a refill. Then he said, "Samuel, it must be something of grave importance if you are taking the risk of being seen by the likes of me in public. How long has it been? Can we still consider ourselves friends? Pardon my insolence, it is Sir Parson now, is it not?" A fake smile found its way onto the man's smooth face.

"Yes, it is Sir Parson and has been for some time now. You know that, Florence. You are a man that knows much. In fact, that brings me here to answer your question. I have questions of my own that a man with your talent may be able to aid me in figuring out."

"And here I was thinking my old friend just wished to join me for a bit of breakfast. Now, what kind of talent makes me more suited to work something out a knight of kings cannot?" Florence's tone had a hint of mocking to it. "But, by all means, make your inquiries and I will see what this humble sword can do to help his old friend."

"Thank you," Samuel thanked the serving girl as she put down two cups of wine. "And some of what he has, if you please? I hear it is exceptional this morning." He put down enough coin to cover both their meals.

"Here to buy my words, Samuel?" Florence asked.

"No, not at all," the knight replied. "Just paying an old debt, that is all."

For the first time, they shared what resembled a friendly memory. However fleeting, death came quickly for that memory.

"Your question? Ask it," Florence said, taking another bite.

"A nobleman was killed a few nights ago, and the killer left no evidence of his deeds. Guards on duty that night said they saw no one enter nor leave their master's quarters. Sounds to me like the work of a man skilled in the art of assassination." The knight looked for a reaction from the man across from him. Florence gave him nothing.

"Why do you feel I can assist you with this? A dead nobleman is none of my concern. Did you properly question his wife? Who knows what part she may have played in it. Maybe she and one of his guards plotted against him. I know noblemen do not become as wealthy as they do without making a few enemies. Did you question some of them?"

"I did. Only one stood out to me," Samuel said as he looked over his breakfast that arrived at the table. "A baker that you and I used to visit as boys were one of this nobleman's victims as you would call them."

"Then there you have it. Why bring these questions to me? Sounds to me you have found your man." Florence smiled and raised his cup.

"That would be ideal if this man had the skills in which to accomplish such a feat. But he would have to have been able to do all this with a broken arm."

"How did the baker come to be in such a state? I never thought baking was such a taxing occupation." Florence leaned in to hear more of the tale of the baker and his misgivings.

"The nobleman had him beaten when he refused to sell his bakery to him for much less than what it's worth. He gave the baker a week to rethink his offer."

"Did our baker take the nobleman's low-ball offer, after all?" Florence asked, now well invested in the conclusion of this tale his old friend was relaying.

"He never had to make that decision," Samuel replied.

"Oh?" Florence leaned back in his chair. "Why is that? Did the nobleman change his mind about purchasing the bakery? That is great news. We do so love the bread the old man makes. We should go purchase some when we are through here. If Sir Parson can spare more of his time for an old friend."

"That is the thing. The nobleman was killed the night before he was to return to hear the baker's decision. Lucky for him, I guess."

"Lucky, indeed," Florence said as a wicked smile crossed his face.

Those words were the last exchanged between them. They sat in silence as they ate their breakfast. Samuel smiled when he realized he had not been lied to by his boyhood friend. The breakfast was truly exceptional.

"I told you," Florence said as he saw his friend devour the sausages and eggs like when they were boys sitting down at their first meal of the day. Their long silence turned into stories of the past. Which were better times for them. A time when they were boys playing at swords, not men that lived by them. They even shared a laugh or two and drank to games well played.

With plates empty and stomachs full, they took that walk that Florence suggested and left the ears of the room behind them. When Florence teased about leaving the sweet smells of the castle, he was not jesting. The streets in that part of the city were now as plumed as the parts of the city where the rich and nobles spent their coin.

Where the lucky baker's bread shop was, you first had to walk through some tough areas. In this part of the city, one man would be seen there to keep the peace. The other, there to end the men that disturbed the little peace they enjoyed. However, seeing men like them together and not at odds, brought about a bevy of confused gazes.

As boys, they would both wander into this area even after being told by their fathers how dangerous it was for them. Instead, they found themselves welcomed, fed, and befriended by the other children. When they got older and their training began, Florence was sent to learn how to kill as a Kishi, and Samuel's father had him trained by knights. It had been years before they saw one another again and when they did, they were both different men. They remained friends, but events set them on different paths that made it hard for them to stay that way.

The baker that knew them as boys smiled when he saw them and presented them with their known selections before either of them had the opportunity to ask.

"Now that we are away from peering ears and eyes, why did you truly seek me out? It was not to ask me about a fat dead nobleman that you would have killed yourself if you did not stand here, Sir Parson. Tell your old friend what would force you to come all this way from your sweet-smelling castle to the fowl-smelling slums to find me?" Florence pulled off a piece of his pastry and waited for the knight's answer.

"What have you heard about this boy calling himself Sanch, Son of Lackshin?" Samuel asked with dead eyes.

Franklyn Thomas Jr

About the Author

As a young boy from the Island of St Croix, Franklyn Thomas Jr. grew up learning of life from two worlds spoken in two different tongues. Leaving his home at a young age, he was suddenly plunged into a world that spoke English.

Learning a new language was difficult, but he caught on quickly. When Franklyn returned home after a long day of speaking English, he was relieved to be home speaking his native tongue.

Franklyn started to read stories of knights and their adventures. Later, he delved into the dark tales of Edgar Allan Poe, which inspired him to pick up the pen.

In his mind, he found words with lives all their own, and for them to live, others must read them and give the words a chance to live in their minds and imaginations as well.

You may find the way he writes far from conventional—spending almost all his life speaking two different languages daily influenced his writing style. As you read, you will find both of his worlds now living as one

.

www.ingramcontent.com/pod-product-compliance
Lightning Source LLC
Chambersburg PA
CBHW070451120726
47910CB00003B/1006